RESTORING WHAT WAS LOST

BARBARA HINSKE

CASA DEL NORTHERN PUBLISHING

ALSO BY BARBARA HINSKE

Available at Amazon and other fine retailers in Print, Audio, and for Kindle

The Rosemont Series

Coming to Rosemont

Weaving the Strands

Uncovering Secrets

Drawing Close

Bringing Them Home

Shelving Doubts

Restoring What Was Lost

No Matter How Far

When Dreams There Be

Novellas

The Night Train

The Christmas Club (adapted for The Hallmark Channel, 2019)

Paws & Pastries

Sweets & Treats

Snowflakes, Cupcakes & Kittens

Workout Wishes & Valentine Kisses

Wishes of Home

Novels in the Guiding Emily Series

Guiding Emily

The Unexpected Path

Over Every Hurdle

Down the Aisle

Novels in the "Who's There?!" Collection

Deadly Parcel

Final Circuit

Connect with BARBARA HINSKE Online
Sign up for her newsletter at **BarbaraHinske.com**
Goodreads.com/BarbaraHinske
Facebook.com/BHinske
Instagram/barbarahinskeauthor
TikTok.com/BarbaraHinske
Pinterest.com/BarbaraHinske
Search for **Barbara Hinske on YouTube**
bhinske@gmail.com

This book may not be reproduced in whole or in part without written permission of the author, with the exception of brief quotations within book reviews or articles. This book is a work of fiction. Any resemblance to actual persons, living or dead, or places or events is coincidental.

Copyright © 2020 Barbara Hinske.

Cover by Elizabeth Mackey, Copyright © 2020.

All rights reserved.

ISBN: 978-1-7349249-1-6

Library of Congress Control Number: 2020914819

Casa del Northern Publishing

Phoenix, Arizona

*To Lisa Burns Coleman—my insightful advisor,
right hand, partner-in-crime, and now beloved friend.
This journey is more joyful with you.*

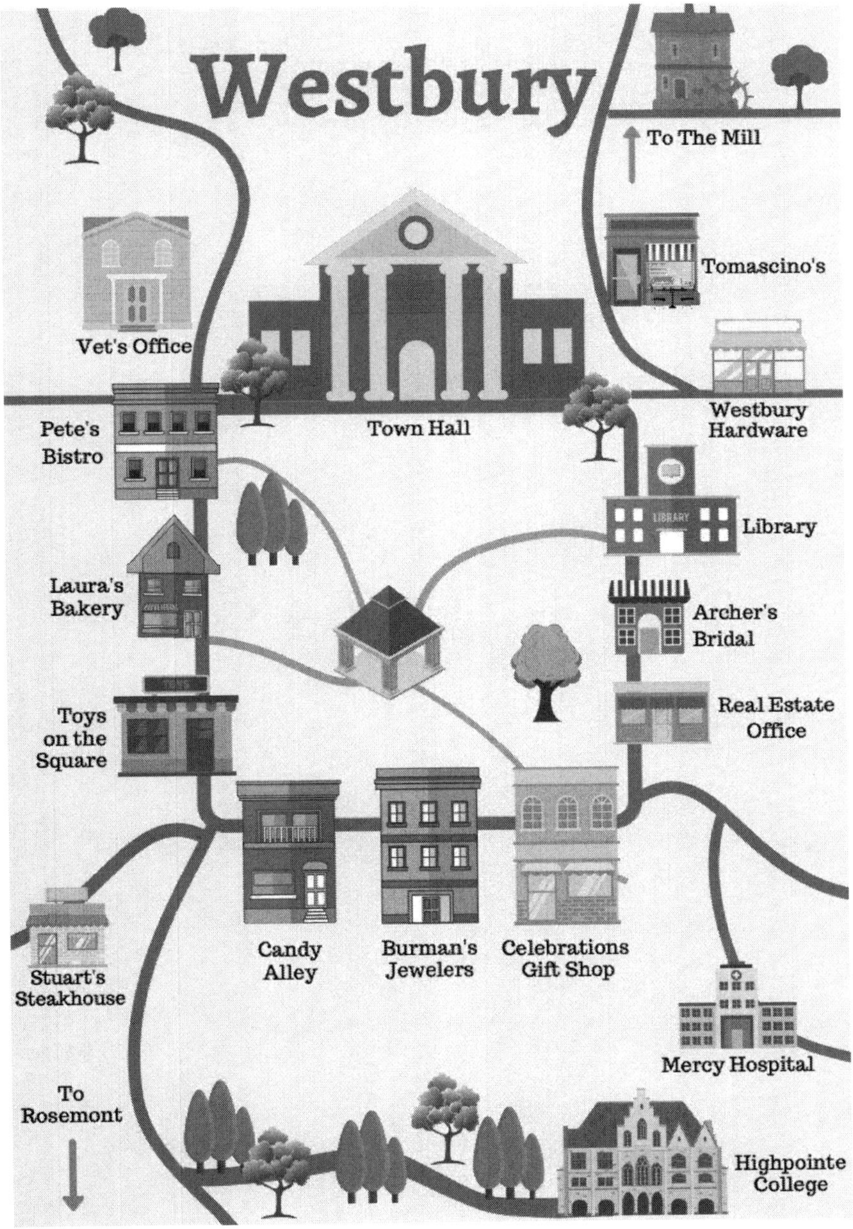

Westbury
To The Mill
Tomascino's
Vet's Office
Town Hall
Westbury Hardware
Pete's Bistro
Library
Laura's Bakery
Archer's Bridal
Real Estate Office
Toys on the Square
Candy Alley
Burman's Jewelers
Celebrations Gift Shop
Stuart's Steakhouse
Mercy Hospital
To Rosemont
Highpointe College

CHAPTER 1

Maggie Martin pushed her disheveled chestnut hair off her face and wound her way through the crowd of police officers congregating on the steps of Highpointe College Library. As president of Highpointe, she was given access that the officers would have denied to anyone else.

Police cruisers idled along the drive, in front of the imposing Romanesque facade of the library, their flashing red lights slicing across the brick and glinting off the dark glass of the arched windows before disappearing into the night. The low rumble of their engines underscored the urgency of the scene.

She approached Dean Anthony Plume as he stepped off the bottom step. The English literature professor staggered, his trim gray hair in uncharacteristic disarray. She caught his arm, steadying him. He stared at the retreating taillights of the ambulance that had just departed.

"What happened?" Maggie asked.

Anthony faced her. "It's all my fault," he said, his eyes wild and expression distorted. "He almost killed her."

Maggie recoiled and tightened her grip on his arm. "Who?"

"Sunday Sloan." A moan escaped his lips. "I was almost too late."

"What are you talking about?"

"That man—the one they took away in the ambulance. He was trying to kill her."

Still bewildered, Maggie looked into Anthony's eyes. "Why would someone want to kill one of our librarians?"

Anthony brought his hands to his temples and swayed on his feet.

"Let's get you someplace where you can sit down." She touched his shoulder, and he winced. "You're hurt, aren't you?"

Maggie began to lead Anthony to a low stone wall at the base of the steps when an officer intercepted them.

"We'd like to take your statement, sir. Can you come to the station?"

"He's hurt," Maggie said. "He needs medical attention."

"I'm fine," Anthony said to the officer and spun to Maggie. "I'm responsible for all of this." His voice cracked, and his words tumbled out. "I'm a gambler and got in over my head. I started stealing rare books from the collection that Hector Martin left the college library when he died."

Maggie brought her hand to her heart. Her life was intersecting with Hector Martin's, again. She'd inherited Rosemont from her late husband, Paul Martin, who was one of Hector's heirs. Moving to Rosemont when Paul died had dramatically changed the trajectory of her life.

Anthony paused to draw a deep breath. "It was supposed to be the perfect crime—nobody was going to notice they were missing, and nobody was supposed to get hurt. But I sold them to a man named Nigel Blythe—the man who just tried to kill Sunday."

The officer stepped forward. "You need to come with me."

Maggie addressed Anthony. "This is very serious. You shouldn't say anything else until you've hired an attorney."

"I don't care. I want to tell you everything." He looked at Maggie. "You trusted me, and I betrayed that trust. I'm so sorry." He rattled on. "Nigel killed Hazel Harrington when she was in charge of the rare books. She was getting suspicious about the thefts. He was here to do the same to Sunday. I had to stop him."

Maggie gasped.

The officer clutched Anthony's right arm.

"You can tell us all about it at the station." He stepped forward, bringing Anthony with him.

Anthony raised his voice. "He was going to kill Sunday by pushing her off the second-floor landing! I couldn't let that happen." A sob escaped his throat. "Too many people have suffered on account of me."

"Don't say anything else, Anthony," Maggie said, following them. "Wait for your lawyer."

"I'm done waiting. For once in my life, I'm going to do the right thing and tell the truth."

The officer opened the back door of a police cruiser and placed his hand on the top of Anthony's head as the professor lowered himself into the seat.

***

John Allen gave his wife's hand a reassuring squeeze as he pulled into the parking lot of police headquarters. A line of police cruisers idled in front of them. He and Maggie watched as Anthony was removed from the backseat of one of the vehicles and led into the building.

Maggie turned to her husband. "You can let me off here."

"What are you talking about? I'm going in with you."

She put her hand on his arm. "I'll probably be here all night. You've got a full schedule of surgeries in the morning."

John opened his mouth to protest.

Maggie raised her hand to stop him. "I can't tell you how much I appreciate your coming with me to the library, John. But we can't have Westbury's favorite veterinarian too tired to function at the top of his game. I'll be fine on my own." She pointed toward the front of the building where a young man and woman were climbing the steps to the entrance. "Josh and Sunday are here. I'll get a ride home with Josh."

John turned to his beloved wife. "I guess you're right. I have to get some sleep. My schedule tomorrow is packed."

"You need to hire another vet—your workload is off the charts."

"I know, I know." He sighed heavily. "I'm working on it. Go ahead, but keep me posted. And don't go straight to the college when you're done here. You'll need some sleep. Highpointe can do without its president for the morning."

"I promise," Maggie said, leaning over to kiss his cheek.

"Text me when you get home if I've already left for the animal hospital."

"Of course," she said as she got out of the car. She made her way through the tangle of police cars and entered the utilitarian, slump block building, large block letters stamped in stone dominating the double glass doors: WESTBURY POLICE DEPARTMENT.

Josh and Sunday were huddled together along the wall just inside the entrance. Maggie's efficient administrative assistant had a cell phone to his ear. She'd be sad to see Josh Newlon leave when he completed his graduate studies in college administration.

Maggie joined them.

"They want to question me," Sunday said, "and Josh insists that I have a lawyer with me when I talk to them." She shifted her weight from foot to foot, swaying unsteadily. "He was going to kill me! He fell off the landing, and ..."

"Josh is absolutely right. You shouldn't be talking to us, either."

"You don't think I had anything to do with this, do you?"

"I most certainly don't. We haven't worked together for very long, but I don't think my rare book librarian is involved in anything criminal. Still, you shouldn't say anything to anyone without your attorney being present." She patted Sunday's hand reassuringly. "My daughter is a lawyer, and she'd tell you the same thing."

"That's who he's calling. Susan. She helped him find his birth mother."

"I remember. Susan arranged the meeting between Josh and Lyla."

Josh rested his tall, athletic frame against the wall and stabbed at his phone screen to end the call. "Susan said she'll be here in half an hour."

"Good," Maggie said.

Sunday sagged against the wall and put her hands to her head. "I can't believe what just happened."

Chief Andy Thomas approached them. "Ms. Sloan?"

Sunday nodded.

"We'd like to take your statement."

"My ... my lawyer will be here soon," she said. "Susan Scanlon. I'd like to wait for her."

"That's fine. Let me put you in a private room until she gets here. Anthony Plume has provided a detailed statement. We just want to corroborate what he said." He regarded her carefully. "Looks like you need to sit down. I'll get you some water, too."

"That'd be nice." She pushed herself away from the wall.

"Just Ms. Sloan," the chief said when Josh began to follow her. "You can stay out here—with Maggie."

"Can't I sit with her?" Josh asked.

"It's okay," Sunday said. "I'll be fine. You should go home and get some sleep."

"I'm not leaving here without you."

"I can use your help while we're waiting for Sunday," Maggie said. She glanced at Chief Thomas and raised an eyebrow. "I suspect that Dean Plume won't be available to teach his classes tomorrow?"

"I can't comment on an ongoing investigation, but that's a safe assumption for now—and for the foreseeable future." He put his hand on Sunday's shoulder and steered her to the steel door that separated the waiting room from the interior of the police station. He waved his keycard over the keypad, the door lock clicked open, and he escorted Sunday inside and out of view.

Josh pointed to a row of molded plastic chairs, where he and Maggie each took a seat. "Who was that other guy who walked out of the library—the one you were talking to? An officer put him in a police car pretty fast. I didn't get a good look at him. What'd you say his name was?"

"Anthony Plume."

"Dean of English literature?"

Maggie nodded.

"The guy you put on the Friends of the Library Committee?"

"That's the one."

"Do you think he was part of whatever was going on with the guy that they took out on the stretcher?"

"I'm afraid so."

"The police aren't treating him like the hero who saved the day."

Maggie shrugged. "I don't know what happened in there, but I do know we've got to cover Anthony's classes." She pointed to Josh's phone. "Can you pull up the school calendar on that thing so we can see if he's got anything scheduled for tomorrow?"

Josh's fingers began flying across the screen. "Yep. A second-level class at eleven o'clock."

"Does he have a graduate assistant?"

Josh scrolled down on his screen and nodded.

"Can you find contact information for this grad student?"

"Her college email is linked on the screen."

"Great. Email this: Dean Plume will be unable to attend his eleven o'clock class. Please conduct the class and contact President Martin's office for further instructions."

Josh arched his brows at Maggie. "This is going to get the rumor mill going."

"I think the morning news will accomplish that—in spades."

Josh typed the email and tapped send. "Done."

"What about the rest of the week?"

"He's got a bunch of committee meetings. All within the department. I think he spent most of his time on administrative duties."

"We've lucked out there. It'll make his absence easier to work around."

"You don't think he'll be questioned and released?"

Maggie bit her lip. "No. I think Dean Anthony Plume won't be returning to Highpointe."

"What else can I do to help?"

"Set up a meeting between me and the chairs of the English department. For late tomorrow afternoon."

"In your office?"

Maggie nodded as Susan pushed open the door to the waiting room, allowing a blast of frigid air to precede her. She adjusted her oversized, dark-rimmed glasses on the bridge of her nose.

Josh and Maggie leaped to their feet.

"Mom! What are you doing here?" Susan blurted, unwinding a scarf and allowing her thick blond hair to cascade around her shoulders. She lifted a hand. "Never mind. Of course, you'd be here. Where's Sunday?"

"They put her in a room to wait for you. She was pretty shaken up."

"I'd tell you both to go home, that it'll be a long night and I'll call when I've got information to share, but I suspect that neither of you would listen to me."

Maggie and Josh nodded in unison.

"Let me get in there and do my job." She looked into Josh's eyes, and her expression softened. "Don't worry. You did the right thing by calling me. We'll get this sorted out."

Susan walked to the receptionist, seated behind bulletproof glass, and proffered her credentials before being admitted into the station.

CHAPTER 2

❦

Maggie paced in front of a window overlooking the police headquarters parking lot. Three cars came around the side of the building. She recognized Chief Thomas's car in the lead, his lights flashing as his vehicle entered the street and picked up speed.

"I wonder where they're going," she said to Josh.

He rose to join her at the window. The inner door to the waiting room opened, and Susan and Sunday walked out.

"Nigel Blythe is out of surgery and has regained consciousness," Susan said. "The chief is on his way to question him."

"Makes sense," Maggie said.

Josh held out his arms to Sunday, and she sank into them. "Are you all right?"

"Yes," Sunday mumbled against his shoulder.

"Anthony confessed to everything. Sunday's account of what happened in there corroborated his statement," Susan said.

Eyes wide, Maggie and Josh looked at Susan.

"Reader's Digest version: Nigel Blythe realizes Sunday has

discovered that Highpointe's stolen books are being sold out of Blythe Rare Books, his bookshop in London. So Blythe orders Anthony—who's been selling him the rare books to cover his gambling debts—to kill Sunday. When Anthony won't do it, Blythe arrives to do the deed himself. But what does Anthony do? He follows Sunday and foils a hitman's attempt to run her down in a parking lot by putting his own car in harm's way, sending him straight to the hospital with a concussion!"

"Anthony saved my life—twice today," Sunday interjected.

Susan continued. "Anthony knows Blythe won't stop, so he leaves the hospital—against doctor's orders—and takes a cab to the library. The only cars in the lot are Sunday's and Blythe's, and the library is locked. So Anthony breaks in through a basement window and runs upstairs to find Sunday struggling with Blythe on the second-story landing. Anthony attacks Blythe, who tries to push him over the railing—" Susan paused and looked at Sunday.

"I grabbed the bust of Alfred, Lord Tennyson, from that niche on the landing and hit him on the back. I wanted to break his grip on Anthony." Sunday raised both hands and splayed her fingers. "Nigel released Anthony but lost his footing—the landing was coated with something slippery. It all happened so fast. One minute he was sliding toward the railing—his arms flailing, trying to regain his balance—and the next he was tumbling over it and onto the marble floor below." She shuddered, and Josh put his arms around her again.

"You did the only thing you could do," Susan said. "Blythe intended to kill you both. The police are satisfied that you acted in self-defense."

"She's not being charged with anything?" Josh asked.

"No. Nothing at all," Susan replied.

Maggie turned to Josh and Sunday. "Why don't you both go home and try to rest?"

"The library is a crime scene, and the police will have it cordoned off at least through tomorrow," Susan said.

"I'll send out a college-wide email that the library will be closed until further notice. I'll also call Lyla and ask her to post a sign on the doors before it opens," Josh said.

"Good thinking. Thank you," Maggie said.

"I'll walk you to your car," Susan said to Maggie.

"John dropped me off," Maggie replied.

"Then I'll give you a ride home. I want to talk to you about the fallout that you're sure to face over this."

"What do you mean?" Sunday asked. "The vast majority of thefts happened years before either President Martin or I were on campus."

"I understand," Susan said, "but you were here when they were discovered."

Maggie put her hands on her temples. "That's exactly how these things work. And I was the one who appointed Anthony to the Friends of the Library committee." She shook her head. "This is going to be a nightmare!"

"I've got some ideas for how to handle the situation," Susan said.

"It'll be just like the fallout from the fraud and corruption scandal at Town Hall." Maggie moaned.

"Not this time," Susan said. "You've got people who will have your back." She moved to the entrance. "The best thing we can all do right now is get some sleep. All hell is going to break loose soon enough."

***

Susan stepped into the house from the garage, took off her shoes, and laid her purse on the kitchen counter. She looked at the digital clock on the wall oven: four fifteen. With any luck, she'd be able to get a couple of hours' sleep before her day exploded into activity.

She was padding her way quietly across the kitchen when the baby monitor crackled. She hesitated. Julia, please don't be awake, she thought. I'm exhausted.

Everything was quiet. Julia should be asleep for another hour, at least.

Despite her fatigue and better judgment, Susan slowly pushed open the door to her daughter's room and moved noiselessly to the side of the crib. Cooper was curled, nose to tail, under the crib in his usual spot. The golden retriever opened an eye as she approached and thumped his tail once.

Susan stared at her daughter's peaceful form, snug in her footed flannel onesie. She was stepping back from the crib when Julia rolled over and opened her eyes wide. She stared at her mother, then pushed herself into a sitting position. A smile lit Julia's face.

No! Now I'll never get back to sleep. Susan picked up her daughter and gave her a quick hug. "It's not time to get up yet," Susan whispered. She laid Julia back in the crib. Why, oh why, had she disturbed her?

Julia popped back up.

"No, sweetheart, time to go back to sleep." Susan walked to the door.

Cooper got to his feet and stretched, keeping his eyes trained on Susan.

Julia began to whimper. When Susan disappeared from view, Julia began to wail.

Susan paused in the hallway. Please stop, she thought.

Julia's cries became louder and more insistent.

Susan sighed heavily. She had awakened Julia and shouldn't let the baby's crying disturb her husband. Running Westbury's busiest orthopedic surgical practice, Dr. Aaron Scanlon was chronically sleep-deprived. She returned to her daughter's room.

Julia's cries filled the space. Susan reached for her.

"I'll take her."

Susan jumped at the voice that had snuck in behind her.

"Sorry," Aaron said. "You've been gone way longer than expected. I don't have to be at work until ten. Go back to bed, and I'll take care of Julia this morning."

"Really?" Susan covered her mouth to stifle a yawn.

Aaron picked up the now-quiet Julia. He leaned over and kissed his wife. "I've never known you to have a middle-of-the-night emergency," he said. "What happened?"

"You won't believe it," Susan said. "Come with me while I get out of these clothes, and I'll fill you in."

Cooper followed, stretching out at the foot of their bed. Aaron rubbed Julia's back while Susan recounted the events of the evening.

"That's incredible! Who would have thought this rural midwestern town would be so full of intrigue."

"That's for sure," Susan said, throwing back the covers and getting into bed. "It's always interesting, though. And, once again, my mother seems to be in the middle of it all."

"Surely this won't affect her much, will it? Other than finding someone to take Plume's place?"

"Don't count on that," Susan said.

Cooper rested his nose on the side of the bed. Susan patted the spot next to her, and he launched his eighty-five-pound body onto the bed.

"The board of trustees will come under tremendous scrutiny, and they'll be looking for someone to blame," Susan said. "It's usually the college president."

"That's not fair. This wasn't Maggie's fault."

"I'm afraid that won't matter." Susan settled into her pillow.

"Is there anything you can do about it? Can Alex help?"

Susan pushed herself onto her elbows. She regarded her husband. "You know, I think your brother could be tremendously helpful. That's a great idea! Alex knows everybody in town from his days as a prosecutor and now as Westbury's mayor."

"He'd do anything for your mom."

"There are others, too."

"Like?"

"Frank Haynes. Tim Knudsen. Just for starters." Susan threw her legs over the side of the bed.

"What are you doing? I thought you were going back to bed."

"Not anymore, I'm not. I'm wide awake now."

"What can I do to help?"

"Can you make coffee? I'll send some emails. Organize talking points. Then hit the phone."

"It's way too early to call anyone."

"You're right. I'll wait until six to call Alex. He's an early riser." She shoved her feet into her slippers. "He'll probably be done with his morning run by then."

"You're sure things will get as bad as all that for Maggie? You're not overreacting?"

Susan patted her thigh, and Cooper reluctantly abandoned his spot on the bed. She kissed her daughter as she slipped by Julia and Aaron. "I wish I were. Trust me—this is going to be a disaster."

CHAPTER 3

Lyla Kershaw peered through her windshield at the tidy bungalow. A cheerful twig wreath hung on the dark gray front door, which was flanked by vibrant orange pots. In a few weeks, spring would be upon them, and she knew Sunday would fill them with vibrant annuals.

Lyla checked her reflection in her rearview mirror. Her shoulder-length auburn hair was streaked with gray. She had considered visiting her salon to cover the gray, but she liked what she saw in the mirror: a woman comfortable in her mid-fifties, still fit and trim.

She took a steadying breath. Josh's call about the events at the library last night had startled her. Why would anyone want to kill Sunday? She and the young librarian had worked together since Sunday had come to the library. They'd formed an easy camaraderie on Sunday's first day that had deepened into a close friendship over the years. Now that Sunday and Josh were seeing each other, Lyla couldn't be happier.

She blinked rapidly as emotion welled up in her. Lyla still

couldn't believe her great fortune in reuniting with the son she had given up for adoption—and that this son was actually Josh Newlon. They'd become friends while taking a painting class together before they learned they were mother and son. Her life was overflowing with joy, and Lyla wasn't going to let anything derail that.

She picked up her cell phone from the passenger seat and hovered over the redial button. She'd been trying to reach Sunday since she'd hung up with Josh. When Sunday hadn't picked up, she'd gotten worried and driven over.

She unbuckled her seat belt and got out of the car. She made her way up the driveway that ran along the house to the detached garage, searching for any movement or light peeking through the closed plantation shutters. Was she being ridiculous? It was so early. Maybe Sunday was asleep. Lyla didn't want to wake her friend.

The house was dark. She was heading back to her car when, through the shutter slats of a rear window, she saw Sunday's silhouette moving in a darkened room.

Lyla stepped toward the window, raised her hand, and waved.

Sunday opened the shutter, and the two women stood looking at each other through the glass. Sunday pulled the crocheted throw that hung from her shoulders tighter around herself and motioned to the back of the house with her head.

Lyla nodded and began walking.

Sunday waited in the open doorway. She stepped aside and motioned for Lyla to follow her into her kitchen.

Lyla laid a gentle hand on Sunday's back. The young woman turned to her. Lyla threw her arms wide, and Sunday stepped into them, gasping and sobbing. Lyla held her friend in a strong embrace until Sunday's breathing calmed.

Sunday pulled back and wiped her eyes with both hands. "Sorry about that," she said in a shaky voice.

"Nonsense," Lyla said. "You've got nothing to be sorry about. I'd be doing the same thing in your shoes."

"Josh told you?"

Lyla nodded. "As much as he knew."

"I'd like to ... tell you everything," Sunday said, beginning to tremble again, "but I can't right now. I just can't."

"Of course not," Lyla said. "There's time for all of that, later. Or you never have to tell me, for that matter. I'm here because I'm worried about you and didn't want you to be alone. I tried to call, but you didn't pick up, so I decided to come and check on you."

Sunday pushed her hair out of her eyes. "My phone must be in my purse. I dropped it by the front door when I got home and went upstairs to change into my pajamas." She looked down at the black flannel pants with comical penguins marching across the fabric. "I actually thought I was going to get some sleep."

"Did you?"

"I crawled into bed, but my mind kept replaying everything in a loop as soon as I shut my eyes. It was like I was watching a horror film on a continuous feed, and I was at the center of it all."

Lyla led Sunday to the kitchen table and urged her into a chair. "I can only imagine how terrifying that was."

"I gave up on sleep and came downstairs. I thought I'd go back to bed once it was light out." Her voice cracked. "Maybe it wouldn't be so scary then."

"That's an idea." Lyla looked at the counter. Eggs, bread, and butter were laid out next to the stove. "Are you hungry?"

Sunday shrugged. "I thought if I ate something, it might help me sleep."

"Good plan. Let me scramble these eggs and make you some toast."

"Have you had breakfast?" Sunday asked. She looked at the clock on the stove. "It's not even six. Make yourself some, too. Join me."

"I will," Lyla said, lighting the burner under the pan and cracking four eggs into it. "We'll eat, and then you can try to get some sleep. I'll stay here until you wake up."

"You don't have to do that. I'm not a baby. I'll be fine—"

"You're not being a baby—you've suffered a serious trauma." She placed bread into the toaster and pushed the lever down. "I think you should see a counselor to help you cope with what's happened."

Sunday lowered her gaze to her hands in her lap. "I don't know about that."

Lyla gave the eggs a final stir and slid the pan off the hot burner. "You can decide all of that later—after you've slept." She buttered four thick slices of sourdough bread and placed them and the fluffy eggs onto two plates. She brought them to the table and took a seat opposite Sunday.

"Eat what you can," Lyla said.

Sunday tried—and failed—to smile. She picked up her fork. "You'll need to go to work when we're done."

"Nope. The library's closed today for … for obvious reasons. I've got my laptop in the car and am going to work remotely." She tapped the tabletop. "From right here. I'll stay all day so you can get some sleep."

Sunday opened her mouth to protest.

"Or we can pack you up, and you can come to my house," Lyla continued. "Wherever you feel better."

Sunday took a bite of her toast. "You're the best friend anyone could ever have."

Lyla beamed. She felt the same way about Sunday and knew that her son was smitten with this lovely woman. Hopefully, one day, Sunday would be her daughter-in-law.

CHAPTER 4

"Mommy can't take us to school." Five and a half-year-old Nicole Nash found Frank in his home office placing orders for supplies for Haynes Enterprises, the fast-food franchise holding company he owned and now ran with the help of his wife, Loretta.

"I know, sweetheart," Frank said. "Marissa said she'd help you with your breakfast and get you dressed." He didn't take his eyes from the screen. "I need to get this order placed, and then I'll drive the three of you to school."

Nicole didn't move away. "Why is Mommy so sick?" she asked in a small voice. "Is she dying?"

Frank swiveled his chair to face her, opening his arms to her. "Of course not! Mommy's got morning sickness, is all. She'll be fine—probably in a few weeks."

Nicole threw her arms around the stepfather she adored. "The baby's making Mommy sick? Is the baby sick, too?"

"The baby is fine," Frank said. "Your mother and I are going to the doctor at the end of the week for a special test called an ultrasound. We'll bring home pictures of what your brother or sister looks like in Mommy's tummy. Would you like that?"

Nicole moved her head up and down against his shoulder.

"Nicole?" Marissa called from the hallway.

"She's in here with me," Frank called back.

Marissa appeared in the doorway. "Come on, Nicole. You've got ten minutes to eat and get your clothes on. I'm in high school now, and I can't be late." She made a sweeping motion toward the door. "Get going!"

"You don't have to yell at me," Nicole said.

"I'll drop you off first, Marissa. If anyone's going to be late, it'll be her," Frank said as Nicole scampered away. "She's worried about your mother."

"I know," Marissa said. "Morning sickness doesn't sound like it's any fun. Mom's fine, though, isn't she?"

"Completely."

"I'll round up Sean, and we'll be ready to go."

"You've been a tremendous help through all of this, Marissa. Your mom and I appreciate it more than we can say."

Marissa blushed. "Thanks. I'll let you finish so we can get out of here."

CHAPTER 5

Maggie looked at the six faces turned to her and felt a surge of warmth. The senior members of the English department who crowded around the small conference table in her office were a capable and committed lot. She leaned forward in her chair. "I can't tell you how impressed I am that you've already made a plan to cover Dean Plume's absence."

"The graduate student you emailed last night has been in several of my classes and contacted me early this morning," said a gray-haired man with a ruddy complexion. "Anthony's arrest was also all over the news this morning."

"By the time we got in, we all knew that we'd have to divvy up his work to keep the department running," a woman said. "We don't want any students—or the reputation of the department—to be affected."

Maggie lifted the stack of papers the woman had handed to her when the group arrived. "When did you have time to get all of this decided—much less put down on paper?"

"We canceled our lunch plans and met to work this out. By the time we had to break at two, we'd settled on everything."

Maggie's tired smile radiated around the room. "As I said, I'm most impressed. And grateful that you've taken this on."

The man seated to her right lifted the lid from the cut-glass candy dish in the middle of the table. He helped himself to a piece of Werther's Original candy and passed the dish to the person next to him.

"We figured you'd be busy with other aspects of ... whatever this is," another woman said.

"I'm sorry I can't say more," Maggie began when she was interrupted by a knock on the door.

Her administrative assistant pushed the door open without waiting for an invitation. "Excuse me, President Martin," he said.

Maggie drew her brows together. Josh never addressed her by her title. "We're almost through—"

An imposing man in an impeccable suit pushed past Josh.

Maggie got to her feet.

The chairman of the board of trustees ignored the others and spoke directly to Maggie. "The trustees would like a word with you. Now."

Maggie inwardly bristled. Who did he think he was, barging in on her like this—treating her like a truant child? She calmly smoothed her skirt.

The members of the English department remained motionless.

"How nice to see you. Certainly." She turned to Josh. "Would you show the trustees to our boardroom? And would you mind making coffee?"

Josh nodded.

The members of the department began to gather their things.

"We're almost done with our meeting," Maggie said to the trustee in clipped tones. "I'll be with you in a few minutes."

The trustee turned on his heel and strode out of the room. Josh followed in his wake.

"We can finish up later," said one of the professors.

"I don't think you should keep them waiting," said one of the women, giving Maggie a worried look.

"As I said, I'll be with them when we're finished here. Your time is valuable, especially now that you're all taking on more responsibilities." She pointed to the papers. "I think you've considered everything. I approve of your plan. Don't hesitate to contact me if issues arise as you begin to implement this. I don't feel the need to meddle in the way you run your department, but I want to help if you need me."

Maggie stepped to the door of her office and shook every hand as the professors filed out of her office. She inhaled slowly, then went to her desk. She knew from her late husband's tenure as president of Windsor College, an impromptu visit from the board of trustees was never good news. Pulling her lipstick out of her desk drawer, she swiped on a fresh dash of color and checked her hair in her hand mirror. She might be exhausted from her sleepless night, but she didn't need to look it.

***

Josh looked up to find Maggie striding toward his desk.

"They're in there," he nodded his head toward a room down the hall.

"How many of them?"

"Nine."

"That's all of the trustees." She raised her eyebrows. "They all made time to come here—on such short notice?"

Josh nodded.

"What's the tone in the room?"

He shifted uncomfortably in his chair and opened his mouth to speak.

"Never mind. I can guess." She sighed heavily. "Susan warned me." She glanced at the bleak expression on Josh's face. "Don't worry about me. I've been through worse—especially as mayor of Westbury."

"I put coffee and water in the room. Do you think you'll need anything else?"

"No. Thank you. That should do it. It's after five—you can leave now."

He shook his head. "If it's all the same, I'm staying right here until they leave."

"You don't have to do that. I'm sure you didn't get any more sleep last night than I did. Go on, get out of here. I can handle this on my own." Maggie held her head high as she walked to the conference room.

Josh watched the door close behind Maggie before he picked up his cell phone and scrolled to Susan's number.

She picked up on the third ring.

"You just caught me. I was about to pack it in for the day. What's going on?"

"I think the you-know-what has hit the fan—just like you predicted."

"Why do you say that?"

"The entire board of trustees just showed up here—unannounced—and demanded to see your mom."

Susan sucked in her breath. "You're right. That's not good. What did Mom do?"

"She was in the middle of a meeting with members of the English department. The chairman of the board barged right in and demanded to see her. She told him she'd be with him when she was done."

Susan chuckled. "Good for her. She's not one to let herself be bullied."

"You should've seen his face when he left her office after being told to wait." Josh lowered his voice. "Furious. I think she made things worse for herself."

"Don't worry about my mom. She knows how to handle herself."

"She's in there with them now. I just thought you'd want to know."

The line remained silent.

"Susan?"

"I'm here," she said. "Just thinking. Are you heading home now?"

"No. I'm going to stay until they leave. In case Maggie needs me for anything."

"Thank you, Josh. That's very thoughtful of you. I think I'll swing by, too. See you soon."

CHAPTER 6

Sean heard a familiar "woof woof" coming from the end of the hallway on his right. The kennels of Forever Friends, Westbury's no-kill animal shelter, were at the other end of the building. It must be Dodger. He headed down the hall in search of the dog and his master.

"Hey, David," Sean said to the tall, lanky teen.

Sean knelt to greet Dodger, the mid-sized mixed breed who was David Wheeler's constant companion.

David had adopted the one-eyed dog from Forever Friends after his father's jailhouse suicide. William Wheeler's convictions for fraud and embezzlement while he was mayor of Westbury had demoralized David. His father's death had devastated him.

The grief-stricken teen had landed in the juvenile court system after stealing from his high school. Glenn Vaughn, his court-appointed mentor, had been a godsend. The older man not only recognized the boy's pain, but also his potential, and wanted to help. Glenn was the one who insisted that David get a dog.

As often happens with rescue dogs, it was hard to say who saved whom. Dodger brought purpose and happiness back into David's life, and David brought safety and tenderness to the abused stray's. Together, they learned to trust again and discovered the joys of serving others as a therapy dog team.

Dodger touched his cold nose to Sean's cheek and swiped his tongue over the boy's ear.

Sean laughed and reached in his pocket for a dog treat. "Daisy won't mind if I give you one of hers," he said. Then he noticed that David hadn't taken his eyes off his computer screen. "What're you looking at?"

David glanced up and grinned at the seventh grader. David had been showing him the ropes around Forever Friends so that Sean could step into David's shoes if David went away to California to become a guide dog trainer. Like David, Sean was hard-working, responsible, and had an instinctive rapport with animals. "Come around and see," David said. "I'm watching videos of service dogs in action. It's incredible."

Sean stood behind David and leaned over his shoulder.

"This one shows a Lab-golden mix calming down a veteran with PTSD. He was having a panic attack."

The two boys watched the video with rapt attention.

"Cool," Sean said.

"I'm going to learn how to train guide dogs," David said, "if I get admitted to the program."

"You will. Dad says you're a shoo-in."

"What'd I say?" Frank asked from the doorway. The dimly lit hallway behind him could have been in any office building, but the faint, earthy smell of dogs identified the location.

"That David is going to get into that guide dog training school in California."

"Without a doubt," Frank said. "Are you worried about that, David?"

David shrugged. "I haven't heard back from them. They're supposed to contact me to schedule an in-person interview."

"I've never seen anyone with a more intuitive connection with dogs," Frank said. "Or a better trainer. How long ago did you apply?"

"A week ago."

"Give it time. I'm sure you'll hear from them soon." Frank turned to Sean and held up a stack of papers with his right hand. "I've got what I need. Let's go. Your mother hasn't felt good all day, and I'm going to make dinner, but we have to stop by Highpointe first."

Sean reluctantly tore himself away from the video. "How long will that take?"

"I've got to feed and walk the dogs," David interjected. "We're almost full here. Can Sean help me? I'll bring him home when we're done. Shouldn't take more than an hour. Will that work?"

Frank studied Sean. "I think that'd be fine. Do you want to stay here?" he asked his stepson. He could see by the expression on Sean's face that he did.

"Sure," Sean said. "If I'm going to take over for David when he's in California, I need to start training now. David does a lot around here."

Frank suppressed a smile. "That he does. Thank you, David. Why don't you—and Dodger—stay for dinner? The only thing I know how to cook is steak, and I have an extra one."

David's eyes lit up. "I'd love to." He rose and motioned for

Sean to follow him. "Let's get started, so we won't be late for dinner."

***

Mayor Alex Scanlon plucked a speck of lint from his suit coat and smoothed his impeccably cut hair as he waited at the entrance to the Highpointe College administration building. He checked his watch. The others would be there soon.

He was reading email messages on his phone when someone touched the back of his shoulder. He turned to see Frank Haynes.

The two men regarded each other warily.

"Thank you for calling me, Alex."

Alex shrugged.

"I know you still don't trust me, but I've changed." He glanced to the ground, then looked into the distance. "I'm not the same man that got involved with Delgado and his cronies. I'm here because Maggie had a lot to do with changing my life for the better."

"I agree with you on that score."

"I've got a wife and stepkids that I love. And"—his voice cracked—"Loretta and I are expecting."

Alex brought his head up. "I hadn't heard." He hesitated, then extended his hand. "Congratulations."

Frank took his hand. "Thank you. I'll do anything I can to show support for Maggie."

"I hope we can prevent any of the negative ramifications that may come her way from all of this," Alex said.

The men turned at the sound of their names. A tall, elegantly dressed woman was approaching them.

"How did you find out we were meeting?" Alex asked Councilwoman Tonya Holmes.

"Seriously?" Tonya scoffed. "You think you can keep a secret in this town? I came with Pete Fitzpatrick. He's parking the car."

"I thought that Pete, as chairman of the Westbury Merchant's Association, might want to be here," Frank said.

"Good idea." Alex nodded his approval.

"I was having a late lunch at Pete's Bistro this afternoon when Pete got the call from Frank," Tonya said.

"Did you tell anyone else?" Frank asked.

"I checked in with John at the animal hospital. Judy Young was scheduled to bring in her cat this afternoon. He said he'd mention this meeting to her."

"Sheesh," Alex said. "We may as well have hired a blimp to fly over town with a banner. Judy is the modern-day equivalent of the town crier."

Tonya chuckled. "I wouldn't deny that."

"Here come the reinforcements," Frank said, pointing to the parking lot across from the administration building.

The three of them watched as Pete, along with the octogenarian couple, Glenn Vaughn and Gloria Harper from Fairview Terraces, and Maggie's oldest and dearest friends in Westbury, Sam and Joan Torres, made their way to them.

"Anyone else en route?" Frank asked.

"Just Councilman Tim Knudsen," Tonya said. "I might have mentioned this when I ran into him at Town Hall." Her eyes sparkled. "Judy will come as soon as she closes up Celebrations."

"What's the plan?" Pete asked when he joined them.

Alex held up his hand as Tim Knudsen and Susan Scanlon

came around the corner, followed closely by Judy. "I'm glad we're all here to support Maggie," he said.

"What's all this about?" Sam asked. "I read an article in this morning's paper about a long-running theft of rare books from the Highpointe Library. The investigation's ongoing but they believe most of the books were stolen more than ten years ago."

"Apparently there was an altercation in the library last night that left one man in critical condition." Pete added.

"I heard this afternoon that the man in the hospital was trying to kill a librarian," Judy supplied, "and that there was a professor involved."

Gloria gasped. "At our college library?"

"What does this have to do with Maggie?" Joan looked to Alex and then Susan.

Susan sighed. "You know how these things go. The school will be criticized for negligence for not securing the collection before thefts occurred. And someone's going to have to take the blame. I warned Mom."

"That's ridiculous," Glenn said. "Why do you think that's what's going on?"

"The entire board of trustees showed up about an hour ago," Susan said. "The chairman of the board stormed into Mom's office, interrupting a meeting she was having with the English department, and summoned her into the boardroom with the trustees."

Tim sucked air through his teeth. "That doesn't sound good."

"I'd like to be our spokesperson, if that's okay," Alex said. "We don't know exactly what's going on with Maggie right now, but we want the board to know that she has wide support throughout the community. We're not going to stand by and let them make her into their political scapegoat."

"I agree," Susan said. "Our presence when they emerge from this meeting will speak volumes. Since I'm her daughter, they won't listen to anything I have to say. Alex—as the Mayor of Westbury—will be the most persuasive person to address them."

"Are we all agreed?" Alex asked.

The group nodded.

"I'd like to give them a piece of my mind if they're going after Maggie," Judy huffed. "I've known most of those trustees my entire life. Their fancy jobs and expensive suits don't intimidate me."

"There'll be time for that later," Alex said. "Not now, all right? We don't want to make things worse for Maggie." He held Judy's gaze.

"Oh, all right. I'll keep my mouth shut."

"Thank you," Alex said. "Let's get in there."

The group of supporters entered the building and found Josh waiting for them outside Maggie's office.

"The boardroom is down the hall, second door on the right." Josh led the way.

They lined up in the hallway outside of the boardroom. They didn't have long to wait.

Seven unsmiling men and two stern-looking women filed out a few minutes later. Maggie brought up the rear. Her countenance appeared calm and unruffled, but those who knew her well could tell by the set of her shoulders that she was angry.

Maggie's eyes widened as she took in the sight of her friends, waiting in the hallway.

Alex stepped forward and addressed the man he recognized as chairman of the board. "Good afternoon," he said. "We represent a cross-section of the citizens of Westbury. We've known President Martin for years, and many of us—myself included—

worked with her to uncover and repair the fraud and corruption at Town Hall that almost bankrupted Westbury."

The trustees stood in steely silence.

"We understand that Highpointe College is beginning to deal with its own scandals and criminal activity. We're here to show our support for President Martin and our confidence in her ability to bring the college through this challenging time." Alex looked at each trustee in turn. "You could have no better person at the helm to lead the college right now."

"We're not in a position to discuss this with you," the chairman said. He spun to Maggie and glowered at her. The set of the man's shoulders changed when he turned back to Alex. "Thank you for your concern. President Martin has the support of the trustees at this time."

He brushed past Alex and made his way to the exit. The other board members followed.

When the door closed behind them, Maggie flung her arms wide. "I cannot believe you did this. Talk about a sight for sore eyes!"

"We all love you," Gloria said. "You saved Fairview Terraces from foreclosure when you were mayor. Glenn and I would have lost our home without your help."

"We've got your back," Sam said. "No one is going to dump on you."

Tears welled in Maggie's eyes as she looked at the gentle face of the first person she'd met in Westbury, on that fateful evening when she'd been snowed in at the stately manor home known as Rosemont. Sam had been taking care of Rosemont for her late husband, Paul, and had opened the house for her. She'd planned to take a quick look at the place before putting it up for sale. All that changed after the first night she spent in the house that would become her home and lead her into a new life. She'd surprised her adult children when she had uprooted her life and moved to Westbury, where she'd known no one. It had proved to be the best decision she'd ever made.

Sam had become her handyman and, later, her confidant and encourager as she coped with Paul's infidelities and betrayals. Both she and the Windsor College trustees learned after Paul's death that he had been embezzling funds while he was president of the college. She'd settled Paul's debt to the college for the amount of his life insurance policy. Her negotiations with the Windsor trustees crowded her mind now. That situation shed light on what to expect from the trustees in her current plight.

"Was it brutal in there?" Susan asked.

Maggie shrugged. "About what I expected. They're concerned about covering their own behinds."

"Typical," Frank said.

"Nothing I haven't seen or dealt with before," Maggie said. "Still, you can't know how uplifting it was to see you all standing here when I walked out."

"You should've seen their faces," Pete said. "They were shocked."

"Were they going to remove you as president?" Tim asked.

"Not today," Maggie said, "but they were hinting at it."

"We're all here for you," Tonya said. "Don't forget that."

"And I couldn't be more grateful. There's still a lot of work—"

"Maggie," Josh interrupted her. "I just took a call for you from Chief Thomas."

All eyes spun to the young man.

"Nigel Blythe died—in the hospital—fifteen minutes ago."

CHAPTER 7

Josh put his hand on the vase of tulips riding on the passenger seat to steady it as he turned the corner onto Sunday's street. He pulled to the curb and breathed a sigh of relief at the sight of the familiar car in Sunday's driveway. He should have known that Lyla would have gone to check on her.

He'd been trying to reach Sunday all day, to no avail, and had grown increasingly worried. Maggie's meeting with the trustees had run late, and he was beyond anxious to leave by the time he finally reached his car. He had almost been too impatient to stop at the supermarket, but the lot wasn't full, and he was in and out with his purchases in under ten minutes. He wanted Sunday to know he cared, and the small fuzzy teddy bear that was sitting in the floral section, holding a book under its arm, was perfect for a librarian.

Josh grabbed the flowers and the bear and dashed to Sunday's front door. He was about to knock when Lyla opened it.

She grinned when she saw what he held in his hands. "Look at you! Those are lovely," she said, eyeing the tulips. "My favorite."

"I hope she'll like them."

"Of course she will. Let's put them on the kitchen table. Come in."

He followed her to the kitchen. "I also got this," he said, wiggling the bear. "Do you ... do you think it's too childish?"

Lyla put her arm around his shoulders and squeezed. "It's adorable, and she's going to love it."

Josh looked around. "Is she here?"

"She's upstairs, taking a shower. I came over early, and she'd been too upset to sleep. I made us some breakfast, and she went back to bed after she ate."

"That was awfully nice of you."

Lyla raised an eyebrow at him. "I've been very fond of this girl for a lot longer than you have. I was concerned about her. I brought my laptop and worked here all day while she slept."

"Are you staying the night?"

"No. She woke up about thirty minutes ago and said she felt much better. She asked me to wait while she took her shower, and then I was going to go home."

"Do you think she should be alone?"

"She'll be just fine alone," Sunday said, rubbing her wet hair with a towel as she entered the room.

Josh and Lyla turned to her.

Josh experienced the jolt he always felt when he looked at Sunday. Her hazel eyes that shone violet in daylight were dark against her damp blond hair. Her face, unadorned by makeup, was luminous. She smiled at Josh, and his heart expanded.

"I was wondering how you were. I tried to call."

"I put my phone on silent and slept all day," Sunday said. "Lyla's orders."

"I'm glad," Josh said. "Best thing you could have done." He pointed to the vase of tulips. "I brought you these. I wasn't sure if you'd like them or not."

"Are you kidding? I love spring flowers. They're beautiful." She touched his elbow. "That was very thoughtful of you."

Josh took the teddy bear out from under his arm and handed it to her. "I got you this, too."

Sunday laughed softly.

"I thought it looked like a librarian bear."

She hugged the bear to her chest and nuzzled it with her chin. "She is, indeed. I love her. I haven't had a teddy bear in years."

Lyla looked between the two of them. "I think this is the perfect time for me to get going."

"I thought we were going to get takeout when I came downstairs," Sunday said.

"I just remembered that I can't," Lyla said. "I've got a … a neighbor I should visit in the hospital."

Sunday rolled her eyes. "Are you sure?"

"Positive." Lyla snatched her coat from the back of a kitchen chair and headed for the door. "Why don't the two of you order dinner?"

"I'd like that," Josh said quickly.

Lyla turned back to them, one hand on the door handle. "My offer still stands. If you decide you don't want to stay here tonight, just give me a call. My guest room's always made up and ready."

"That won't be necessary," Sunday said. "I'm fine now. Thank you for being here this afternoon. It helped."

Lyla and Josh exchanged glances. "All the same, the offer's open."

"Thank you," Josh mouthed before Lyla turned and went out the door.

"Can I keep you two ladies company tonight?" he asked, glancing at the bear still clutched to her chest. "How about I order a pizza, and we watch a movie? Your choice of both."

Sunday held the bear out at arm's length. "What do you think, Miss Marian? Should we let him stay?"

"You've named her already?"

"It's the logical choice."

Josh furrowed his brow.

"After the librarian in The Music Man," Sunday said. "One of my favorite movies of all time."

Josh shrugged.

"You've never seen The Music Man?"

"Nope."

"It's a classic. I have a copy around here somewhere." She placed Miss Marian on the coffee table and opened a trunk she used as an end table. "It's time to correct this deficit in your education. We'll watch it tonight." She looked at him over the lid of the trunk. "Are you sure you meant it when you said I could pick?"

Josh nodded his agreement. If he could sit close to her on the sofa for two hours, he didn't care what they watched.

CHAPTER 8

David Wheeler scooted past Dodger and dumped the contents of a plastic bin of outdated records into the shredder bin. He was happy that John Allen, DVM, was modernizing Westbury Animal Hospital by putting all its patient records online. The file room would now become an additional surgery. If David accomplished his dream of founding a service dog training school in Westbury, the animal hospital would need the extra treatment capacity.

Sean approached him, carrying a dilapidated cardboard box, torn and stained, its flaps frayed. "This isn't full of papers," he said. "We can't put this stuff in the shredder bin."

Sean set the box on the ground and opened the flaps. Collars of every size and description were stuffed into the box.

David knelt and began to rummage through them.

"Do you think these belonged to pets that … that they had to put to sleep? Or that died?" Sean asked.

"That'd be my guess. They must have kept them in case their owners wanted them back." David pulled out a red plaid collar with a heart-shaped tag and read the name. "Sunny. And there's an address and phone number, too."

"Should we just toss them?" Sean asked.

David pursed his lips, thinking. "Not yet. At least not the ones with tags. Maybe we can contact the people who live there—see if they owned the pet and want the collars back." He looked at Sean. "What do you think?"

"If it were Daisy or Snowball or Sally, I'd want their collar back," Sean said. "I'll help you find them," he offered. "If they've moved, maybe we can track them online."

"That's a great idea." David high-fived the boy. "Good thinking."

They continued to pull collars out of the box and sort them. All but two had tags.

"What's that red cloth thing at the bottom of the box?" Sean asked.

David plucked it out and shook it. He held a red winter coat by the hem. He shifted it around in his hands until he grasped it by the collar.

"It's small," Sean said, eyeing the coat.

"It's a woman's coat. Looks old."

"What's that shiny thing?"

"It's a pin." David fingered the piece of jewelry on the lapel. "Looks like a fancy bow with a bunch of diamonds in the center. My great-grandmother wore stuff like this."

"Do you think it's valuable?"

David shrugged. "I have no idea. Let's give it to John. He'll know what to do with it."

"We're still going to find the owners of the dogs that belonged to these collars, aren't we?"

"We sure are. I'll let you tell John about our plan since you found the box. He'll be impressed."

Sean stood up straighter, and David could tell the boy was pleased by this opportunity to shine in front of John. David felt a surge of warmth for his young friend. He'd learned a thing or two about how to treat other people from Glenn Vaughn. Glenn had been endlessly kind and supportive of David as his court-appointed mentor.

David handed the coat to Sean. "Let's go find John."

***

John watched his wife place her laptop on the desk in Rosemont's library and toe off her pumps as she grasped the back of the chair. Maggie stifled a yawn. "I really should spend another couple of hours working," she said, her shoulders sagging.

John patted the spot next to him on the sofa. "I think you've done enough work for one day."

Maggie scooped Blossom up from her usual spot next to John. The cat squeaked in protest, and John held out his hands to take her from Maggie. "She's always liked you best," Maggie said as she flopped down and tucked her slim frame under her husband's arm. "After everything that's gone on over the last few days, I want to veg out in front of the TV for an hour and then go to bed."

John drew her closer. "I think that's an excellent idea." He picked up the remote. "I'll bet you're not hankering to watch sports."

"I don't want to interrupt if you're watching the game."

"I'll record it and watch it later if I feel like it." He clicked the remote. "If I know you, you'd like to watch one of those home renovation shows."

Maggie kissed his neck. "You're so smart. And you're interested in them too, aren't you?"

"That's a deep, dark secret, okay?"

"You've got it." Maggie signaled for Eve to join them. Her terrier mix rose from her bed in front of the fireplace, stretched, and hopped up next to Maggie. Eve never declined an invitation to cuddle.

Maggie stroked her faithful companion and sank into the cushions, then quickly leaned forward. "What's that red thing draped over the arm of the chair by the French doors? It looks like a coat."

"It is," John said. "David and Sean found it stuffed in the bottom of a box of old collars when they were cleaning out the file room."

"There's something sparkly on it."

"That's why I brought it home," John said. "I wanted to show it to you. It's a very fancy pin."

"Someone must have left their coat behind. Can you find the owner?"

"That's highly unlikely. The box it was buried in was shoved in a corner of the file room. It probably hasn't been opened in over ten years—maybe even twenty years or longer."

Maggie began to rise.

"Don't get up," John said. "I'll bring it to you."

He retrieved the coat and handed it to Maggie.

She ran her hand over the fabric and noted the label. Her eyes grew wide. "This says it's a Christian Dior." She held out the coat so he could read the label.

"Wow," John replied. "Even I've heard of Christian Dior. Do you think this is the real thing? Aren't there a lot of knockoffs out there?"

"I have no idea," Maggie said. "I'll have to do some research. Anita Archer at Archer Bridal might know."

John pointed to the pin. "What do you make of this?"

Maggie sucked in her breath. "It's stunning."

"Do you think it's real? Like ... those are diamonds?"

Maggie took the coat to the desk and switched on the lamp, clicking the three-way bulb to its brightest setting. She fished a magnifying glass from the lap drawer and began studying the pin.

Clear baguette-cut gems lined the double-looped bow, and an arc of marquises surrounded a cluster of round stones in the center. Maggie counted them. "Seven rounds and eleven marquises. I'm no expert, but I'd guess they were each at least a half carat."

John shrugged. "I'd have no idea."

Maggie continued her inspection. "The color and sparkle on these stones are breathtaking."

"Do you think they're real diamonds?"

"Again, I'm no expert, but I think they might be." She set the magnifying glass on the desk and removed the pin. "The fastener is a double pin fitting." She held out the pin to John. "These two pins pierce the fabric. Fine brooches are made this way because they're more secure and hold a heavy pin—like this one—in place on a garment."

"You seem to know a lot about this."

"Only because I'm interested. A pin like this—if these are real diamonds—would be way out of my price range."

"You may have one of these pins now. I can't imagine that we'd ever be able to find the person who left the coat at the hospital."

"If this is as valuable as I think it might be, we should try to find the owner."

"How much do you think it's worth?"

"If these diamonds are real, I'm guessing at least thirty or forty thousand dollars."

John whistled softly.

Roman, who had been sleeping on the hearth rug, lifted his head off his paws.

"And if this pin was made by a major jeweler, the value could be much higher."

John and Maggie stared at each other.

"I think this was a very good week for David and Sean to find this coat," John said. "Now, you have something fun to focus on."

Maggie shrugged. "I've got to come up with a plan to restore our stolen rare books to Highpointe's library. That's my first priority."

"Understood," he said. "This pin has been sitting, undetected, for years. It can wait a while longer."

She set the pin on the desk and ran her fingers over the stones. "It's beautifully finished," she said. "No sharp or jagged edges. It feels like quality." She looked up at John. "I think I could find time to take this to Harriet at Burman Jewelers. She'll know if it's real."

"Excellent plan," John said.

Blossom hopped onto the desk and sauntered over to the pin. She cautiously extended one paw and swiped at the shiny object, sending the pin flying off the desk.

John lunged and caught it before it hit the floor.

"Well done," Maggie said. "I'm impressed."

"I guess I haven't lost all skills as a wide receiver."

"I'd have had such a crush on you in high school," Maggie said. "A jock and a smart guy, too."

John blushed. "If I'd have met you in high school, I'd never have let you marry that idiot Paul Martin."

Maggie kissed his cheek. She took the pin from him and replaced it on the lapel, folding the coat carefully so that the pin was hidden on the inside. "No point in advertising it," she said.

She walked to the sofa and picked up her phone. Maggie scrolled to her calendar and her countenance lightened. "I have an opening in my schedule day after tomorrow. I'll drop by Burman's then." She grinned at John.

"That's my gal. Always making time for the important things."

"Are you making fun of me?"

"No! Not at all." He put his arms around her. "I'm thrilled that you've got this distraction."

Maggie yawned again.

Eve and Roman circled at their feet.

"I'm too tired to watch television now. And these guys"—she pointed to the two dogs—"think it's time to go outside and then head for bed."

"I'm bushed, too," John said, turning off the TV. He and Maggie linked arms and walked out the kitchen door. They huddled together in the cool night air, watching the dogs race into the back garden, awash in moonlight.

CHAPTER 9

Maggie and Sunday hunched over Sunday's laptop, perched on the small conference table in Maggie's office.

"To the best of my knowledge, this is a comprehensive list of the volumes I believe are missing from our rare book collection," Sunday said.

Maggie rose and walked to her window overlooking the quadrangle. Sidewalks crisscrossed the lawn that was wakening from its winter dormancy. Students laden with bulging backpacks hurried along to afternoon classes. She put her hands on the small of her back and stretched. "We can't tell when the books might have gone missing?"

"Other than the Tennyson volume that started our investigation and our Gone with the Wind volume, no." Sunday sighed heavily. "The others may have been missing for decades. Hector Martin donated his collection in the seventies. They sat in boxes in the basement of the library for years. When they were finally placed on shelves, they were out in the open. We didn't have the Hazel Harrington Rare Book Room secured until a year ago."

"And some might not have been stolen. They could have been taken out and simply not returned."

"That's true," Sunday said. "It happens."

"This list gives us a place to start. I'm not sure how we'll ever find any of these volumes—much less recover them. I'll need to give this list to the trustees. They've been hounding me."

"I'm so sorry that I can't give you something more definite," Sunday said. "It's very unfair that they're blaming you."

"I'm the one who appointed Anthony to the Friends of the Library Committee." Maggie clawed her hand through her hair. "I let the fox into the hen house, as it were."

"There's no way you could have known what he was up to," Sunday said. "At the time, he seemed like the best, most logical choice to help me."

"Just try telling that to the trustees."

"Maybe we can get some of the books back. I'd like to go through the inventory of Blythe Rare Books," Sunday said. "Some of these may still be in the shop."

"I'd like that, too," Maggie said. "The fact that it's located in London makes it difficult."

"Nigel was the sole proprietor. I wonder what's happened to the shop, now that he's died."

"I asked Chief Thomas if he could find out for us," Maggie said.

Both women turned at the sound of a loud knocking on Maggie's office door.

"Come in," Maggie called.

Josh pushed the door open, and Chief Thomas stepped into the room.

"Speak of the devil." Maggie smiled at the chief as she rose to meet him. "Were your ears burning? We've been talking about you."

"Only good things, I hope," he replied.

"Always," Maggie assured him. "You remember Sunday, don't you?" Maggie swung her arm in Sunday's direction, and the young librarian began to get out of her chair.

"Sit, please," the chief said. "Of course, I remember. I'm glad you're here. You'll both want to hear this."

Sunday sank back into her seat, and Maggie pulled out the chair next to her. The chief joined them.

"Nigel spoke to the police before he died."

Maggie and Sunday remained silent, waiting for him to continue.

"He said that he killed Hazel Harrington—and that he tried to kill," he swung to Sunday, "you. He also indicated that Anthony Plume wasn't involved in Hazel's murder or your attempted murder."

Sunday gave a tight-lipped smile. "Anthony may have stolen books, but he risked his life—twice—to save mine."

"So it appears," the chief said.

"Poor Hazel. All this time—and no one knew. Have you told her family?"

The chief nodded. "They're shocked and upset."

"I need to reach out to them. What about the stolen books?" Maggie asked. "Did he mention them?"

The chief shook his head. "Nigel died after he uttered those few confessions."

"What'll happen to his bookstore?" Sunday asked.

"I just spoke to my counterpart in London," he said. "Blythe Rare Books remains closed for business. The hospital gave me the phone number of Nigel's next of kin—a cousin who lives in Nottingham."

"Did this cousin inherit the shop?" Maggie asked.

"He inherited everything," the chief said. "Nigel never married. He had no children and no siblings. His cousin hasn't had any contact with Nigel for decades and was horrified to hear what Nigel confessed to."

"I can imagine," Sunday said.

"I filled him in on our suspicion that Nigel was selling books stolen from the Highpointe College Library."

"What did he say to that?" Maggie asked.

"He seemed stunned by the whole thing," the chief said. "Said he wanted to talk to his solicitor and that she'd need to confirm what I was telling him, but that he'd cooperate with us in restoring anything to the college that you can prove was stolen."

"That's very reasonable," Maggie said.

"That's what I thought," the chief said. "He gave me the phone number of his solicitor."

"Have you spoken to her?"

"Deidre Hyde-Jones said that her client has instructed her to work with us. She said that he's elderly and frail and won't be coming to London to sort this out. He's leaving it to her," the chief said. "She's requested a list of what we believe may be in the shop. She'll also go through the old ledgers to see if she can ascertain whether any of the books were sold."

"That's promising," Sunday said. "We just went over a spreadsheet containing details of all the books we suspect were stolen."

"Can you forward that to me?"

"Sure," Sunday said. "I'd like to go over it one last time, and then I'll send it to you."

"Deidre said she doesn't know anything about rare books, so she's hired an expert in the field to help her. The plan is to sell off the inventory and close the store," the chief continued. "She intends to do this in the next few months. She asked if someone from the college could go through the inventory at the bookstore with the person she's hired."

"We can send you back to London," Maggie said to Sunday. "If you feel like you're up to it."

The chief looked at Sunday. "How are you doing in the aftermath of that horrible night in the library?"

"It was rough at first, but Josh and his mom—she's one of my coworkers and a close friend—have been wonderful the past couple months. They've been keeping track of me. I'd be lying if I said I'm not still rattled by it all, but I'll be all right." Sunday turned to Maggie. "I'd love to go back to London."

"If you're sure. It sounds like this might be a big undertaking. How long do you think you'd have to be gone?"

Sunday tapped her chin with her index finger. "Ten days? Maybe longer. Let me get this spreadsheet into the chief's hands, and then I'll make arrangements."

"We've got a solid plan," Maggie said, relief evident in her voice. "And I've got something concrete to report to the trustees." She rose and walked to the door, followed by the others.

"Thank you for coming to deliver the good news in person," she said to the chief before redirecting her attention back to Sunday. "Let me know as soon as you've made your travel arrangements," she said.

Maggie was smiling as she shut the door behind them.

CHAPTER 10

"Where are we headed?" Sunday asked as Josh merged onto the winding rural highway that skirted the Shawnee River.

"You'll see soon enough."

"Very mysterious, aren't we? Am I dressed properly? You said to wear layers, but that we'll also be somewhere fancy. What does that mean?"

"Is the suspense driving you crazy?"

"A little bit," Sunday admitted.

Josh slowed his car and swung onto the long driveway to the town's most venerable restaurant, The Mill.

Sunday leaned forward in her seat as the imposing stone building that had served as the local sawmill a century ago came into view. "It's so handsome, isn't it? Look at those beams and the gables on the roof. They didn't cut corners back then, did they?"

Josh parked and looked up at the structure. "I'm glad they

made it into a restaurant and inn—saved it from the wrecking ball."

"This place is so ..." She searched for the right words.

"Solid and enduring," Josh supplied.

Sunday nodded.

"Since you're going to be gone for the next two weeks, gallivanting around London—"

"I won't be gallivanting. I'll be holed up in a dusty old bookstore, culling through the inventory"—a smile crept across her face—"and loving every minute of it."

"I wanted to make our last date before you left memorable." He walked around the car to open her door. "I don't want this rare book expert to sweep you off your feet."

Sunday tucked her hand into his elbow as they walked toward the inn. "Are you worried about that?"

"I'd be worried about any man you were going to spend two weeks with—discussing something you both love."

"We don't even know if this expert is a male or female." She arched her brows as she looked at him.

"There's that," Josh said. "I jumped to conclusions."

"This expert is probably one of the other rare book sellers in London, and most likely is a thousand years old."

They rounded the building and stopped to look at the skating rink set up on the riverbank. The late afternoon sun had sunk below the horizon, and stars were beginning to emerge in the night sky. A handful of skaters circled the ice.

Sunday sucked in the crisp air. "That looks like so much fun."

"Good. I'm glad you think so because we've got an hour before our dinner reservation, and I thought we could go skating."

Sunday shrieked. "For real? Brilliant!"

Josh grinned and led her to the skate rental window. They gave the teenager behind the counter their shoe sizes and took the skates to a bench at the edge of the rink.

"Seriously, this is a genius idea."

Josh finished lacing his skates and stood, holding out his hand to her. "I take it you can skate?"

"Roller skate. I've never ice skated before, but it can't be all that different." She stood and stepped onto the rink, immediately losing her footing.

Josh caught her and slipped his arm around her waist to steady her.

Sunday laughed. "Okay, I'm wrong. It's way different than roller skates."

"Just hang onto me. I'll steer us."

Sunday tightened her grip on his arm, and Josh pushed off. They glided forward together.

"You're good," Sunday said.

"I played ice hockey in school. I should have asked if you could skate before we came out here, but I got the idea to surprise you from Maggie."

"This was her suggestion?"

"I asked her for ideas for a romantic evening before you went away. She said John brought her here, as a surprise, on their first date."

"That's so sweet."

"I figured if it worked for them, it could work for us."

Sunday relaxed and leaned into a turn.

"See? You're getting the feel for this."

Sunday swept her hair off her face. "A-plus for John Allen—and for Josh Newlon. This is the most romantic way to start an evening."

They circled the rink in an easy rhythm, arm in arm, until it was time to go in to dinner.

The maître d' placed them at a window table overlooking the river. The night was clear, and the moon transformed the river into liquid silver.

They dined on salmon and steak, mushroom risotto, and asparagus. Sunday filled Josh in on her travel arrangements and her hopes that she'd find some of the college's books on the shelves at Blythe Rare Books.

"I know it's a long shot, but it'd help appease the trustees," Josh said.

"Are they still hounding Maggie about this?"

"The chairman calls her every single day for an update."

"For crying out loud! That must be annoying."

"You know her. She puts a brave face on everything, but I know it's starting to wear her down."

The waiter approached and asked if they would like coffee with dessert.

Sunday shook her head. "Neither for me."

"Coffee for me," Josh said. "I always want coffee with cherries jubilee."

Sunday rocked back in her seat. "Cherries jubilee?"

"I ordered it ahead," Josh said. "Do you like them?"

Sunday grinned. "Of course I do! Who doesn't?"

The waiter turned to her again.

"In that case, I'll have coffee, too."

"Very good. Cream and sugar?"

They both shook their heads no.

Josh leaned over and took her hand in his. "I know we haven't been dating very long. The attempt on your life brought things into sharp relief for me. I've been thinking about you—about us—ever since."

Sunday brought her other hand to rest on top of his.

Josh held her gaze. "I love you, Sunday Sloan."

Sunday swallowed the lump in her throat.

"If it's too soon for you to feel the same way about me, I can wait. I'm certain about what's in my heart."

Sunday ran her eyes over his face. "That night in the library woke me up, too. I love you, Josh."

"I wanted you to know before you left," Josh said.

"It feels so good to say it!" she replied. "And don't worry about the rare book expert. My heart belongs to you."

Josh leaned across the table and kissed her. They broke apart when the waiter clamored up to their table with the cart bearing the cherries jubilee. Their faces flushed—whether from the heat of the flaming dessert or the depth of their newly professed feelings, they couldn't say.

CHAPTER 11

Maggie set her purse on the corner of Josh's desk while she put on her coat. "Have you heard from Sunday?"

"She texted from JFK while she was changing planes." He looked at the digital time readout on his computer screen. "She's been in the air for hours and should be approaching Heathrow. She'll be on the ground soon."

"Good. Will you text me when you hear from her?"

"Sure," Josh said, looking quizzical.

"I know, I know," Maggie said. "I'm treating her like she's one of my kids and not one of my employees." She grinned sheepishly. "Indulge me, okay?"

His face softened. "Of course."

"I'm running a personal errand," Maggie said. "If any of the trustees call, just say I'm out and will be back within the hour. I don't want to talk to them on my cell phone. There's nothing I have to say to them—or that they have to say to me—that can't wait."

"I agree completely."

Maggie picked up her purse and slung it over her shoulder.

"Why don't you take an extra half hour?" Josh called after her. "You deserve it."

Maggie waved over her shoulder and kept going. She emerged from the double doors of the entrance to the administration building and stepped lightly down the broad stone stairs. The sun warmed her face, and the crisp air held the first promise of spring.

She headed toward the parking lot when she came to the bottom of the stairs, then stopped. Town Square was only a twenty-minute walk from campus. Maggie tilted her chin to the sky and didn't spot a cloud in sight. After being cooped up all winter, the first fair day of spring held an irresistible allure. Josh was right. She could afford to be gone from her office for another thirty minutes. She'd walk to her destination.

Maggie lengthened her stride, thankful that she'd chosen to wear sensible flat shoes that morning. A light breeze brushed across her hair and skin. Birds lined up on an electrical wire, twittering and chirping to each other.

Her spirits were soaring when she pushed open the door of Burman Jewelers. The engagement and wedding rings in the long glass display cases gleamed under the halogen can lights. Harriet was handing a receipt to a man dressed in a well-tailored suit. "We'll have your watch repaired and cleaned, and back to you in a week."

"Thank you," the man said. "That's my favorite timepiece. My wife says it's my lucky watch. She swears that I win all my cases when I wear it to court."

Maggie stepped to a counter and examined gold earrings on a turnstile display.

Harriet beamed. "She does, does she? Well, we wouldn't

RESTORING WHAT WAS LOST

want our favorite lawyer to be without it. When does your next trial start?"

"A week from Wednesday."

"You'll have it by then," she said. "I'll make a note of the date and follow up myself."

"Much appreciated," he said, turning to leave. He saw Maggie standing to one side and nodded to her, his face flushing before he strode out the door.

Harriet looked at Maggie, and both women burst out laughing.

"His wife thinks it's his lucky watch?" Maggie asked, abandoning the earring display.

"Men can be very superstitious," Harriet said. "You learn these things when you're in my line of work. What brings you in today?"

Maggie reached for her purse.

Harriet held out her hand. "Let me have that wedding ring of yours. It's not sparkling like it should. I'll put it into the ultrasonic cleaner."

Maggie tugged the large diamond ring off her finger and placed it into Harriet's palm. "Thanks. I've been so busy I haven't had time to clean it."

"I'd rather you brought it in here, anyway. Gives me a chance to see you." She put the ring into the cleaning bath that stood ready for use behind the counter.

Maggie pulled a ziplock bag from her purse and removed an item wrapped in a paper towel. She carefully unwound the paper towel and laid the brooch on a small velvet tray on the counter.

Harriet gasped. She tore her eyes away to look at Maggie. "Where did you get this? Was this in your family?"

Maggie shook her head. "John found it."

"What?"

"It's real, isn't it?"

Harriet placed her jeweler's loupe against her right eye to examine the brooch.

Maggie waited, scarcely breathing.

Harriet began to nod. "Yes. Without a doubt, these are real. Based on my cursory review, I'd say that they are all very high-quality diamonds. Clear and colorless." She peered at Maggie. "You say John found it?"

Maggie filled Harriet in on the details.

"So, you have no idea who this belongs to or how long that coat's been sitting in the box?"

Maggie shook her head. "Just that it's been decades. John thinks it might have even been there when he purchased the animal hospital from the estate of the previous veterinarian, after he died."

"If that doesn't beat all," Harriet said. "The two of you have a real knack for finding valuable things, don't you? All of that priceless vintage silver in Rosemont's attic and now this?"

"I know." Maggie tucked her hair behind her ears. "It's hard to believe. What do you think it's worth?"

Harriet picked up the pin and flipped it over, scrutinizing the back. She drew in her breath sharply when she came to the clasp and moved it slowly back and forth under the loop. She leaned back and called for her husband.

"I'd like Larry to see this," she explained as he emerged from the workroom behind the retail showroom.

"Hi, Maggie," Larry said, coming to her side and giving her a hug. He looked at his wife, who stood motionless, the pin in her hand. "What've you got there?"

"Come see for yourself," Harriet said, holding out the pin to him.

He focused on the item in her hand for the first time, and his step quickened. "Let me take this into the back room."

Maggie leaned toward Harriet as he slipped out of view.

"You think it's really valuable, don't you? Did you find a jeweler's mark?"

"Let's see what Larry thinks."

They didn't have long to wait.

Larry emerged, holding the brooch carefully—almost reverently. "This is quite the piece of jewelry you have here, Maggie," he said.

"Sean Nash found it in an old lost-and-found box at the animal hospital," Harriet said.

Larry emitted a low whistle. "Doesn't that beat all."

"My words, exactly," Harriet said.

"For heaven's sake," Maggie broke in. "The suspense is killing me. Tell me about it."

Harriet and Larry looked at each other. "Tell her, honey," Harriet said.

"You have a diamond brooch, set in platinum. An appraisal would give you a better idea, but my guess is that the total weight of the diamonds is in the neighborhood of twenty carats. They are all exceptionally fine stones. Everything about them is exquisite."

"What would the value be?"

"There's one other factor to consider," Larry said. He looked Maggie directly in the eye. "This brooch was made by one of the most famous—and highly sought after—jewelers in the world."

Maggie held her breath.

"Van Cleef & Arpels. The fitting is stamped with their name and stock number."

"I've heard of them," Maggie said. "They're like Harry Winston and Cartier."

"In that league, yes. You've made the find of a lifetime."

"Any idea of the value?"

"I'd need to appraise the stones and do some research, but my best guess is that it's worth in the neighborhood of one hundred thousand dollars."

Maggie took a step back. "We've got to find the rightful owner," she said. "We've got to try."

"There are registries for lost and stolen jewelry," Harriet said. "Do you want us to search them and make inquiries? This is a very distinctive piece. It's a long shot, but we might come up with something."

"Yes. Thank you." Maggie said. "Can I leave it in your safe? We don't have it insured."

"I was going to suggest that," Larry said. "You'll need an appraisal to get it insured, anyway."

"You said that it was pinned to a red coat with a Christian Dior label," Harriet said. "I've lived here all my life and am wracking my brain, trying to think who might have been here in the seventies with the kind of money to own a coat like that. If only my mother were alive. She would know."

Harriet and Maggie looked at each other and grinned.

"If anybody in this town knows," Maggie said, "or can figure out who to ask—"

"—it's Judy Young," the two women concluded in unison.

***

Maggie emerged from Burman Jewelers into the soft sunshine of the early spring day. The stately trees that lined Town Square across the street were beginning to bud, enveloping the treetops in a fuzz of vibrant green. An elderly man walked a portly dachshund that was tugging at its leash to sniff the dormant grass. In only a few more weeks, the square would be full of joggers on the paths and kids playing Frisbee. Ice cream vendors would be hawking treats from brightly painted carts.

She loved the square in springtime. Inhaling deeply, she filled her lungs with fresh air. She was glad for this break in her routine.

Maggie set out for Town Hall on the far side of the square. She hadn't properly thanked Alex for dropping everything and turning up to support her when the trustees had summoned her into that meeting. It would be nice to tell him in person.

She crossed the plaza that led to the main entrance to Town Hall. The building was constructed of bricks ranging from rich terra cotta to deep burgundy. The front was decorated with three identical rosettes of purple brick, a lasting testament to the expertise of the bricklayers from a bygone era. The symmetrical rows of windows were capped with chiseled stone eyebrows. The effect was solid and grand, reflecting the prosperity of Westbury at the turn of the twentieth century. Maggie's heart beat faster. The clean lines of today's municipal buildings didn't convey the timeless grandeur of these older gems.

She climbed the steps. Sometimes it didn't seem real to her that she had been elected mayor of Westbury and had worked in this very building until she'd taken the post as president of Highpointe College. She'd been a write-in candidate, elected after Alex had been critically injured in an auto accident on the eve of an election he'd been favored to win. Now he was finally serving in the position he'd coveted for years, having won the last mayoral election by a wide margin.

Maggie crossed the lobby, smiling and exchanging greetings with municipal workers she remembered from her time in office, and took the elevator to the top floor.

The reception desk was not staffed, and a sheet of paper in a plexiglass frame directed her to register her presence on the computer screen provided and take a seat. Someone would be with her shortly.

Maggie scowled. Had Westbury's administrative offices done away with a receptionist? Is this how visitors were treated? She stepped around the desk and made the familiar trip down the hall to the mayor's suite of offices.

She pushed open the door and was surprised to see that the desk that had been occupied by her assistant was no longer in place. The door bearing the placard Mayor of Westbury was closed. She knocked firmly.

"Yes," Alex called gruffly.

Maggie pushed the door open and stepped inside.

"Maggie," he cried, rising from his desk and coming to her. "I didn't get notified that you were here."

They hugged, and Maggie stepped back. "I didn't type my name into that screen thing you have out there."

"Ah … that explains it. We get a message when someone's here to see one of us. It's a great system."

"We had the same thing when I was here. It was called a receptionist. A real, live, friendly human being." She peered at him over the top of her glasses and cuffed him playfully on the shoulder.

"Our system works just fine. Usually." He motioned for Maggie to sit in one of the chairs in front of his desk. "You can't fight progress."

"I see you don't have an administrative assistant, either," she remarked.

"I'm self-sufficient, with the benefits of modern technology."

"I know you're doing a great job—and I'm sure you're saving the taxpayers money—but don't forget that receptionists and assistants can be your eyes and ears. Town Hall is a gossipy place, and that screen out there," she pointed over her shoulder toward the lobby, "won't keep you informed."

"That's true enough," he conceded. "I'll think about that. I'm sure you didn't stop by to school me on how to manage my office."

"No," Maggie said and arched an eyebrow. "That was a bonus. I'm here to thank you for your support with the trustees. I can't tell you how much I appreciated it."

"You're welcome. I've always got your back. You know that, don't you?"

"I do. I haven't heard from the chairman this week. I think they're finally done worrying about this."

"They're not."

"What're you talking about?"

"I've been meaning to talk to you. I've received calls from the chairman of the board and several of the trustees." Alex drew a deep breath. "They're scared that the thefts of these rare books will tarnish the college's reputation. If word gets out, they think it'll have a chilling effect on bequests to the college."

"Oh, come on. The vast majority of the thefts happened decades ago."

"Most of the trustees have been serving on the board for decades. They're afraid this whole thing is going to make them look bad—maybe even subject them to liability for poor management."

"What are you saying?"

"They want a scapegoat, Maggie. They're on a witch hunt—and they've set their sights on you."

"I thought we'd gotten past all that. I've been president of Highpointe for less than a year. It makes no sense."

Alex cleared his throat. "You did appoint Dean Plume to the Friends of the Library Committee."

"So what! His being on the committee didn't make it possible for him to steal books."

"Maybe not, but you have to agree—it looks bad."

Maggie rocked back in her chair. "You don't think I had anything to do with those thefts, do you?"

Alex reached toward her, and she recoiled. "Of course I don't. You should know better than to ask me that. I just wanted to make sure you realize how serious this is getting."

Maggie leaned forward, putting her elbows on her knees, and cradled her head in her hands. "I can't believe this is happening to me."

"I'm on your side," Alex said. "But they're coming for you, Maggie. Make sure you're ready for them."

CHAPTER 12

Sunday turned up her collar against the sudden cloudburst and bent her head into the wind. The morning had been dry and balmy when she'd set out for Blythe Rare Books, just a mile from her hotel. Rush-hour traffic was inching along, and she'd figured it would be faster to walk. What she hadn't factored into her decision was London's ubiquitous rain.

She hurried along the pavement with her fellow pedestrians, most of whom wielded umbrellas that afforded her no protection and only impeded her progress. Her hair was soaked by the time she spied the familiar sign on the door.

Sunday pushed against the handle, but the bookshop was locked. She rapped on the doorframe.

The rain came down harder, and Sunday raised her arms to shield her head. She cursed under her breath. The solicitor was supposed to be here. Where was Deidre Hyde-Jones?

Sunday raised her hand to knock again when she heard the

deadbolt click. The door was thrown open, and a tall, trim man reached for her elbow and drew her into the shop.

"Good heavens, you're soaked!" he began and stopped short, raking his hand through his thinning hair and peering at her over the top of his half-moon glasses. "Sunday?"

Sunday brushed her wet hair off her forehead and out of her eyes. Water dripped from her chin.

He pulled her farther inside and shut the door against the inclement weather.

She lifted her face to his, and a smile chased away her gloomy expression. "Robert!"

"Deidre told me the college was sending someone to go through the inventory. I assumed it would be one of the local rare book dealers, armed with a list." He pointed to a stack of papers on the counter where an old-fashioned cash register and a telephone sat. "I never dreamed that they'd send you over here."

"She didn't tell you I was coming?"

"No. It's a complete surprise. A very welcome one," he said. "Let me take your coat, and I'll get you a towel to dry your hair."

"Thank you." Sunday unbuttoned her trench coat and handed it to him. "Now I know why the English always carry their umbrellas. I won't make that mistake again."

Robert handed her a towel, and she began rubbing her hair. "Deidre didn't tell me you'd be here, either," she added. "I'm delighted I'll be working with you. This day got off to a bad start, what with getting caught in the rain, but your being here makes everything better." Her smile warmed the room.

Robert flushed at the compliment. "Let's get you a cup of tea before we begin. We can't have you coming down with pneumonia."

"I'm sure that won't happen," she replied, "but I'd love one. You can tell me how long you've been working with the estate and fill me in on what you've been doing since we met at the London rare book conference last year."

He led her behind the counter into a tiny room that housed a small sink and cabinet. An electric tea kettle and mugs sat ready to be put into service. Robert filled the kettle and plugged it in. He filled a tea strainer with loose tea from a canister bearing foreign-looking stamps. The faint scents of strong tea, cloves, and nutmeg hung in the air.

"I'm still working at Cambridge, so I've been squeezing my duties to the estate of Nigel Blythe into the weekends. The university is on break next week, so I'll be able to spend as much time with you as you need."

"Do you think we can finish in a week?"

"I've already been through all of the books," he said. "I wanted to make it easy on whoever was representing the college." The kettle began to whistle, and he poured the boiling water into the teapot.

Sunday inhaled the fragrant cloud of steam. "I'd forgotten how wonderful tea smells."

"I agree. Bracing, as they say. I know you Yanks love your coffee—I like it, too—but there's nothing like a perfectly brewed cup of tea."

He poured the rich brown liquid into two mugs and handed one to her. "I'm afraid I don't have any cream, but there's sugar in that dish." He pointed to the right of the kettle.

"Black is fine for me." She brought the mug to her lips and sniffed. "What have you found? Are any of the college's books still on the shelves out there?" She gestured to the interior of the shop behind her.

"There are quite a few that I believe came from Highpointe's collection," he replied. "Whoever made all of those notations on your inventory about the condition of the books along with any identifying characteristics did an excellent job. Very meticulous."

Sunday closed her eyes briefly. "The credit for that goes to our former librarian, Hazel Harrington."

"Is she—?"

"The woman Nigel murdered because she'd become suspicious?" Sunday sipped her tea. "Yes."

"Tragic. I can't fathom greed that drives someone to such extremes."

Sunday bit her lip, purposely not filling him in on how close she'd come to also becoming Nigel's victim.

"I've made two stacks of books for you to go through. One is a group that I feel certain belongs to Highpointe. I figured we could start there and go through them quickly. The other stack are ones I have questions about. I figured that the two of us could study them and try to agree on whether they had been stolen from Highpointe or not."

"Sounds like an efficient way to go about it."

"When we're done, I figured you'd want to go through the rest of the shop to make sure I hadn't overlooked something."

"I can't imagine you've missed anything."

"There's a lot of inventory out there," Robert said. "I'll want you to double-check what I've done."

"Do you know if Deidre made any progress on obtaining the old records of what's been sold from the shop?"

"Three large boxes arrived at my home in Cambridge last week. I haven't had a chance to look at them. I'll turn to that when I go home."

Sunday drained her mug and set it in the sink. "Thank you. I'm completely restored."

Robert stood. "We've got a big job ahead of us. Let's get started."

CHAPTER 13

Frank held the car door open for Loretta as she dabbed at her lips with a tissue.

She lifted miserable eyes to her husband. "There's nothing in my stomach. I can't stop these dry heaves."

"I'm so sorry, sweetheart."

She swung her feet onto the pavement.

Frank offered his hand, and she placed hers in it, hoisting herself out of the car. "I thought this morning sickness would be better by now."

"It's not, is it?"

Loretta shook her head.

"Do you think everything's alright?" Frank put his arm around her waist and guided her into her doctor's office.

"We'll know soon enough," she said. "The ultrasound should show us if the baby is fine. As long as he—or she—is good, I can endure this."

Loretta sank into a chair in the waiting room, and Frank

signed them in at the reception desk. He'd no sooner sat next to his wife than the nurse called Loretta's name.

They followed her down a long corridor. The nurse stopped to weigh Loretta and took her temperature, pulse, and blood pressure. She made notes on an electronic tablet and smiled at Loretta. "Everything's perfect. How are you feeling?" she asked as she showed them into the room where the ultrasound was to be performed.

"I'm still suffering from morning sickness," Loretta replied. "Twenty-four seven."

The nurse cocked her head and looked at Loretta carefully before noting the file. "Let's see what the ultrasound says. The technician will be in shortly. Change into this," she said, handing Loretta a paper gown, "and sit on that table." She motioned to Frank. "Your husband can hover on the other side of the technician." She closed the door.

"Did you see the look she gave me?" Loretta asked. "Do you think she's worried about something?"

"You're imagining things, honey," Frank said. He'd noticed the same look but didn't want to admit it to Loretta.

The door opened, and a technician entered. "Good morning," she said. "Do you want to find out the sex of your baby today, or would you like us to keep that a secret?"

Frank and Loretta looked at each other.

"We want to know," Loretta said.

"Then let's get started," the technician said. "Just lie back." She began the procedure that she performed dozens of times each month.

***

Frank slid behind the wheel and sucked in a breath through his teeth. He withdrew the handkerchief from his coat pocket and wiped his eyes.

Loretta leaned toward him and ran her hand along his arm. "Are you okay, honey? I know it's a lot to take in." She raised her brows as she studied his profile. "It's definitely not the news we were expecting. Are you … happy about it?"

"Am I happy?" Frank's voice cracked as he choked on his words. "I'm overjoyed. I never thought I'd have a child of my own." He shifted to face her in the car. "Don't get me wrong—I love Marissa, Sean, and Nicole like they're my own. I was completely happy."

"I know that, Frank. You're a wonderful father to them."

"But when you got pregnant, and I knew we would have our own little boy or girl, I thought I couldn't be happier."

"And now … ?"

"Now, I'm going to have a son and a daughter!"

"You're pleased? You'll be supporting a family of seven. You'll have gone from being a bachelor to being the father of five in a very short period of time."

"Are you kidding? It's the best news! I feel blessed beyond my wildest dreams." He took her face in his hands. "I have the kindest, smartest, most beautiful wife, three great stepchildren, and now this." He kissed her tenderly.

"Twins are a lot of work," Loretta said. "Don't kid yourself. Things are going to be very hectic at our house."

"I'll hire a bookkeeper. You won't have to work at Haynes Enterprises anymore."

"I love my job. I don't want to quit."

"Then we'll hire a nanny to help at home."

"That would be nice."

"In fact, let's hire one right away. The doctor said your hormones are what's making you so sick. They're at high levels to support twins. Sounds like your morning sickness may not go away."

Loretta rested her forehead against his. "If I'm not going to feel better, I'd like to hire a nanny."

Frank drew back and looked into her eyes. "How are you feeling about this?"

"A bit overwhelmed, actually."

"You're not happy?"

"Of course, I'm happy," Loretta said. "But I've also cared for three newborns. I've got a better idea than you do of how … challenging this next phase of our life is going to be."

"It'll be fine," Frank said. "Don't worry about a thing. We've got this."

Loretta squeezed his hand. "How shall we tell the kids? Everyone does these big gender reveals on social media these days, but I think that's all nonsense. I say we just tell them at dinner."

Frank swung his face quickly to his window.

"What have you done?" she asked.

"I may have gone to that toy store—"

"The one where you bought all those toys when Nicole was so sick?"

Frank faced her and a flush began to creep up from his collar.

"And?"

"I might have picked up a giant pink and a giant blue teddy bear. Just to be prepared." A sheepish grin spread across his face. "I think those social media posts are nice."

"Frank Haynes—you are full of surprises." She leaned over

and kissed him. "Looks like you've got us covered. We'll use both of them."

"I'm going to have a baby, and I want everybody to know about it," Frank said, wiping at his eyes again. "Make that two babies."

CHAPTER 14

"I said I'll take care of the dishes." Maggie snatched the dishtowel and china serving bowl from John's hands. "You're being too rough with it."

John took a step back. "What're you talking about?"

"You're hurrying because you want to go watch some stupid game on TV. This belonged to my grandmother, and I love it." She glared at him. "You're going to chip the rim."

"We've been using that bowl—and I've been drying it without incident—since we were married." He rocked back on his heels and studied her.

Maggie placed the bowl carefully in its place in the hutch and gave him a wide berth as she hung the dishtowel on its peg.

Eve went to her mistress and placed her front paws on Maggie's shins, wagging her tail and whining.

"Get off," Maggie snapped, stepping back so that Eve's paws landed on the floor. "You went out before dinner. That's enough."

"What's going on with you? You've been prickly with me all week, and I've never seen you be short with Eve."

Maggie hung her head and brought her hands to her temples.

John crossed to her, putting his hands on her shoulders.

"Have I done something to upset you?"

Maggie looked up at him. "No. Of course not."

"Then what is it?"

"Just something that Alex told me. It's stupid, really. Go watch your game. Eve here needs to go out."

Maggie bent and patted her beloved terrier mix. "I'm sorry, girl," she murmured into the soft fur on the top of Eve's head. "Mommy's sorry."

Eve thumped her tail softly and licked her mistress's face.

"The game can wait. Let's take the dogs out, and you can tell me everything."

Maggie stood as John whistled for Roman. All four of them headed through the kitchen door to the back lawn. The dogs raced down the hill ahead of them, heading for a cluster of birds pecking in the grass for food. The dogs barked and chased as the birds found safety in the trees, chirping their disapproval at being disturbed.

"Now, what did Alex have to say that's gotten under your skin?"

Maggie filled him in on her conversation in the mayor's office.

"How could they possibly blame this on you?" John was incredulous. "Couldn't he be misinterpreting what he's heard?"

"That's what I thought, at first. But the more I think about it, the more I realize Alex may be right. College trustees are like politicians—always trying to spin things to their advantage."

"You dealt with the trustees of Windsor College after Paul died, didn't you?"

"Yes. They were as unhappy at the prospect of being accused of lax oversight as they were that Paul had embezzled from the college. That's why I was able to settle Windsor's claim against Paul's estate quietly for the amount of his employee life insurance policy." She shivered and hugged herself with her arms. "They wanted the whole issue to go away without it ever seeing the light of day."

John ran his hands up and down her back. "That proves it. You've dealt with trustees successfully in the past, and you'll do it again now."

"From your lips to God's ears," she said. "I'm sorry I've been so curt with you all week. I didn't realize I was doing it."

"No need to apologize," John said. "I understand you were upset." He rocked back and looked at her. "Promise me that you'll tell me about anything that's bothering you, okay?"

"I promise," she said. "I know you're so busy at work, and you need to relax and unwind—in front of a game on TV—when you get home. I didn't want to unload on you."

"That's what I'm here for," John said. "Your problems are my problems. I may not have a solution, but I know that sharing a concern makes it less of a burden."

Maggie placed her palm against his cheek. "You're right about that. Thank you."

"Why don't you concentrate on making plans for when Mike and Amy and the girls are here for their spring break? You love having them at Rosemont. That'll make you feel better."

"You're right. I can't wait to see them." Maggie blew out a breath. "You really think it's nothing to worry about?"

"I do. You can handle those trustees. There's no way they can blame it on you."

***

Maggie lifted the lid from her mocha latte as she walked along the wide sidewalk to the administration building. She inhaled the comforting aroma of coffee as she sipped. The frothy milk clung to her upper lip. She rarely allowed herself this caloric indulgence, but she'd awakened in a good mood. After her talk with John about the trustee issue, she felt like a small celebration was in order. She had been worrying about nothing. Maggie smiled.

The sun was still low over the horizon, and the campus buzzed with students hurrying to their first class or getting in an early jog.

A young man cupped his mouth with his hands and called to a girl ahead of him on the path. The girl turned around, shielding her eyes from the sun and scanned the crowd for him. He ran to her, and they fell into each other's arms and kissed, oblivious to those around them.

Maggie's smile faded at the sound of her phone ringing. She set her coffee down on the low wall leading to the administration building steps and churned through her purse.

"President Lawry," she answered, "what an unexpected pleasure! How are you?"

"Ex-president," came the familiar voice. "I'm just fine. And please, call me Ian."

"How's your wife? Has she been well enough to make those trips you wanted to take when you retired?"

"She has. We spent the summer visiting friends all over Europe and had a wonderful time."

"I'm so glad to hear it," Maggie said. She reached for her coffee, then set it back down again. Something in the tone of his voice told her this wasn't a social call. He had a purpose for making it, and she feared she wasn't going to like it. "Will you be going anywhere this summer?"

"We've got plans to be in the Irish countryside for three weeks and then spend a week in Cornwall."

"John and I honeymooned in Cornwall," Maggie said. "You'll love it. The people are kind, and life moves at a much slower pace. Very relaxing."

"That's why I'm calling. I'm hoping we still get to go."

"Why wouldn't you?"

"Kevin Baxter called me this morning."

"He's one of Highpointe's trustees."

"Yes," Ian replied. "He's a huge contributor to the college and has the longest tenure on the board."

"What did he call you about?" Maggie swallowed her rising panic.

"He wanted to know if I'd be available to come back—as an interim president."

Maggie gasped.

"He's intimated that they're going to terminate your contract over this issue concerning the stolen rare books."

"You've heard about that?"

"I've read the coverage in the newspaper, and he told me what he knew."

A woman Maggie recognized from the payroll department gave her an odd look as she walked by on her way to the entrance. Maggie abandoned her coffee and moved to a spot out of public view. "What did you say to him?"

"That they had no grounds whatsoever to terminate your

contract and that I wouldn't talk to him at this time about an interim position."

"Thank you," Maggie replied.

"You've got my support, Maggie, and you always will. They're trying to make you the scapegoat."

"I'd heard that."

"If they do force you out, I would step back in. I love Highpointe, and I'd do anything to protect it, but I don't want that to happen. You need to fight these guys, Maggie."

"I'm not sure how."

"You do it by being you, Maggie. The strong, smart, honest woman who stood up to Chuck Delgado and his mob cronies when they were embezzling from the town and the town workers' pension fund. Councilwoman Holmes may have gotten the ball rolling on the fraud inquiry, but you got the job done. You can handle these trustees."

"You know them better than I do," Maggie said. "What should I expect?"

"They're sometimes pompous and overbearing, but except for Baxter, they're decent. Baxter is the one you have to watch out for."

"I understand he has a drinking problem," she said.

"That and a bad temper."

Maggie straightened her spine. "Sounds like I need to find out a little bit more about Kevin Baxter."

"It couldn't hurt. Know thine enemy and all that."

"Thank you for the call, Ian," Maggie said.

"You've got this. I have every confidence in you."

"That means the world to me."

"If you need someone to talk to—someone to run things by—just give me a call. I'm always happy to listen."

"I appreciate that, more than you know." Maggie made her

way back to the sidewalk. "I'd better let you go. I have some digging to do. And you can continue making plans for your trips to Ireland and Cornwall."

"That's the spirit."

"I'll send you a copy of our favorite guidebook to Cornwall. I think you'll enjoy it."

CHAPTER 15

Tommy Acosta spotted David coming up the walkway and answered the door before David had a chance to ring the bell. "Hi. You lookin' for my sister?"

"Is she here?"

"Doing her homework. She's in a bad mood," Tommy said. "Grace yelled at me twice to keep it down."

"She's trying to get valedictorian, and that essay she's working on is pretty important, buddy. It could be the deciding factor."

"Whatever." Tommy said while rolling his eyes, doing a perfect impression of his big sister. "Come on in. I'll go get her."

"That's okay," David said. "Dodger's in the car with me." He pointed to the curb with his thumb. "I only need a minute. Tell her it's important."

"You can bring Dodger in! We can play video games." Tommy's eyes were pleading. "We haven't hung out for a while."

David cuffed Tommy's shoulder. "I know, buddy. I can't right now. I just need to see your sister."

"Okay." Tommy trudged to the stairs.

David paced on the porch. Grace hadn't been happy about his decision to apply to the Guide Dog Center instead of Highpointe College. He wanted, one day, to become a veterinarian, but he wanted to learn to train guide dogs first.

He took the letter out of his jacket pocket and unfolded it. Just the sight of it made his spirits soar. After so many years of disappointments, his dreams were coming true.

The front door opened, and Grace stepped onto the porch in a tattered pair of sweatpants and a T-shirt, her long strawberry-blond hair piled on top of her head in a messy bun. She wore no makeup. To David, she was the most beautiful girl he'd ever seen.

"It's cold out here. I should have grabbed my jacket."

David pulled her to him. "It's okay. I'll keep you warm." He rubbed her arms.

She buried her face in this chest, and he rested his chin on top of her head.

"Tommy said it's important. What's up?"

David took a deep breath. "I got my letter."

"From the Guide Dog Center?" She leaned back so she could look into his eyes. "You got in, didn't you?"

He nodded, a smile spreading across his face.

"That's wonderful! Congratulations!" She hugged him tightly.

"You mean it? I know you wanted us both to be at Highpointe together."

"Of course I mean it. I know I was upset when you first told me you wanted to go away to learn to be a guide dog trainer, but I've had time to get used to the idea." She put her hand on his cheek. "This is what you want to do. And watching you with animals? It's what you're meant to do. You've got a gift, David.

A gift that should be developed. You can do so much good for so many people." Grace looked aside. "I was being selfish when I wanted you to stay with me."

David released the breath he'd been holding. "I'm so happy you feel this way." He leaned down and kissed her. "I love you, Grace. I hope you know that. This training is part of what I want to do with my life."

"I understand."

"I want to start a service dog training school right here in Westbury. There's a growing need for everything from diabetes alert dogs for children to PTSD service dogs for veterans to guide dogs for the blind. Frank says I can start a school in the Forever Friends building, and he'll help me get funding for a larger operation when I'm ready for it."

"I'm happy that you know what you want to do with your life."

"I'll only be gone a couple of years," David said. "Once I get this up and running, I'd still like to get my degree and become a vet."

"What does John Allen say about that?"

"He thinks having guide dog training on my resume will help me get into veterinary school."

"I'm glad you want to come back to Westbury," she said. "I'll be busy with my classes. You know me—I'll be knee-deep in homework. I'm already planning to take eighteen credits this fall. I'll probably get better grades if my hunky boyfriend isn't there to distract me."

She smiled, and David felt the familiar jolt.

"What did Frank and John say?"

"The only other person who knows is my mom."

"I'll bet you're anxious to tell them. They'll both be so happy for you." Grace shivered and leaned up to kiss him. "I love you. Now get out of here and spread your good news."

***

The smell of dogs and disinfectant assaulted David's nostrils as he and Dodger entered Westbury Animal Hospital by the employee entrance. He'd performed enough odd jobs for John that, even though he didn't work at the hospital, he was afforded this privilege. He would make a copy of his letter, scribble a note of thanks across the top, and leave it on the busy veterinarian's desk.

He'd accomplished his task and was slipping back out the door when Juan, the senior vet tech at the hospital, called his name.

"What are the two of you doing here today?" Juan asked.

David stopped. Juan had been the first person to encourage him to turn his interest in dogs into a career. "I was just leaving a note for John," David said.

"Is something wrong with Dodger?"

"No. He's fine. I wanted John to be one of the first to know," he straightened his shoulders, then continued in a rush, "that I've been accepted into a school for guide dog trainers."

"That's fabulous!" Juan clapped him on the back. "I'm so happy for you. John'll be delighted. Why don't you tell him yourself?"

"I didn't want to interrupt him."

"Nonsense. He'll want to hear this from you. Let me check his schedule." Juan consulted the tablet he was carrying. "Look at this. He's with Frank Haynes and Sally right now. They're in for a routine checkup. Why don't you tell both of them at once?"

"Are you sure?"

"Positive. Follow me."

Juan led David and Dodger to a closed door that was labeled Exam Room 3. He knocked, then pushed the door open.

John and Frank were shaking hands as Sally lay at Frank's feet. They turned to the door.

"Wait until you hear the good news," John said, still pumping Frank's hand. He swung back to Frank. "Are you telling people?"

Frank nodded and addressed David. "Loretta and I are expecting twins—a boy and a girl."

David stepped through the doorway. "What? That's incredible. I'm so happy for you."

John bent to greet Dodger, and Frank pulled David into a hug. "You'll be a sort of honorary uncle," he said, "being the best man at our wedding, and all."

"That'll be awesome," David said.

"This is a day for big things," Juan said. "David's got something to share, too. I caught him leaving a note on your desk. I told him you'd want to hear it from him."

John and Frank looked at David.

"I got into the Guide Dog Center's training program," he blurted out. "As long as I pass the interview, I'm in."

Both men rushed to congratulate him.

"There's no question that you'll do fine in the interview," John said. "I'm thrilled for you."

"When do you leave for California?" Frank asked.

"Week after next. My mom's going to book the trip. She's coming with me."

"Terrific. Let me know if you need any," Frank searched for a tactful way to phrase his next sentence, "help with anything. Anything at all."

"Mom says we've got the trip covered. It's the tuition that I'm worried about."

Frank and John exchanged a look.

"Don't worry about that," Frank said. He gestured to John with his head. "We've got ideas. Let us figure out how to pay for it."

David blinked hard. He didn't know what he'd done to deserve such kindness from these two men.

"I think they're a couple of others that will want to hear this news in person," John said.

"Glenn Vaughn and Sam Torres," David said. "I'm on my way to see them next."

CHAPTER 16

"There's no record of the pin on any of the registries," Harriet said. She scanned the list in front of her. "We've heard from everyone we reached out to. We also called our counterparts at some of the jewelers in the wealthier neighborhoods of New York City. No one is aware of anyone who lost this pin, or had it stolen."

"Thank you for going to all this trouble," Maggie said, pressing her phone to her ear. "Where does this leave me?"

"The owner of a gorgeous and valuable Van Cleef & Arpels brooch, I would say," Harriet replied. "I'm happy for you."

"I'm not prepared to accept it's mine," Maggie said. "Surely, there couldn't have been many people with a pin like that in Westbury."

"It does seem unlikely. I'd suggest you have us appraise it so you can insure it."

"Okay. Prepare the appraisal. I'll insure it, but I'm going to look for the owner."

"One more thing," Harriet said. "You said it was pinned to the lapel of a coat that had a Dior label in it?"

"Yes."

"Why don't you take the coat to Anita Archer? Her grandmother founded Archer's Bridal, and her mother worked as their chief seamstress until the day she died. Anita might remember if Archer's made any alterations to the coat. They would have been the only place in town anyone would have taken something of that caliber."

"That's the plan," Maggie said as she hung up. Visiting Anita Archer about the mysterious brooch and designer coat would make a nice break during her stressful day at the college.

***

Anita Archer heard the bell tinkle as someone opened the door to Archer's Bridal. She was alone in the shop because both of her cousins had taken the afternoon off to attend their grandchildren's music program at the local elementary school. She carefully removed the pins she was holding between her teeth and set them and the bodice of the bridal gown she was letting out onto the large worktable.

"Coming," she called as she stepped through the curtain that separated the showroom from the workroom in back. Her eyes searched for her visitor among the mannequins draped in gowns of satin, chiffon, and lace.

"Hi, Anita," Maggie called, stepping out from behind a lace and tulle gown with an enormous skirt and train. "This dress is incredible," she said. "I couldn't resist taking a closer look."

Anita beamed. "It is, isn't it? That's a ball gown style. It's a classic, and we sell a lot of them."

"Isn't it hard to maneuver around at the reception wearing this?"

"That's why so many brides buy two dresses—one for the ceremony and one for the reception."

"Seriously? That's a thing now?"

"It is. And a trend that bridal shops are grateful for."

"I'm sure." Maggie smiled at Anita and stepped to a display case that showcased bridal headwear.

"What can I help you with?" Anita followed her. "Is someone in your family getting married?" Her words came faster. "We love working with the Martin family here at Archer's. It was an honor to do your wedding and your daughter's."

"And we loved everything you did for both of us," Maggie said, setting a shopping bag on top of the display case. "No one's getting married. Harriet Burman and I thought you might help me figure out something that's a bit of a mystery."

Anita stepped closer. "I'd be happy to do that."

Maggie withdrew the red coat from the shopping bag and held it out to Anita. "Do you recognize this?"

Anita picked up the reading glasses that hung from a chain around her neck and fixed them on the bridge of her nose. She scrutinized the garment, pausing to examine the label. Her eyebrows shot up to her hairline.

"Christian Dior?"

"Do you think it's real? Not a knockoff?"

"I'm certain of it," Anita said, rubbing the fabric between her thumb and forefinger. "This is quality fabric." She held out a seam to Maggie. "The stitching is hand done. And perfect."

Maggie examined the seam.

"Was it in your family? Maybe your mother's coat?" Anita asked.

"No. Nothing like that. I grew up in a very modest home. My mother could never have afforded anything like this."

"Did you buy it online?" She held the coat out in front of Maggie. "It's in wonderful condition, and the color would be lovely on you. I'm sure I can alter it to fit you perfectly."

"Actually, that's why I'm here. To see if Archer's ever altered this coat before."

"Not since I've been in charge of the shop," Anita said. She looked at the garment. "My guess is that this is from the sixties. My mother or grandmother may have made alterations on it at that time, but I didn't start working in the shop until the early eighties."

"They never mentioned it?"

Anita shook her head. "Why do you ask?"

Maggie told Anita how the coat had been found at Westbury Animal Hospital.

Anita blew out a breath in a rush. "That's one for the books, isn't it? Someone leaves a Dior coat—with an expensive brooch—behind and never tries to find it?"

"That's what we're thinking," Maggie said. "We're trying to find the rightful owner, but all we're coming up with are dead ends."

"If Harriet and I can't help, that leaves only one other person in town."

"Judy?"

"Who else?" Anita replied with a smile. "Something tells me that Judy may have an answer for you."

CHAPTER 17

Glenn gripped the porch swing and pushed himself up. He moved to the top of the steps and watched the boy he'd come to love like one of his grandsons and Dodger, the dog that was David's constant companion, striding along the path toward him. "To what do we owe this pleasure?" he asked as David came up to him.

"Thanks for letting me stop by," David said.

"You're always welcome here," Glenn said. "No invitation necessary, although the fact that we knew you were coming gave Gloria a chance to whip up a batch of chocolate chip cookies."

David followed Dodger's lead and sniffed the air. "They smell amazing."

"You'll be taking most of them home with you." Glenn patted his stomach. "I'll have a few, but the last thing I need is six dozen cookies." He extended his arm. "Come on in. Gloria's anxious to see you."

Glenn rested his arm on David's shoulders, and the two made their way into the house.

"Is that Sam's truck at the curb?"

"Yep. He's fixing the laundry room faucet."

"I'd like Sam to hear what I've got to say," David said. "Could he join us?"

"Sure. I'll go get him. Gloria's waiting for you in the kitchen."

David walked into the kitchen, where Gloria was pulling a tray of cookies out of the oven.

"Perfect timing." She set the tray on a trivet and pointed to a bowl of batter. "This recipe makes a lot. Being the mother of nine, I never figured out how to make small amounts of anything."

David grinned and leaned in to kiss her cheek. "No worries, ma'am. I can handle all you've got."

She lifted a cookie off the tray and held it out to David. The warm cookie bent in on itself, and chocolate dripped off the sides.

David popped the entire cookie in his mouth.

Dodger barked and wagged his tail, looking expectantly from David to Gloria.

"These aren't good for you," she said, patting him on the head, "but I've got something you'll like." She reached for a small white canister on her counter that was decorated with paw prints and withdrew a dog treat.

Dodger squirmed in excitement.

"Here you go." Gloria tossed the treat to Dodger, and he caught it in midair.

"You don't even have a dog," David said.

"No, but someone we love does." Gloria handed him another cookie as Sam and Glenn entered the kitchen.

"Don't tell Joan I said this, but you make the best chocolate chip cookies in the county," Sam said.

"Is that a hint, Sam Torres?" Gloria placed cookies on a plate and handed it to Sam. "Help yourselves."

"Now, what's this big news you've come to tell us?" Glenn asked.

David straightened his shoulders. "I've been conditionally accepted into the training program at the Guide Dog Center. In California. I've got to go out for an interview, but assuming that goes okay, I'm in."

Glenn grabbed David by the shoulders and hugged him, patting his back. "I'm so proud of you, son. That's wonderful news!"

"Terrific," Sam said. "Nobody's worked harder or deserves this more than you."

David stepped back and looked at both of them. "You don't think I'm being foolish to put college off while I learn to become a guide dog trainer?"

"Not at all," Glenn said. "I think you're fulfilling your destiny."

"You can go to college later," Sam said. "I agree with Glenn. You're a natural with dogs, and you'll be learning something that can dramatically improve a lot of lives. You can't ask for more than that."

"Thank you," David said. "I'm really excited about it. It's what I want to do, but I don't want to make a bad decision."

"Listen to your gut," Gloria said. "Do what you love. You'll never go wrong that way."

"I can't tell you what your support and encouragement mean to me." David's voice cracked. "You both saw the better side of me when I was … after my dad—"

Sam stepped forward and put his hand on David's shoulder. "We know, David. And look what's become of you. You proved us right."

Gloria pulled more cookies out of the oven. She took a pitcher of milk from the refrigerator and set it on a tray with a fresh plate of cookies. "Why don't you three go sit at the table?"

"I should get back to that faucet," Sam said.

"I have something else," David said. "And it involves you."

Sam raised an eyebrow.

"Both of you," David said as a smile spread across his face.

"That sounds intriguing," Glenn said, carrying the tray. "What've you got up your sleeve?"

Sam pulled out a chair and sat. The others followed suit. "Have you heard? Frank and Loretta are expecting."

Gloria gasped and joined them at the table. "Are you sure?"

David nodded. "I just saw Frank, and he told me. As a matter of fact, they're having twins."

"Twins!" Gloria exclaimed. "Oh, my word!"

"That'll be a big change in the Haynes household," Glenn said.

"How's he holding up?" Sam asked.

"He's over-the-top excited," David said.

"Do they know what they're having?" Gloria asked.

"A boy and a girl."

Gloria clapped her hands together. "Praise be. That's wonderful. This day has brought nothing but good news."

"I'll say," Glenn said. "I'm happy for him."

"How does this involve both of us?" Sam asked, pointing at Glenn and then back to himself.

"They're going to need a room for the babies," David said.

"A nursery!" Gloria called, closing the oven door.

"And you know that Frank isn't the least bit handy around the house?" David asked.

Sam laughed. "That's an understatement. He means well, but I'm always over there fixing something he's worked on."

"Exactly. So I was thinking that I could paint and do the—" he looked over at Gloria, "nursery for them. I'm not sure what all is involved, so that's where the two of you come in. You could teach me anything I need to know."

"We'll do more than that," Glenn said, looking at Sam, who nodded his agreement. "We'll help with the work."

"We can do it together," Sam said. "It'll be fun."

"I'll put the crib—cribs—together," Glenn said. "They're not as easy as they look. They never come with all the hardware you need."

"And I can make baby blankets," Gloria said. "I'd better get started on them. Do you know what colors Loretta's picked out?"

David raised his palms over his head. "No idea. I just thought that this was something nice I could do for them. Frank's been good to me."

"It's a very nice thing, son. I'm proud of you for thinking of someone else while you've got all these other things going on in your own life," Glenn said, his voice catching.

David flushed.

"This is going to be fun," Sam said. "The three of us will make a great team."

"Joan and I are in on this, too," Gloria said. She looked at Sam. "I know that wife of yours will want to knit them something."

"I'm sure you're right."

"When will you tell Frank and Loretta?" Gloria asked David. "We've got to get cracking."

David took another cookie and washed it down with milk. "I'll get to it right away, ma'am."

"You're a very nice boy," Gloria said. "You can take all those cookies home with you." She retrieved a ziplock bag and handed it to David. "I've got to call Joan."

CHAPTER 18

Josh Newlon slammed the crosswalk button with his fist and jogged in place, waiting impatiently for the walk symbol. He'd overslept and probably should have forgone this morning ritual, but a stormfront was moving in and today would be his last chance to run for a while. He had fifteen minutes to get home, shower, and get to class.

The signal changed, and he sprinted off the curb without checking for traffic. He didn't see the white minivan making a left-hand turn. The van's driver's side corner collided into Josh's body and sent him flying into the windshield of a compact car waiting at the light.

Josh stared into the startled eyes of the driver before he lost consciousness and slid off the hood onto the asphalt.

***

The drivers of the minivan and the compact reached Josh at the same time.

"Oh, my God. I didn't see him," the driver of the minivan cried, wringing her hands.

"He's breathing," the other driver said, kneeling over Josh. He looked at the twisted body on the pavement, limbs sticking out at improbable angles. "Looks like his left arm and leg are broken."

Drivers from other cars that witnessed the accident approached. "I've called 9-1-1!" one of them cried, waving their phone in the air.

A siren could be heard in the distance, growing louder.

Josh moaned and tried to move.

"Help's on the way. Stay still. You're going to be all right. They'll be here any minute."

A fire truck, lights flashing, pulled into view with an ambulance behind it.

Paramedics sprang out of the ambulance. One of the drivers huddled around Josh signaled to them.

"What've we got?" asked a paramedic as he dropped to his knees next to Josh.

"He was jogging and ... and I didn't see him," said the anguished minivan driver. "I was making a left turn and hit him."

Another paramedic joined them, and the two men worked together in a practiced fashion, assessing Josh before preparing him for transport.

"I'm so sorry," the woman said as she leaned toward Josh.

"Everyone step back," another paramedic said, rolling a gurney into place. "You can make your statements to the police. We've got to get him to the hospital."

The paramedics completed their triage and placed Josh onto

the gurney. He groaned as they hooked up an IV bag and loaded him into the ambulance. They were shutting the doors when the driver of the compact spied Josh's wallet on the pavement. He scooped it up and rushed to the back of the ambulance.

"Wait," he said, holding the wallet out to one of the paramedics. "You'll need this. For identification."

The paramedic took the wallet. The doors shut, and the ambulance sped off.

***

Lyla paced the emergency room waiting area. She caught the toe of her shoe on the leg of a chair and stumbled into a woman who had just succeeded in quieting a screaming infant. The baby startled and began to wail. The woman huffed at Lyla in exasperation. "I'm so sorry," Lyla murmured, and forced herself to sit. She lowered her head to pray, but her thoughts raced, and she couldn't calm them enough to formulate even a simple supplication. Her God knew what was in her heart. That would have to be enough.

Her hands began to shake, and she put her arms around her waist. It didn't help. She rose and resumed pacing.

The woman at the desk who'd taken her information called to her. Lyla hurried over.

"Let's put you in a quiet room," she said, motioning for Lyla to follow her.

Lyla swallowed her rising panic. "Is he ... ?"

"Your son is in surgery and stable," the woman said. "You're going to be here for a while, and we like to do this for family members when we can." She opened the door to a tiny room, dimly lit by a fluorescent fixture with only one bulb that hadn't burned out. The room was furnished with two straight-backed chairs and a chrome and glass end table. An empty tissue box sat on the table. "You can have some peace and quiet in here. Is there anyone you'd like to call to sit with you?"

Lyla brought her head up. Her first thought had been Sunday, but she was in London. She needed to call Sunday. "No. I'll be fine."

The woman closed the door behind her.

Lyla fished her phone out of her purse and checked the time. What was she going to tell Sunday? There wasn't any point in calling her until Josh was out of surgery and she had more information about his condition.

She was putting her phone back into her purse when she remembered that Josh worked for Maggie. Should she call Maggie and tell her about the accident? Maggie would be positive and encouraging. She also might have suggestions for how Lyla should break the news to Sunday. She searched the college's directory on her phone and placed the call.

"This is Maggie Martin," came the voice on the other end of the line.

"Maggie," Lyla said, her voice cracking. She tried unsuccessfully to stop herself from sobbing.

Maggie waited.

"I'm … I'm sorry." Lyla's breathing was uneven. "It's Lyla Kershaw. From the library."

"Lyla. What's happened?" Maggie asked.

"Josh has been in an accident." Lyla's words came out in a rush. "He was hit by a car while he was out jogging this morning."

Maggie gasped.

"He's in surgery right now. They told me he's stable."

"Mercy Hospital?"

"Yes. I wanted you to know that he won't be in to work for…" Her voice trailed off.

"Do you have anyone with you?"

"No." Lyla's voice was small.

"I'm on my way. It'll take me fifteen minutes to get there."

"You … you don't have to do that."

"Of course I do. Hang on. I'm praying for you both."

Lyla hung up and brought the phone to her chest. She was grateful for three things: that her son was alive, that he'd picked her as his next of kin, and that Maggie Martin was on her way.

CHAPTER 19

Sunday popped the remaining bite of scone into her mouth and licked a dollop of lemon curd off her finger. She looked across the white linen-clad table at Robert. "I guess that wasn't very ladylike, was it?"

"Maybe not, but it was only sensible. Lemon curd is not, in my opinion, something to be wasted."

"I'm glad you agree." Sunday sank into her upholstered chair and examined the domed glass ceiling of the Thames Foyer. The Savoy Hotel had been serving high tea since the late eighteen hundreds in much the same fashion. Silver sparkled on every table amid champagne flutes and graceful bone china. Tiered trays of delicate tea sandwiches and miniature desserts —true edible masterpieces—stood on sideboards flanking the room.

Sunday had tried one of each of the four varieties of tea sandwiches and had just finished her second scone. The currant scone with clotted cream and strawberry jam had been delicious, but she preferred the plain one she'd slathered with clotted cream and topped with a generous dollop of lemon curd.

A waiter unobtrusively removed their plates, brandishing a silver, pencil-like half-cylinder, which he used to deftly whisk away any errant crumbs. He'd no sooner stepped away when another waiter placed a tray of desserts in front of them, each bite-sized pastry more elaborate and appealing than the next.

Sunday groaned. "I shouldn't. I'm stuffed, but I'm going to try one of each."

"You must," Robert said. "I insist. Otherwise, what's the point?"

"Precisely," Sunday said. "Who knows when I'll ever be back here for tea again?" She leaned forward and pushed the dessert tray toward him.

Robert shook his head. "Ladies first."

Sunday's fork hovered over the tray before she finally selected a small caramel-covered oval, topped with a meringue dome dotted with pistachios and pomegranate seeds. "This looks exotic," she said. "I'll start here."

Robert took a lemon square on a ginger graham cracker base, dusted with confectioner's sugar. He topped off both of their cups of tea, and they savored every mouthful while the pianist played Broadway show tunes.

"This is magical," she said, smiling at Robert over the rim of her teacup. "I can just imagine what it must have been like at the turn of the nineteenth century—the women in their floor-length dresses, with lace at their throats and billowy puff sleeves, and the men in cut-away coats."

"I'm sure it was very grand." Robert looked around the room and nodded approvingly. "Even as relaxed as today's dress codes are, people still put on their finery to come to tea at the Savoy."

"That they do," Sunday said. "I'm so grateful to you for bringing me here. What a perfect way to end our week."

"You've worked so hard, getting things sorted out at the shop."

"We wouldn't have finished if you hadn't organized everything before I got here."

Robert looked aside and shrugged.

"I mean it," Sunday said. "The credit goes to you. I should be the one taking you to tea, not the other way around."

"Nonsense. It's my pleasure." His expression grew serious. "After what you've told me about that night in the library—when Nigel tried to kill you—I think you deserve something nice."

"It's still surreal to think about all that." Sunday sat up straighter in her chair. "But that's over now. All we have to do is pack up the books I'm sending back to Highpointe to return to our library."

"I'm glad we both agreed on which ones are rightfully yours," Robert said.

"Do you think I'm crazy to want to bring the most valuable ones home with me in my luggage?" Sunday grew serious. "Now that we're this close to recovering them, I don't want to tempt fate."

"Not at all," Robert said. "If it were me, I'd put the most valuable ones in my carry-on and tuck it safely under the seat in front of me."

"I'm not being paranoid?"

"I don't think so. We'll get the books ready to go in the next day or two. When do you fly home?"

"I'm on a red-eye, day after tomorrow."

"Your timing is ideal."

Sunday's phone began to chirp in her purse. She lunged for it, almost knocking over the teapot. "Sorry," she said with a rueful smile. "I should have put this on silent."

Her smile faded as she looked at the read-out. "I'm sorry," she said. "It's from Maggie, the college president. I'd better take this."

Robert nodded as Sunday rose to exit the tearoom as she accepted the call. He watched her wind her way among the crowded tables.

"Maggie," Sunday said into the phone.

"It's Lyla. I'm using Maggie's phone because my battery is almost dead."

What could be so urgent that Lyla would be calling her on Maggie's phone?

Robert saw Sunday stumble. She recovered her footing and disappeared from view.

"What's going on?" Sunday tucked herself into a quiet spot in the hallway.

Lyla drew a deep breath and launched into the explanation she had rehearsed with Maggie.

"He's out of surgery, is that what you said?" Sunday pressed the phone against her ear. "It's hard to hear you."

"Yes." Lyla raised her voice. "They said they couldn't complete everything because his blood pressure dropped too low. They'll have to go back in tomorrow if he's well enough."

Sunday felt the icy grip of fear. "He's going to be all right, isn't he? He'll … he'll recover, won't he?"

"They think so. The next few days will be critical."

"Where is he now? Have you seen him?"

"He's in the recovery room. They'll take me back when he wakes up. I'll only be able to see him for a few minutes."

"Can I talk to him?"

"I don't think so."

"Should I come home?"

It took all of Lyla's will power to keep her voice steady. "Yes. As soon as you can."

"I'll get the first flight home. I won't finish everything I came here for. Do you think Maggie will mind?"

"She's here with me at the hospital. We talked it over, and she agreed you need to come home now."

"I'll text you my flight information." Sunday inhaled deeply. "Tell Josh to hang on. Tell him I love him."

Sunday turned back to the foyer and devoured the distance to their table.

Robert caught her eye and rose abruptly. He removed enough pound notes from his wallet to pay their bill, along with a generous tip, and left them on the table.

Sunday leaned in and told him what she knew, managing to keep her composure.

"I'm sorry I have to leave you in the lurch," she said, trying to keep her voice steady and hold back the tears that threatened to engulf her.

"Nonsense," Robert said. "I can take care of the books. We'll sort that out later. Right now, we need to get you a flight."

"Thank you for understanding."

"Call your airline to see if you can rebook your ticket," he directed. "I'll take you back to your hotel and wait while you pack up. With any luck, you can get out of here tonight. I'll take you to the airport."

They reached his car, and Robert held the door for her.

"I'd like to say all this isn't necessary," Sunday said. "But I'd be grateful for your help. I'm feeling very scattered and a little frantic right now. It's hard to think about anything but Josh."

"Don't worry. I'll see you safely on your way."

Sunday tapped on her phone, searching for the airline's number.

"I'll keep Josh in my prayers, too," Robert said. "I think your young man is going to be fine."

CHAPTER 20

"You can drop us at curbside check-in." Jackie Wheeler leaned forward from the backseat of John's Suburban. "No need to park and go in."

"I'm picking up Sunday Sloan in half an hour," John replied. "I'm going inside to wait for her, anyway."

He approached the ramp to the airport parking garage.

"Isn't she that librarian who was in the newspaper recently? The one that guy tried to kill?"

"That's her."

"Wasn't there something about old books being stolen from the college library?" David asked from the seat next to John.

"Yes. She's been in London getting some of them back for Highpointe. Her trip's been cut short because her boyfriend was seriously injured. He got hit by a car while jogging." He pulled his car into a numbered parking spot. "Sunday's very shaken up about it and took the first flight home. Maggie didn't want her to have to hassle with retrieving her luggage and hailing a cab. I'd already blocked out my calendar this morning, so I could take the two of you to the airport. It made sense that I'd pick up Sunday."

"That's very kind of you," Jackie said. "For both David and me, and for Sunday. I couldn't believe you made time for us."

"I wanted to see this guy off in style," he said as he reached over and patted David's shoulder. "One day, maybe you'll get your DVM and become my partner. In the meantime, I think learning to become a guide dog trainer is a terrific idea."

David's skin reddened from his collar to the tips of his ears.

"Frankly, I'm jealous," John continued. "I would love to have learned to do that."

They got out of the car. John opened the hatchback, and he and David removed their luggage.

"Thanks for taking care of Dodger while we're gone."

"Roman and Eve will have a blast with him," John said. "Don't worry about a thing."

"I just hope I do well enough in my interview."

"It's as much about you being impressed with them and their facility as it is about them liking you. Don't lose sight of that. This needs to work for you as much as it does for them," John said.

"That's what I told him," Jackie said as they entered the terminal and walked to the board listing arrivals and departures. "I'm more concerned about the financial aid package. We're getting our feet back on the ground after the foreclosure, but we'll need student loans."

"I've told David, and I want to reassure you—Frank and I are going to cover anything you can't handle. Don't worry about that."

Jackie looked at her hands and swallowed hard. "That's so kind of you. Whoever would have thought that Frank would be helping us. Except for Forever Friends, he never did anything for anyone else."

"People can change," John said, locating Sunday's flight in the arrival column. "Her flight's arrived—almost half an hour ago. It's early." He spun around, searching the crowd. "I'd hate for her to be waiting for me."

"Does she have your cell phone number?"

John's phone rang, as if on cue. He held out the screen to Jackie. "Sunday Sloan" appeared on the screen. He squeezed David's shoulder and mouthed the words, "Good luck," as he swiped to answer the call.

Jackie and David entered the TSA check-in line.

John sped off in the opposite direction. He brought the phone abruptly to his side and waved his arm over his head in a large arc.

Sunday raised her hand back in recognition. Her heavy carry-on bag slipped off of her shoulder and onto her elbow, almost knocking her off balance. She blew her hair off of her face and tugged the bag back onto her shoulder.

"Let me take that," John said, catching up to her.

She relinquished it without argument.

"How was your flight?"

"Fine." Sunday fell into step next to John. She caught her heel on one of the wheels of her rolling suitcase and nearly tripped.

"I'll take that one, too," John said, seizing the handle. "You look exhausted."

They turned and walked toward John's car. "How's Josh?"

"He's ..." John pulled her out of the flow of pedestrian traffic. "He's in surgery again."

Sunday swallowed hard. "Is it just the operation they planned to go back in to do today?

"Yes. That's all."

Sunday's eyes brimmed with tears. "He's going to be all right, isn't he?"

"Of course he is."

"I'm so scared for him."

"I know, but you don't need to be. Josh is young and strong. He'll pull through this just fine."

Sunday fumbled in her coat pocket and pulled out a crumpled tissue. She blew her nose. "I'm sorry. I don't know why I'm carrying on like this."

"Because you care about him, and you're dead-tired from a long trip. Maggie and Lyla told me to take you straight home so you can get some sleep. Josh should be in recovery in about three hours. They'll call you, and you can go to the hospital then."

Sunday shook her head as he was speaking. "I couldn't possibly sleep. I want to go straight to the hospital."

John looked into her eyes. He knew it would be pointless to try to convince her otherwise.

"Do you mind hanging on to my luggage for me? Or I can take it into the hospital with me …"

"I don't mind one bit."

Sunday quickened her pace. "Thank you. I don't want Lyla to be waiting alone, either."

"No worries on that score. Maggie is with her, along with several others you may—or may not—know from this town."

Sunday's countenance lightened. "If there's one thing I've learned about Westbury, people show up for each other."

CHAPTER 21

Sunday opened the door to the surgical waiting room of Mercy Hospital. The space was packed. She spotted Lyla and Maggie and started toward them.

Lyla looked up at her and stood, coming toward her with open arms. Lyla and Sunday embraced, propping each other up, for a long while.

Lyla finally drew back and held Sunday at arm's length. "What are you doing here? We didn't expect you until later."

"I couldn't go home to sleep," Sunday said. "I want to be here when Josh wakes up."

"That'll be hours yet," Lyla said. "We just got word that he's out of surgery."

"And?" Sunday held her breath.

"It was a little touch and go," Lyla said, her voice cracking, "but they don't have to go back in again. Now all Josh has to do is heal."

"Thank God. I've been so scared. That long plane ride, with

no information, was torture. I was terrified that I'd turn on my phone when we landed and find a message—"

Lyla ran her hands up and down Sunday's arms. "I know. It must have seemed like the flight would never end. You didn't get any sleep, did you?"

Sunday shook her head no. "I'm exhausted, but I had to come straight to the hospital. I didn't want you to wait alone."

"As you can see, I've got lots of people to keep me company."

Sunday looked at the sea of faces now focused on them. "I guess you do."

"Do you know everyone?"

"Not well, no. Just Maggie."

"Let me make introductions," Lyla said.

Sunday nodded as Lyla introduced her to what seemed like everyone in the waiting room. Joan Torres looked like a distant cousin of hers, so she'd be easy to remember, and she recognized Judy Young from Celebrations, her favorite shop in Westbury, but the other names came and went in a blur. What she did gather, as Lyla gently pushed her about the room, was that everyone she was introduced to clearly cared about Lyla and Josh, which was a small comfort and bolstered her spirits.

She turned to Maggie who patted the empty seat next to her. She sat and Lyla sat next to her.

Sunday leaned close to Maggie. "Thank you for letting me come home early."

"You had to."

"I'm sorry I didn't bring any of the books back with me."

"That's not important right now," Maggie assured her.

"We finished our work. Robert was super-helpful."

Maggie opened her mouth to tell Sunday that she didn't have to discuss the fate of the college's stolen books right now but stopped herself. Sunday needed something to take her mind off of Josh.

"That's wonderful news," Maggie said quietly. "What's the next step?"

"I was going to pack the most valuable volumes in my carry-on bag and box up the rest. I planned to bring it all with me on the plane. Now I'll have to figure out how to get the books back here safely."

"How many volumes are there?"

"Eighty-one."

Maggie rocked back in the molded plastic chair. "That many? I'm amazed."

"We were, too. Robert says the inventory in a rare book store doesn't turn over very fast."

"Makes sense. I guess it wouldn't be like a regular bookstore. These aren't current bestsellers."

"Exactly. It would have been so easy to bring them back with me." She looked at Maggie and frowned. "When Lyla called, I decided I needed to get back here as fast as possible. My choice was a flight that boarded in four hours or one that wouldn't leave until the following afternoon."

"You did the right thing by coming home on the first one." Maggie said. "I'm surprised you made your flight since you had to grab your things from your hotel and get yourself all the way out to Heathrow. London traffic is no joke."

"Robert took me back to the hotel and waited while I packed, then drove me to the airport."

"That was nice of him."

"I didn't have time to stop and pick anything up, not even the most valuable books," Sunday said apologetically.

"Of course not. Don't worry about that. We'll work something out. Maybe this Robert person will be able to help."

A tall, thin woman in scrubs stepped into the waiting room. Maggie and Sunday watched as Lyla rose and walked over to her. Lyla glanced back and motioned for Sunday to join her.

The woman removed a surgical mask from her face. "He's taking longer than expected to come out from the anesthesia," the doctor said.

Sunday drew in a sharp breath.

"This isn't uncommon, and we're not worried," she said, but her eyes signaled a different message. "We're monitoring him closely. I wanted you to know. When he's able to have visitors, we're only going to allow one or two of you." She scanned the group staring at her with anxious eyes. "You may want to tell these folks they can go home."

The doctor retreated through the door to the recovery room.

Lyla and Sunday clasped hands.

Lyla addressed her friends. "The doctor said Josh is taking a bit longer to wake up than expected. Nothing to worry about. Only Sunday and I will be allowed to see him. She recommends that the rest of you go home. There's no reason for you to stay." She tried to smile.

Judy looked from Joan on her right to Gloria on her left, then returned her attention to Lyla. "We're not going anywhere."

"I'm staying put," Tonya said. "I'll call George. He can wrangle the kids today."

Nancy Knudsen joined in. "We'll leave when you do," she said.

Lyla's vision was fuzzy with tears as she made her way back to her chair.

An hour and a half later, a nurse approached them. A smile

lit her face, and tension ebbed from the group waiting for news. "You're here for Josh Newlon?"

Every head bobbed in agreement.

"He's awake and doing much better."

The group heaved a collective sigh of relief.

"Can we see him?" Lyla took Sunday's arm, and they stood.

"The doctor said he can only have one visitor. It'll have to be quick. You're his mother?"

Lyla nodded. "And this is his girlfriend."

"Are you Sunny?" the nurse asked.

"Sunday," she said.

"Ahhh ... my mistake. He can only whisper, but he was asking for you."

Sunday's heart flooded with happiness, and she beamed with delight.

"You go," Lyla said.

"You're sure?" Sunday squeezed Lyla's hand.

"Positive." Lyla looked into Sunday's eyes and added softly, "We almost lost him, Sunday. Whatever my boy wants right now, that's what I want, too."

"Follow me." The nurse began to walk away, and Sunday followed.

"Tell him I love him," Lyla said as Sunday stepped out of view.

***

The nurse drew aside a curtain and told Sunday where to stand.

Josh lay on his back, hooked up to tubes and wires, surrounded by machines and monitors. The medical apparatus beeped, and their lights blinked steadily.

The nurse busied herself checking readouts and making notes on a tablet.

Josh's eyes were closed. Sunday found his hand lying still on the bed and gently placed it in her own, making sure not to disturb the oxygen monitor on his fingertip. She bent and brought her lips to his hand. A tear rolled off of her cheek and onto the sheet.

When she stood, his eyes were open and trained on her.

"I love you, Josh. Lyla said to tell you that she loves you, too," she said. "I'm so sorry this is happening to you. You're going to be all right. Don't worry. Everything's going to be fine."

Josh squeezed her hand with an almost imperceptible pressure.

Her smile shone like a beacon in the dim space.

Josh closed his eyes and slept.

CHAPTER 22

Maggie deliberately slowed her pace as they rounded the corner and stepped onto the sidewalk that skirted Town Square. It felt good to be stretching her legs after spending so much time in the hospital. Roman's stride was long and quick, forcing Eve into a trot to keep up with him. Her smaller companion was already panting. Maggie had thought about bringing Dodger, too, but decided that three dogs would be too much for her to handle. She steered the dogs toward Laura's Bakery, where she knew Laura would have a full water bowl by her door for all of her canine friends.

Roman waited patiently while Eve lapped up her fill before he took his turn at the bowl.

The sun glinted off the plate glass, rendering it more mirror than window. Maggie placed her face against her hands, cupped against the glass, and peered at the window display. Trays lining the bottom of the case held colorful fruit tarts and intricately iced cookies in the shape of butterflies that would be at home in any French patisserie. Cakes decorated with buttercream flowers in shades of rose, yellow, and cream were displayed on tiered stands. Pies took center stage on a two-level stand. She leaned to the left to read the small sign under one of the pies. Coconut cream—one of John's favorites. She'd stop in on the way home to pick up a pie for dessert. John deserved a treat for spending his free time shuttling people to and from the airport.

Maggie was placing a call to the bakery to reserve one of the pies when the door opened, and Laura Fitzpatrick stepped onto the pavement.

"Maggie!" Laura cried. "I thought that was you, peering in my window. It's been ages." The young woman secured an errant wisp of her dark hair that had escaped her hairnet.

The two women embraced. "I know. Way too long," Maggie said.

"You're so busy," Laura said. "I can't keep up with you."

"I'm busy? How about the town's best baker who's married to our favorite restaurateur, not to mention the mother of a preschooler."

"First-grader, actually," Laura said.

"What? Where does the time go? You'll be empty nesters before you know it."

A smile played at Laura's lips. "That day may be a little farther off than we thought."

Maggie clamped her hand to her heart. "Are you saying what I think you're saying?"

Laura grinned. "We're expecting."

Maggie swept her into a hug and held her there. "I'm thrilled for you."

"We'd given up hope, but then …" She shrugged and smoothed her apron over her stomach.

"When are you due?"

"First week of August."

"How are you feeling? You were so sick the first time around."

"I had a little bit of morning sickness, but it's gone now."

"I couldn't be happier."

"I'd better get back inside," Laura said. "Can I give these guys a treat?" She pointed to Roman and Eve, who sat patiently by Maggie's side.

"They'd love that," Maggie said. "And can you save one of those coconut cream pies for me? We're going to walk around the square a couple of times, and I'll pick it up on our way home."

Laura produced two handmade dog biscuits from the pocket of her apron and held them out to the dogs. Roman took his politely, but Eve snatched hers out of Laura's hand.

"Manners, Eve," Maggie scolded.

"She's fine," Laura said, patting Eve. "We're old friends. I'll have the pie boxed up and ready when you get back. Just knock on the door, and I'll bring it out to you."

"Thank you," Maggie said. "And add in a bag of those dog treats. I forgot how much they like them."

Laura retreated into the shop, and Maggie and her companions continued their walk. Squirrels chased each other across the lawn. She watched a bird swoop in and out of a low branch of a tree lining the square, twigs in its beak. She squinted, trying to find the location of the nest so she could check for the appearance of baby birds the next time she and the dogs came this way.

They continued walking in an easy rhythm. Maggie felt her shoulders relax and the tension ease out of her back. She was looking to her far right, observing a young father tossing a delighted toddler into the air and catching him, when Eve yanked her leash out of Maggie's hand, and Roman growled, baring his teeth.

"What in the … ?" Maggie cried as she faced an older man tugging at the collar of a German shepherd who was snapping at Eve.

Eve launched herself into Maggie's arms. Maggie clutched the shaking animal to her chest as Roman settled at her side.

Kevin Baxter pulled his dog back and commanded him to sit. "President Martin," he said. "You need to keep control of your dogs."

Maggie's hackles rose. "My dogs are perfectly behaved, Kevin. You're the one who needs to work with your animal. It's dangerous and irresponsible to be walking on the square with a dog like that."

A vein in Kevin's temple pulsed. "I don't need advice from you on dog training … or anything else." His eyes held a malicious gleam. "As a matter of fact, I think we'll be seeing a lot less of you in the future. We'll be talking about all of that at an upcoming trustee meeting."

"I hope you schedule one soon." Maggie straightened her shoulders and leaned toward him. "I'm looking forward to your full report of what you knew about your nephew's gambling addiction and related problems."

Kevin jerked backward.

"I did some research. I'm sure you disclosed that Anthony Plume is your nephew and that your recommendation of him for a professor's chair was based solely on his abilities as a teacher. You would never have been his champion if you'd known of his prior indiscretions. I'm certain you wouldn't have covered any of that up."

Kevin's face became beet red.

"If the hiring committee had known the truth, Anthony

wouldn't have been offered the job." She narrowed her eyes. "You're the one who let the fox into the hen house, Kevin. If the trustees want a scapegoat to blame for the theft of the books, I think I'm looking at the right person."

Maggie set Eve on the ground and signaled for her dogs to heel. She began to walk, then pivoted back to Kevin, who stood staring at her. "I'll see you at that trustees' meeting. In the meantime, both of you," she wagged her finger between Kevin and his dog, "should enroll in an obedience class." Maggie breathed deeply, savoring the heady feeling of victory. It was liberating to stand up for herself.

She and her dogs continued on their way. Maggie pulled out her phone and placed a call to Laura's Bakery. "Can you add a chocolate layer cake to my order, too? I'll be there in five minutes." It was time to celebrate.

CHAPTER 23

Frank pushed himself onto his elbow and leaned over to watch his wife's rhythmic breathing. Sleep provided her the only relief from her extreme morning sickness, and he loved watching her untroubled face. This time, however, the covers were thrown back on her side of the bed, the sheets rumpled in the spot where she had lain.

He listened for sounds of her in the bathroom but heard nothing. He got up, shoved his arms through the sleeves of his robe, and went in search of Loretta. She hadn't gotten up earlier than him since before she was pregnant.

The heady aroma of coffee greeted him as soon as he entered the hallway. He followed his nose to the kitchen.

Loretta stood mixing pancake batter by the stove. Her hair was piled on top of her head. Long tendrils curled around her face and clung to her neck. She lifted her face to him as he entered, and the smile that spread from her lips to the depths of her eyes made his heart soar. Frank marveled at his luck in marrying this beautiful woman.

"What's gotten into you?" he asked, coming to her side and pulling her into his arms.

She slipped her hands around his neck. "I woke up feeling good this morning."

"No nausea?"

"Not a bit."

"Does that mean you're finally past your morning sickness?"

"I have no idea. All I know is that I'm feeling great today. I wanted to get up and surprise you with a nice breakfast."

"Can I help?"

Loretta shook her head. "I've got this. Just get your coffee and sit here and talk to me."

Frank planted a kiss on her forehead and did as he was told. "What else would you like to do today? Seems like you should take advantage of feeling good."

"I'd like to start planning the nursery," Loretta said. "These guys," she smoothed her hand over her growing baby bump, "will be here before we know it. Can you spare the time to go shopping with me?"

Frank swallowed hard. He loved his wife, but he hated shopping. "What do we have to do? Can't you order stuff online?"

Loretta poured the batter onto the griddle. "I need to see things in person. I want to pick out colors and a theme for the nursery. It's way more complicated now that we're having a boy and a girl. I don't want either pink or blue. That leaves white, yellow, and green, but I'm wondering about purple and orange? Should we go with pastels or primary colors?"

She glanced up at Frank. "You're not listening, are you?"

Frank shrugged. "I'm no good at any of this stuff. You know that."

"Aren't you interested in what we're going to do for our babies?" Her brows knitted together.

"Of course I am," Frank said, trying to stave off the coming storm. "I'll paint and assemble and repair—anything you need."

Loretta rolled her eyes.

Frank took a swig of his coffee. "Why don't you take Marissa and Nicole? They'll love planning the nursery with you." He tried to conceal the hopeful tone in his voice.

The change in Loretta's expression told him he'd hit his mark.

"That's a brilliant idea," Loretta said. "You're sure you don't mind?"

Frank quickly shook his head. "It's Saturday. Why don't the three of you make a day of it? Buy whatever you want, and treat yourselves to lunch, too." Tension eased from between his shoulders.

Loretta flipped the pancakes. "Would you go wake them up and tell them the plan? Celebrations opens in a little over an hour. I'd like to start there."

Frank finished his coffee in one gulp. His wife was feeling better, and he'd gotten out of a day of shopping. This was shaping up to be a fine Saturday.

***

"If this isn't a sight for sore eyes," Judy said as Loretta, Marissa, and Nicole stepped through the door of Celebrations. She came around the checkout counter to greet them. "Congratulations, my dear. Everyone in town is so happy for you and Frank."

"And us, too," Nicole said. "I'm going to be a big sister."

"Yes, you are. And if you're anything like your big sister," she winked at Marissa, "you're going to be wonderful at it."

"Thank you," Marissa said.

"I'm glad to see you up and about, Loretta. I'd heard you've been very sick."

"Today's the first day in a long time that I've felt well enough to leave the house. I thought we'd better get started on the nursery."

Judy stood a little straighter. "I've got a wonderful selection of quilts and crib sheets, and a whole collection of matching decor items—pictures, clocks, toys, books, and stuffed animals, too. Some of them are a bit pricey— "

"Price doesn't matter," Loretta said, uttering one of Judy's favorite phrases.

"If I don't have something in stock, I can order it. How far along are you?"

"I'm in my fifth month."

"Good. High time you got started." Judy led them to the corner of the store dedicated to babies and children. The selection was as large as that offered by the big box retailers, but every item on display was charming and of the highest quality.

Marissa and Nicole began to rifle through the merchandise, oohing and ahhing.

"Don't make a mess of Mrs. Young's displays," Loretta admonished.

"No worries," Judy said. "I can always put things away later. I do it all the time." She recognized the potential for a big sale when she saw it. "Why don't you pile up anything you think you might want over there," she pointed to the counter. "You can go over it all again, later."

Nicole filled her arms with stuffed animals and brought them to the counter.

"We're shopping for the babies, not ourselves," Marissa admonished her much younger sister.

"Frank said the two of you can pick something out for yourselves," Loretta said. "To thank you for your help."

Judy worked hard to suppress her grin.

"Now might be a good time to fill out your registry," Judy said. "Since you're already here."

Loretta swung to face her. "I don't think we'll need to register. We don't have any family here. Nobody's going to buy us gifts."

Judy took Loretta's hands in hers. "Honey, we're your family now."

Loretta swallowed hard. "You've got to be kidding me."

"If you don't want to receive a bunch of stuff you don't want, I'd suggest that we get you registered. Pronto!"

Loretta shrugged. She still didn't believe Judy, but she wouldn't disappoint her.

CHAPTER 24

Maggie reached out and hit the snooze button on her alarm clock. She snuggled back under the covers and reached a hand toward John.

He caught it and brought it to his lips.

"You're awake?" she whispered.

"Yep. Have been for about an hour."

"Why didn't you get up?"

"I didn't want to wake you. Besides, sometimes it's nice to laze in bed."

"I'm glad. You always start your day at top speed."

"Speaking of which, are we going to church, or do you want to go back to sleep? You've spent most of the last two days at the hospital with Lyla and Sunday. Maybe you'd like to lay low today."

Maggie nestled against him. She was drifting back to sleep when a familiar whimper emerged from the basket next to their bed.

"I think Eve's trying to tell us it's time to get up." Maggie yawned.

"I'll take care of the dogs," John said.

"Nope. I'm on it." Maggie sat up and swung her legs over the side of the bed. "I'd like to go to church and see if Judy has time to see me this afternoon."

"Still trying to unravel the secret of the red coat?"

"You make it sound like a Nancy Drew novel," Maggie said, "but yes, I am."

"If we're going to be on time, we'd better hustle. Let's go," he called to Eve in her basket. Roman and Dodger were curled up on the dog bed next to Eve. They stretched and joined John and Eve. "You can jump in the shower, and I'll bring you your coffee."

"You are the perfect husband." Maggie kissed him lightly and headed to the bathroom.

***

"Thanks for coming here to talk." Judy looked up from her computer screen as Maggie approached.

"I always love coming to Celebrations," Maggie said. She placed the bag containing the red coat on the counter and scanned the shop around her. "It's a feast for the eyes. You know how to set up a display like nobody else."

Judy flushed with pleasure.

"Like all those Easter decorations in the front of the store. One of my first purchases in Westbury was that set of Peter Rabbit figurines I bought from you."

"They were perfect as the centerpiece for that Easter dinner you held after the first Easter Carnival at Rosemont," Judy said with more than a hint of pride.

"That carnival brought us all together in a common purpose."

"It sure did. Are you hosting the carnival again this year?"

"We've resolved the issues caused by embezzlement from the town's pension fund. What would be the point of holding it now?"

"There have to be other worthy causes. Everyone in town looks forward to the Easter Carnival. The children will be crushed if you don't have it."

"I'll talk to John about it," Maggie said. "Why are you here this afternoon? I thought you always took Sundays off."

"I try to, but I've got a big order to place." Judy leaned toward Maggie and lowered her voice, even though they were the only ones in the shop. "For Loretta. She and her daughters came in yesterday to order items for the nursery."

"How exciting," Maggie said, surprised that she was genuinely happy for the woman who, in what seemed like a past life, had had an affair with Maggie's late husband. The fact that Paul had fathered the youngest girl, Nicole, had been a bitter pill for Maggie to swallow. All that ceased to matter when the child wound up needing a kidney, and her own daughter, Susan, had donated a kidney to her half-sister. That act of generosity had almost killed Susan when she'd contracted a staph infection in the hospital. Susan had pulled through and now, two years later, the bond the half-sisters shared was palpable. Maggie's resentment of Paul had been replaced with gratitude for the love that Susan shared with her new half-sister. "It's nice that Loretta involved her daughters in making choices."

"That's what I thought, too. You should have seen them. Such nice girls."

"What did they pick out?"

"See the display in that window? With the frog prince and princess?"

"I noticed it on the way in," Maggie said. "The spring green color is so cheerful. The frogs, with their fancy clothes and crowns, are too sweet. I've never seen anything like it."

"I've had so many compliments on it," Judy said. "Almost everyone who walks in goes over to take a better look. I only stock a small number of the offerings in the line. Loretta is going to do the nursery up in it and ordered a bunch of accessories."

"I'm happy to hear it," Maggie said.

"Enough about that. You didn't come in here to talk nursery décor," Judy said. "You seemed sort of—I don't know—anxious at church this morning. What's up?"

Maggie leaned her elbows on the counter, inhaled deeply, and launched into the tale of the red coat and its remarkable brooch. "That's why I'm here," Maggie concluded. "Both Harriet and Anita thought that if anyone in Westbury would have an idea who the coat might have belonged to, it'd be you."

Judy narrowed her eyes and leaned back into her chair.

"What?"

"I'm thinking," Judy said. "I can't put my finger on it, but there's a memory from my childhood. Something with a red coat."

"Would it help to see it? I've got the coat right here." Maggie reached for the shopping bag.

"With the brooch?" Judy sprang out of her seat. "Are you nuts? That's way too valuable to carry around town."

"No, not the brooch. It's tucked away in Harriet's safe." Maggie held up the coat by the shoulders.

Judy inhaled sharply and reached out to touch the coat. The

far-away expression in Judy's eyes told Maggie that she wasn't focused on the fine fabric.

"My piano teacher wore a coat like this when she came to our house for lessons—with a brooch on the shoulder. I always thought it was so pretty."

"Was it this coat?"

Judy studied the garment. "I can't be sure."

Maggie pulled her phone from her purse and scrolled through her photos until she came to a picture of the brooch. She held the screen out to Judy. "Does this look familiar?"

Judy took the phone and studied the photo carefully. "This is exquisite."

"Is this the pin your piano teacher wore on her coat?"

Judy pursed her lips, concentrating on the image in front of her. "It could be." She brought her eyes up to meet Maggie's. "I was only seven or eight at the time. I can't say for sure."

"But this might be her brooch?"

"Possibly."

"Can you tell me her name?" Maggie asked. "I'd like to find her and ask some questions. We should restore the brooch to its rightful owner."

Judy's eyes grew sad. "I can tell you her name, but you won't find her. She died when I was young."

"Even if she's no longer alive, she must have next of kin."

Judy shook her head. "She wasn't married and had no family that anyone ever knew about."

Maggie's smile faded. "I'm sorry to hear that."

"There's one more thing you need to know about Elizabeth Filler," Judy said. "She was murdered."

CHAPTER 25

The sun was just peeking over the horizon when Sunday parked in her usual spot behind the library. The hospital nurses were moving Josh out of the ICU into his new room this afternoon, and Sunday planned to get in and out of work early enough to help him settle in.

She sucked in a deep breath. Hers was the only car in the lot. No one was there to deactivate the alarm at the front entrance. She'd been avoiding that area of the library since the events of that fateful night—when Nigel had attacked her on the staircase and tried to push her off the second-story landing to her death on the marble floor below. Now she always entered through the back, well after the library was open, and took the elevator to her office on the third floor.

If she wanted to be there for Josh this afternoon, she had to do this. She could summon up the courage.

Sunday flung her car door open and forced herself onto her feet. She'd done this dozens of times before. Now would be no different. She would turn off the alarm and head directly to the elevators. She wouldn't even glance at the spot where Nigel had fallen, his body contorted at unnatural angles.

She fumbled with her key. It scratched against the opening. She steadied her hand, and the key finally found its mark. The tumblers clicked into place, and she pulled the door open. The alarm began to beep. Sunday hurried to the keypad and disarmed the system. She flipped on the switches for the bank of lights on the first floor.

To avoid the stairs, she should turn forty-five degrees to her left and walk down the hallway to the elevators. Her office was only a minute or two away on the third floor.

Instead, Sunday walked past the main reception desk into the foyer leading to the central reading room. The halogen lights in the vaulted ceiling created garishly bright pools punctuated by areas in deep shadow. The only sound was the muffled whine of the compressor from the water fountain, cycling on and off. She should go back.

The grand staircase, rising from the ground floor to the landing at the second-story level before it split into two separate sets of stairs leading to the third floor, beckoned. Her gaze swept from the landing, where the struggle had taken place, to the area below where Nigel had landed.

She began to shake and pulled her coat closer around her, even though she wasn't cold. She needed to get out of there.

Sunday inched her way to the foot of the staircase and began her ascent. She couldn't avoid this area of the library forever. Maybe it was best to get her initial visit to the scene of the crime over with now, while the library was deserted. She could take this at her own pace. She didn't want an audience.

She gripped the banister with one hand and forced herself to continue. When the landing was at eye level, she halted. Everything was in place, precisely as it had been before that evening, except for one thing: The bust of Alfred, Lord Tennyson—the one she had used as a weapon against Nigel—was not in its niche. Terrifying memories swirled around her. She turned to run down the stairs when she heard her phone ring.

The call might be from Josh—or the hospital. She sprinted up the remaining steps to the landing and jammed her hand into her purse, withdrawing the phone on the third ring. The screen told her the caller was Robert Harris.

A trembling hand swiped the screen, and Sunday brought the phone to her ear. "Robert," she said in a shaky voice.

"Hello, Sunday," he said. "Robert Harris here. Am I catching you at a bad time?"

"No. Not at all." She tried to steady herself.

"It's just that you don't sound like yourself."

"It must be the connection. I'm fine." She was lying, of course, but hearing his voice was beginning to calm her.

"How's Josh? I've been remiss in not checking in with you sooner."

"He's doing much better," Sunday said. "He's had two surgeries and some ups and downs but should be leaving the ICU today."

"Good. I'm glad to hear it. And how are you doing? You've had a lot to cope with … with Nigel and now this."

Sunday gulped.

"I hope you're taking care of yourself, too. It can't be easy."

Sunday felt tears prick the backs of her eyes. "It's kind of you to ask. I've been doing okay. Until just now."

"What's happened?"

"I'm standing on the landing of the staircase in the library."

"Good heavens. The landing?"

"Yes."

"Why?"

"I didn't mean to. I came in early before the library opened. I planned to go straight to my office, but I couldn't help myself. The stairs drew me to them."

"You walked up the stairs and onto that landing?"

"I did."

"And you survived, didn't you?"

"Well—yes."

"There was no danger lurking there, was there? They're just the same stairs you've used for years."

Sunday's breathing became easier. "You're right about that." She looked around her with fresh eyes.

"I'd say you've done a courageous thing, Sunday."

"Really?"

"You've met a fear head-on. And you've conquered it."

Sunday climbed the second set of stairs to the third floor and walked down the hallway to her office. "Thank you, Robert. You don't know how much I needed to hear that."

"It's funny how things work out, isn't it? I was just calling to leave you a message. I didn't think you'd answer your phone."

Sunday pushed open the door to her office and placed her purse in its usual spot under her desk. "What's up?"

"I'm flying to the States to attend a meeting at Yale. Our libraries have a joint internship program, and I'm Cambridge's designated representative. I've got two days of deadly dull meetings to attend."

"Lucky you," Sunday said.

"I was feeling pretty sorry for myself until I realized I could extend my trip by a few days and bring the books—Highpointe's books that you intended to bring home—to you before I go to New Haven. What do you think?"

"That would be incredibly helpful. And so nice of you."

Sunday's voice reflected the smile on her face. "Will Cambridge let you take the extra time off?"

"I've got buckets of vacation time. I've already cleared this with them. I think I'll come a week early. I wanted to check with you before I booked my flights. I'd like to bring the books to you first thing. I don't want to be touring the country with rare books in my valise."

Sunday chuckled at his word choice. "Perfect plan. I'm not going anywhere, so let me know when you'll be arriving. I'll pick you up from the airport."

"Most appreciated."

"Can you spend a day or two here? I'd love to show you our rare book collection. That is unless you've got other things you'd like to see. The Highpointe College rare book collection isn't in any guidebook. Westbury is charming, but it's not New York, Boston, or D.C."

"I've been to those wonderful cities many times. I was hoping to get a tour of your library. After that, I was going to do some hiking."

"Our countryside's lovely in the spring, if the weather cooperates."

"It's a plan. I'll make my arrangements and send you an email with the details."

"I'll look forward to it. And thank you for your kind words earlier. You helped me more than you know."

"My pleasure." Robert's voice grew soft and tender, and the kind words that came reminded Sunday of her late father. "Be gentle with yourself, Sunday. You've been through a lot. I haven't met this young man of yours, but please give him my very best. I hope all continues to go well for you both."

CHAPTER 26

*L*oretta shifted her weight from side to side in the open doorway of the nursery.

David was rolling the shade of creamy white that she and the girls had eventually selected for the walls. Sean dabbed at a corner with a paintbrush.

Sam glanced up from the pocket door to the adjoining bathroom that he was resetting on its track. "What do you think?"

Loretta tilted her head to one side. She held her arms in front of her, forming a square with both hands. She peered through the square, moving it around in front of her. "I'm not sure. Do you think it reads a bit too gray?"

David swiveled his head over his shoulder.

Sam caught David's eye and gave a slight shake of his head.

"I'd say it's a warm white," Sam said. "Isn't that what you wanted?"

"Yes. It needs to lean toward cream and not gray." She put her hands on her hips. "I just don't know."

Sean stopped cutting in along the baseboard, his brush in midair.

David opened his mouth to speak, but Sam held up a hand to silence him. "Why don't you let us finish the room. You can't tell what you've got until it's all done. If you're not happy with the color," he stepped between Loretta and David, "we can always repaint it."

Sam ignored the sharp intake of breath from behind him.

"Would you?" Loretta brought her hands together. "The girls and I want this room to be perfect."

"We want that, too," Sam said. "We'll let you know when we're done. Live with it for a day or two, and if it's not exactly what you want, we'll redo it."

"Thank you, Sam. I don't know what we would do without you."

"This was all David's idea," Sam said. "I'm just here helping him."

"That's so nice, David. It means the world to us that you're doing this." Loretta leaned over to catch David's eye and patted her heart before retreating into the house.

"What are you talking about?" David asked as soon as Loretta was out of earshot. "This is the color they picked, and it's white. What's all this gray and cream stuff?"

"Don't go getting your knickers in a twist. Women like to change their minds on these things—especially pregnant women."

"That's my mom, for you," Sean interjected. "She changes her mind about stuff like this all the time. Drives Frank and me nuts."

Sam shook his head at the boys. "I've repainted dozens of rooms because the color selected wasn't what the owner wanted. It's always better for the client to be happy than to live with something they don't like."

"I guess that's why you're everyone's favorite handyman," David said.

"Customer relations is important in any business," Sam said, turning back to the pocket door, "including the guide dog training business. If you're serving people, you've got to be focused on making them happy. You'll find that out when you open that guide dog school you're dreaming of."

"That'll be so cool," Sean said. "I want to work there and train guide dogs."

"It'll be a while," David said. "I passed the interview and just got hired as a kennel assistant. I'm on the list for the apprenticeship program. I'll need to work in the kennels for at least six months. The apprenticeship can take three years."

"That's like going to college," Sean said.

"There's a lot to learn," David said. "Training guide dogs is a huge responsibility. People's lives depend on having a properly trained guide. The Guide Dog Center also recommends that I go to college part-time while I'm there."

"Sounds hard," Sean said.

"And like a perfect opportunity," Sam said. "Joan and I are so proud of you."

"I'm excited," David said. He picked up the paint roller. "We'd better get this room painted so your mom and sisters can decide if we get to do it all over again."

CHAPTER 27

"Judy's coming by now?" John asked as he loaded the dishwasher after dinner.

"She's on her way home from Celebrations," Maggie replied, wiping down the kitchen counters. "She said she has old newspaper clippings about the murder of Elizabeth Filler."

"That's her old piano teacher, the one she thinks might have owned the red coat?"

"That's the one."

"I have to admit, I'm interested in what she's found."

"You grew up here. Do you remember anything about the murder?"

"I was away at college and didn't pay much attention to local news." John glanced out the window above the sink and noted the headlights on the driveway approaching Rosemont. "She's here."

"I'm going to bring coffee into the library," Maggie said. "Would you let her in?"

The doorbell chimed, and Eve and Roman began to bark.

John hushed the dogs, and the three of them hurried to greet Judy as Maggie placed a thermal carafe and three mugs on a tray. She poured a dollop of milk into a small pitcher and placed her sugar bowl next to it.

Judy was spreading copies of newspaper clipping on the desk in the library when Maggie entered the room. "That smells heavenly," Judy said. "I hope you didn't go to any trouble on my account."

"It's the least we could do." Maggie placed the tray on the coffee table and came to stand next to Judy. "I can't believe you had time to dig all this up so quickly."

"I can't get that coat out of my mind. I still can't say for sure that it belonged to Elizabeth, but I remember that she was always beautifully dressed. Mom said that she was an English aristocrat who'd fallen on hard times." Judy narrowed her eyes. "I also seem to recall that there were rumors she and Hector Martin were sweethearts. He was much older than she was—and rich—so I'm sure there was a lot of gossip about her being a gold digger."

"I can imagine that would have raised eyebrows in Westbury back then," Maggie said.

"It would also explain the Dior coat and the diamond brooch—gifts from Hector," Judy said. "I remember that my mother had been distraught when Elizabeth was killed and had followed all the news reports. Mom kept a big box of newspaper headlines—Pearl Harbor, Kennedy's assassination, that sort of thing—so I decided to have a look." She tapped the desktop. "And I was right. There're clippings here that span six months. At first, the stories ran every day for almost a month. After that—when the police weren't having any luck finding the killer—they petered out."

Maggie picked up a clipping from the upper left corner of the desk and examined the date of the paper.

"That's the first one," Judy said.

"Piano Teacher Bludgeoned in Apartment." Maggie read the headline aloud, then continued with the article.

"Miss Elizabeth Filler, 51, of Westbury, was found dead in her apartment on West Third Street. The cause of death is blunt force trauma. The neighbor who lives below Miss Filler was not at home at the time of the attack, which the police estimate to have been between six and ten o'clock on Friday night. Cash and several pieces of fine jewelry remained at the scene. Theft has been ruled out as a motive. Miss Filler was a popular local piano teacher and had no known enemies. The police have no suspects at this time. If anyone has information about this crime, please contact the Westbury police."

"Gosh," Maggie said with a shudder. "Sounds like a violent end."

"It was." Judy pointed to the other news reports spread out on the desk. "There're more details in there."

"Did they ever find out who killed her?" John asked.

Judy shook her head. "Not that I remember. A suspect isn't mentioned in any of these articles."

"I'd like to read them all," Maggie said. "But what's the bottom line?"

"The newspaper dug around to see if Elizabeth had some sort of secret life, but they never uncovered any dirt on her. As far as they could find, she was just an unmarried piano teacher, who went to church, lived frugally, and kept to herself. She didn't have many friends, but they couldn't find any enemies, either."

"Any mention of Hector?" Maggie asked.

Judy shook her head.

"That's not surprising," John said. "If Hector didn't want the notoriety, he would have had enough clout to keep his name out of the paper."

"That's true enough," Judy said. "He was the most influential man in this part of the state for most of his life."

"It's shocking that Elizabeth was bludgeoned to death," Maggie said.

"I guess that's why the case was in the news for so long. Everyone was terrified that there was a brutal murderer in our midst who might strike again."

Maggie shivered. "Was there another murder?"

"Nope."

"Is there any mention about a red coat or a valuable brooch?" Maggie looked at Judy, hopefully.

"Not a word. I think the coat you showed me belonged to Elizabeth, but I can't be sure."

"I'd say we're at a dead-end," John said.

"You could check with the newspaper—maybe they've got other articles in their archives," Judy said.

"And I can ask Chief Thomas if they still have an open file," Maggie said.

"You mean a cold case?" Judy arched her brows. "I've watched lots of shows about those on TV."

"Something like that. I don't think they close the case on a murder until it's solved."

"I agree that we should do some additional digging," John said, "but my guess is that we'll wind up with a very valuable piece of jewelry. I think it'll look fabulous on the lapel of one of those fancy business suits of yours."

Maggie glanced at him. "If that pin ends up being ours, I've got a much better plan for it."

John and Judy looked at her and waited.

Maggie smiled back at them and shrugged. "Would anyone like coffee?"

CHAPTER 28

"Let me make sure I haven't missed anything." Maggie flipped through the pages of the report one last time before setting it on the small conference table in her office. "I think I've got it." She gestured to Sunday, seated next to her. "Thanks for preparing such a thorough listing of the rare books that Highpointe is getting back from Blythe Rare Books."

"I'm just sorry I couldn't bring them back myself."

Maggie tapped the report with a forefinger. "This gives me something to tell the trustees. By the time I meet with them tomorrow afternoon, Robert will have delivered the books, and I can say that they are now back in our possession."

"Are the trustees still breathing down your neck and trying to blame you?"

Maggie shook her head and suppressed a smile. "Not anymore. That seems to be a thing of the past."

"Speaking of Robert, I need to leave for the airport in a few minutes." Sunday's phone began to ring. "Maybe that's him, now. His plane might have been early. I should have checked the flight status before I came over here."

She pulled her phone from her purse. "Lyla," she said, a smile spreading across her face as she answered the call.

The smile quickly faded.

"I'll come right over." She punched the screen to disconnect the call and began frantically scrolling through her contacts.

"What's happened?"

"Josh's temperature spiked." She looked at Maggie, and her eyes telegraphed fear. "It was close to one hundred five. They've got it down, but his heart rate is up."

A rivulet of cold sweat trickled down the back of Maggie's neck. Memories of how sick Susan had been when she'd contracted a staph infection after donating her kidney to Nicole flooded her mind. Surely Josh couldn't be septic.

Sunday sighed in frustration as she continued to scroll through her phone.

"What're you doing?"

"I'm looking for Robert's phone number," she said. "I need to go to the hospital. I'm not going to be able to pick him up." Her phone pinged to alert her to a new text message, and she stopped scrolling. She began typing a response to the text.

"Is that him?"

Sunday nodded without looking up.

"Tell him I'll be meeting him in baggage claim."

Sunday jerked her head up. "What?"

"I don't have anything on my schedule this afternoon. I can drive over to pick him up."

"Are you sure?"

"Given the huge favor he's doing us in bringing the books, I don't want to tell him to take a taxi."

"I shouldn't put this on you," Sunday said.

"Don't be ridiculous. Your place is at the hospital with Josh and Lyla." She touched Sunday's arm. "Susan became ill with an infection when she was in the hospital several years ago," she said, omitting just how close Susan had come to dying. "I understand how serious these things can be."

Sunday hesitated, her hand poised above the screen.

"Tell him," Maggie said. "Text me his phone and flight number, and I'll be on my way."

Sunday did as she was told. "Thank you, Maggie. I can't tell you how much this means to me." Her voice wobbled.

"Not at all. Now get out of here."

Sunday headed to the door. "Will you text me when you've picked him—and the books—up?"

"Of course."

Sunday hesitated at the door. "Would you mind bringing him to the hospital? He'll want someone to sign for the books. I could go to your car and check them off myself."

"I can inventory and sign for them," Maggie said.

"It'll be far easier for me," Sunday said. "I know what to look for. I'd like to see this through. It won't take me long. It'll be no problem, unless Josh—"

"Josh is going to be fine," Maggie said, hoping she sounded reassuring. "I'll bring Robert to the hospital so the two of you can deal with the books."

Sunday gave Maggie a thin smile before slipping away.

***

Maggie looked for Robert among the group of people waiting in the baggage claim area. The Cambridge librarian had to be the tall, thin man in the wool trousers and tweed jacket with a sensible trench coat folded over one arm and a backpack slung over his shoulder.

Two cardboard boxes, crisscrossed with strapping tape, slid down the shoot and onto the conveyor belt. Maggie watched as the man pushed past other waiting passengers and pulled first one box and then the other off the carousel. He stood and mopped his brow.

Maggie spun around, searching for a luggage cart. She spied one abandoned by the exit and hurried over, returning with it to the baggage carousel. She pulled out her phone and texted Robert.

The man hovering over the cardboard boxes checked his phone and brought his head up sharply.

Maggie waved to him.

Robert raised his hand to acknowledge her.

"I thought that had to be you," Maggie said, pushing the cart up to him and extending her hand. "Maggie Martin."

"Robert Harris," he replied as they shook hands. "Thank you so much for meeting me."

"Those boxes look heavy," Maggie said.

"They are. I'm still waiting for my suitcase," he said as he placed the boxes on the cart. "I looked, but couldn't find one of these. There aren't any porters, either. I'm not sure what I would have done if you hadn't come along. I wasn't about to leave the books." He pointed to the boxes.

"We're very grateful that you've delivered them," Maggie said. "Sunday's told me how incredibly helpful you've been through the entire process."

"My pleasure," Robert said. "She's a wonderful young woman. It's terrible, what's happened to her boyfriend."

"Josh is a terrific person." Maggie's voice was ragged. "He's my administrative assistant at the college."

"I'm sorry that he's taken a turn for the worse. Is there any update on his condition?"

Maggie shook her head. "Sunday would like us to stop at the hospital when we get to Westbury. She wants to go over the inventory of books with you."

"Surely that's not necessary," Robert said. "You and I can do this. Or it can wait until tomorrow."

"She was insistent," Maggie said. "If you don't mind, I'd like to stop by to see how Josh and his mother are doing. She and Sunday will be cooling their heels, waiting for news from the doctors."

"Of course. I'd like to see Sunday," Robert said. "Maybe going through these books will be a welcome distraction for her."

Maggie took a deep breath. There was something very calming about this Robert Harris. She liked him already.

CHAPTER 29

Sunday stood at the window overlooking the top floor of the parking garage. A young man was struggling to remove an enormous bouquet of flowers from the backseat of a compact car. She watched him as he carefully reinserted into the vase a couple of stems that had been dislodged in the process of getting the bouquet out of the car. She hoped he was visiting someone who was getting better and would be coming home soon. Sunday wrapped her arms around her waist, hugging herself. She hoped that would be her destiny, too.

"Sunday." Maggie called her name as she and Robert crossed to where she was standing.

Sunday smiled as they approached.

Robert opened his arms wide in an uncharacteristically affectionate gesture for a reserved British academic, and she stepped into them.

"Thank you for coming," Sunday murmured. "How was your trip?"

"Fine. Uneventful." He gave a dismissive wave of his hand. "More importantly, how is Josh?"

Sunday stepped back and shrugged. "He's got an infection. They've started him on massive doses of IV antibiotics. We're hoping that the bacteria aren't resistant to them."

Maggie did her best to conceal her alarm. She knew far too much about these superbugs. "Have you seen him?"

"Briefly. He was out of it. I don't think he knew I was there."

"I wouldn't be so sure about that," Maggie said. "Susan later told us that she was aware we were with her, even if she couldn't open her eyes or talk to us."

"I hope that's the case," Sunday said.

"Will you be able to see him again tonight?" Maggie asked.

Sunday shook her head. "Lyla, that's his mom," she told Robert, "is with him now. We're going to the hospital cafeteria when she's done. It's hard to force yourself to eat when you're so worried. We thought we'd both do better if we had some company."

"That's a very wise plan," Maggie said.

Sunday turned to Robert and narrowed her eyes. "You look like you've seen a ghost," she said. "Is anything wrong?"

Robert brushed his hand over his eyes. "It's nothing. You reminded me about someone from a long time ago." He cleared his throat. "I'm sure Josh is going to be fine. He has the advantage of youth in his favor."

"That's what the doctor told us." Sunday said. "Do you have the books with you?"

"Yes," Robert said, "but we don't have to deal with them now. I can come back tomorrow."

"I don't think it'll take us more than twenty minutes to go through them, do you?"

"That should do it. You're familiar with all of them."

"Let's get that taken care of. There's nothing more I can do here, and that will free you up to start your vacation."

"If you really want to."

"I do. You've already done us a huge favor by bringing the books here."

"I'll wait here for Lyla," Maggie said, handing her car key to Sunday. "I'll tell her where you've gone. Maybe we can all meet up in the cafeteria. Are you hungry?" she asked Robert. "Believe it or not, the food at this hospital is surprisingly good."

"I'm fine," Robert said. "Don't worry about me. Let's take care of these books, and I'll get out of your way."

***

"That's all of them," Sunday said, signing the receipt Robert held out to her and handing it back. "The trustees will be thrilled."

"There are some very valuable volumes in there. Nigel must have had many of them for years."

"Thank goodness for that," Sunday said. Her phone chirped, and she scrolled to the message. "Maggie and Lyla are in the cafeteria."

The shadow crossed over Robert's face again.

"Are you sure you're okay?"

"Fine," he said, lifting his suitcase out of Maggie's SUV and closing the hatchback. "Let's get you back to your friend. We don't want to keep her waiting."

"Won't you come eat with us?" Sunday asked.

"I don't think so. I'm exhausted from the trip. If you don't mind, I'll see you back inside and then catch a cab to my hotel."

"Maggie will give you a ride."

"That won't be necessary. She should stay with you and"—he hesitated over the name—"Lyla."

They walked to the entrance, Robert rolling his suitcase behind him.

"The cafeteria is on this floor at the end of the hall," Sunday said. "You don't have to come with me if you'd rather get going." She pointed to a cab that was pulling up to the entrance to discharge its passengers. "This isn't London. If you don't catch that one, you may be waiting a while."

"I'd like to say goodbye to Maggie," Robert said. "I can wait if I have to."

Sunday looked at him. Robert was the consummate gentleman.

They proceeded down the hallway to the cafeteria, a large, open room outfitted with industrial-looking tables and plastic chairs, ringed with steam tables, a salad bar, and a grab-and-go section. The dinner hour was winding down, and only a handful of people remained in the space.

Maggie and Sunday spotted each other at the same time. Sunday started toward her with Robert following behind.

Maggie rose when they reached the table. "Everything in order?"

"It is," Sunday said. "Of course." She smiled at Robert.

"I'll keep the books locked in my office at the college until you're ready to take care of them," Maggie said.

"Did something bad happen to Josh while we were gone?" Sunday asked.

"No. Lyla said that his vital signs have improved. The nurse was very encouraged by that."

"Where is Lyla?" Sunday asked, looking around the cafeteria.

"She went to the ladies' room. She'll be right back."

Robert cleared his throat. "I'm going to head to my hotel. I just wanted to thank you, Maggie, for coming to get me at the airport and to say I enjoyed meeting you."

"I'll give you a ride," Maggie said, reaching for her purse.

"You'll do no such thing. Your presence is needed here, I should say." He extended his hand, and they shook.

"Thank you again, Robert. If there's anything we can do for you during your stay here, please call me."

"Yes," Sunday said. "I'd still like to give you a tour of our library. I'll call you tomorrow."

"If everything is fine here, I'd love that." He nodded to them both and headed to the entrance.

***

Lyla came out of the ladies' room in time to see a distinguished-looking man leaving the cafeteria, rolling a suitcase behind him. She put out a hand to steady herself on the back of a chair. Something about him seemed so familiar.

The intercom crackled, and a male voice announced that the hot food lines would be closing in ten minutes. Lyla shook her head. Stress and fatigue were playing tricks on her. She hurried to the table so they wouldn't miss dinner.

CHAPTER 30

"You're the best babysitter," Susan said to Marissa, who was sitting on a floor mat, naming and handing brightly colored shapes to Susan's giggling baby, Julia.

Cooper abandoned his spot next to Julia, stretched, and padded over to greet her.

Marissa looked up. "Thank you," she said.

Susan bent to place her briefcase on the floor and ruffle the ears of the dog, waiting patiently for her attention. "I'm so glad you take care of her after school. You're going to be a wonderful big sister to the twins, too. I suppose you'll be busy with them, and I'll have to find someone else. I hate the thought of that."

"No," Marissa replied quickly. "Mom and Frank are going to get a full-time nanny. The three of us aren't going to be babysitters. Our job is to be brothers and sisters."

"That's very wise of them," Susan said. "I'm relieved. Are you getting excited?"

"I remember Nicole as a baby, so I know what it's like to have a newborn in the house. Nicole is the one who's really excited about them."

Susan kicked off her high-heeled pumps and sat on the floor. Cooper flopped down next to her and put his head in her lap. She patted him absentmindedly.

Julia squealed in delight and held out her arms to her mother, who scooped her into an embrace.

"I was wondering if I could ask you something?" Marissa looked at Susan anxiously.

"Sure," Susan said.

"Nicole and I have been helping our mom with the nursery. When we were at Celebrations picking out stuff, the lady there got mom to register for things that people could give her if she had a shower—a baby shower."

"With twins on the way, she'll definitely need a baby shower."

"I wasn't sure what that was," Marissa continued, "so I googled it. It sounds like a super-fun party."

"It is," Susan replied.

"I talked to Sophie and Sarah about it, too."

"You're still good friends with my nieces, aren't you? Even though they live in California and you're here."

"It's easy to stay friends if you have a smartphone," Marissa said. "We text all the time. We were wondering—Nicole and me and your nieces—if we could give my mom a baby shower when Sarah and Sophie are in town for Easter."

Susan's eyebrows shot up. "I didn't know my brother and his family were coming to visit."

Marissa shrugged. "That's what they told me."

"I'm sure they're right," Susan said quickly, patting Marissa's

RESTORING WHAT WAS LOST

knee. "And I think that's a terrific idea. Have you decided where you'll have the shower?"

Marissa shook her head. "Sophie thought ... maybe—"

"Here? At my house?"

Marissa raised hopeful eyes to Susan.

"That's a wonderful idea!" Susan cried. "I've got plenty of room, and I love entertaining."

"I was afraid to ask you, but Sophie said you wouldn't mind."

"I'll help you any way I can," Susan said, "but I'll let you girls take the lead on all the planning. How does that sound?"

"We were hoping you'd say that," Marissa said. "Sarah's made a list of what we need."

Susan chuckled. "That sounds like her."

"Can I show it to you? You can tell me if we've left something out?"

"Sure. Do you have it with you?"

"It's on my phone." Marissa rose and retrieved it from her backpack. She opened the document on the screen and held it out to Susan.

Susan perused the list. "You've made a good start. Invitations, food, games, and prizes. The only thing I don't see on here is decorations."

"Gosh ... we'll need those," Marissa said.

Susan handed Marissa's phone back to her. Marissa added decorations to the list.

"I'll cover all of your expenses," Susan said. "You shouldn't have to spend your allowances or babysitting money on this. And I love to cook, so I can prepare the food."

"Sophie said we should order a cake from Laura's Bakery."

"Absolutely. No party is complete without a cake from Laura's. Do you have a date picked out?"

"Sophie and Sarah will be in Westbury the week before

Easter. The carnival will be on Saturday. We wondered if we could have it here that Wednesday evening."

"I wasn't aware that my mom was holding the carnival again. I guess I'm really out of the loop." She gave Marissa a rueful smile. "As for the shower, I don't have anything else planned for that date. I'll call Grace to see if she can babysit. You and I need to be free to do our hostess duties."

"Thank you." Marissa grinned. "I can't wait to tell Nicole."

Susan stood and bent to pick up Julia. "You can head on home now. I'm going to feed Ms. Julia, here, and then it's a bath and bedtime."

Marissa slung her backpack over her shoulder. "I'll add you to our group text about the party."

"Please do," Susan said. "And I need to call that mother of mine to find out what's going on in my family."

"One more thing," Marissa said. "We decided we want this to be a surprise shower."

"That's a fun idea," Susan said. "Do you think you can pull it off?"

"I can keep my mouth shut," Marissa said, "but I'm not sure about Nicole. She means well, but … you never know."

"I've got confidence in that sister of ours," Susan said. "After getting through a kidney transplant, we all know she's a very determined girl."

Marissa opened the front door. "I feel like this is really going to happen, now. I can't wait to see Mom's face when she gets here. Thanks, Susan."

CHAPTER 31

"Note to self," Sunday said. "Don't wait until closing to get dinner in the hospital cafeteria." She scooped her mashed potatoes on top of her dried-out meatloaf.

"I think you made the better choice," Lyla replied, poking at a rubbery piece of cod with her fork.

"I'd be happy to go out and bring something back for us," Maggie said. "None of this looks very appetizing."

Lyla and Sunday shook their heads in unison.

"I'm not hungry," Lyla said, pushing her plate away from her and lifting her too-full cup of coffee. She blew gently across the surface of the steaming liquid.

"This is fine," Sunday said, nibbling at her meatloaf.

"I understand, but you've got to eat. You both need to take care of yourselves, so you can be there for Josh." Maggie pulled up the website of Pete's Bistro on her phone. "I practically lived on takeout from Pete's when I was mayor." She opened the screen to the takeout menu and was passing her phone across the table to Lyla when she looked up and raised her eyebrows.

"Change your mind?" she said to the man approaching their table.

Robert lifted his right hand to shoulder level, a set of keys dangling from his fingers. "I'm afraid I forgot to return your car keys to you, Maggie. I felt them in my pocket as I was getting into the cab."

Lyla jerked back. Scalding coffee slopped out of the cup and onto the table.

Maggie rose and extended her hand to take the keys. "Thank you for coming back."

"Of course," he said, leaning toward her.

Lyla sprang out of her chair, knocking the keys to the floor. She spun to face Robert.

"What …" he began, then stopped in mid-sentence as his eyes fell on Lyla.

Robert and Lyla stood motionless, staring at each other.

Maggie bent to pick up her keys and glanced over at Sunday.

Sunday shrugged.

"Robert," Lyla said in a voice that was barely more than a whisper.

He straightened. "Hello, Lyla."

Lyla put a hand on the table to steady herself.

"You're looking well." A muscle throbbed in his throat. "You haven't changed a bit."

"You're … alive." She choked on the words.

"Of course I'm alive," Robert said. "I recovered when I went home to England. The cancer never came back."

Lyla blinked rapidly. "That's not what they told me," she said softly.

Robert leaned closer to her. "What did you say?"

"Your parents. They told me you died."

He took an involuntary step back. "What are you talking about?"

"I didn't hear from you for weeks after you left the States, and I was so worried. I wrote you every day, but I never heard from you. I came to London to see you. I went to your house. Your father answered the door and told me you were dead."

"I didn't get any letters."

"Why didn't you write to me?" Lyla asked.

Robert clawed his fingers through his hair. "My parents," he shook his head slowly. "They must have intercepted your letters and never posted mine. I wrote you every day, Lyla—some days, more than once."

"They didn't approve of me, did they?" she asked.

"My cancer scared them. They told me they wanted me to stay in England, close to them." He shook his head back and forth. "But this ..."

"What an unspeakably cruel thing to have done." Lyla's voice was hard.

Robert reached for her arm. "God! I never thought they were capable of something like this. How did you manage to get to England? We were both poor as church mice back then."

"I sold my car. I had enough for a round-trip ticket."

Lyla brought her hands to his arms, and they stood, holding each other at arm's length.

"And then my parents told you I was dead."

Lyla nodded. A tear traced its way down her cheek.

"What did you do then?"

"I stumbled back to my youth hostel, collected my suitcase, and came home. I didn't know what else to do."

"My parents lied to us."

Lyla blinked hard.

"Oh, Lyla. I'm so sorry this happened—to both of us."

Her eyes searched his face. "Have you had a good life? Did you marry?"

He smiled a tight-lipped smile. "No. My career has been my life. How about you? I know your son is in the hospital. I'm so sorry about that. Is your husband here with you?"

"I never married, either," Lyla said. "There was never anyone else for me. It was always you."

His breathing became ragged. "Then what about—"

"Josh?" Lyla supplied. She stepped closer to him. "He's your son, Robert."

Robert's eyes grew wide.

"I was pregnant when I went to see you in London. I wanted you to know that I was carrying your child."

Robert stood, breathing erratically. "We have a … a son?"

"Yes."

He drew her into his arms.

"I hadn't heard from you, and I was terrified," Lyla continued. "I thought that if you knew we were going to have a baby, it would give you something to live for."

Robert and Lyla stood, clinging to each other.

Maggie withdrew a wad of tissues from her purse and handed some to Sunday. Both women dabbed at their eyes.

"I can't believe you're here—I've found you," Robert said. "And that I have a son!"

"Wait until you see him," Lyla said. "He's the most wonderful man. We only just met."

"What're you talking about?"

"I put him up for adoption, and we were recently reunited."

"You didn't raise him?"

"No. I had no money and no job. I was grieving for you. I could barely take care of myself, let alone provide a decent life for a child. It broke my heart to give him up." She slipped out of his embrace, and her tears came faster. "I'm so sorry."

"You shouldn't be," Robert said, lifting his hand to her but then curling it into a fist. "My parents are to blame. I'm the one who should be apologizing. We could have—should have—married and raised our son together."

Lyla brought her hand to her cheek.

"Did they know you were pregnant?"

"I was showing. They had to know."

Robert looked away. "I'll never forgive them."

"Are they still living?"

He shook his head slowly.

"I'm sorry you won't be able to ask them why they did what they did."

"I'm not sure it matters. Right now, I'd like to meet my son."

"Yes," Lyla brushed her wet cheeks with her hands. "I think that's a great idea. Let's go talk to his nurse." She motioned to Sunday. "Let's all go."

"I've got to get home, but please give Josh my best," Maggie said. "And don't worry about work tomorrow—either of you."

"Thank you," Sunday said.

Maggie's eyes glistened when she looked at Lyla and Robert. "I'm so happy for you both."

**

"How's Josh doing?" Lyla asked the slender woman sitting behind a monitor at the nurse's station.

The nurse looked up at the three anxious faces in front of her. "You're his mother and girlfriend, aren't you?"

Lyla and Sunday nodded.

"Who are you?" The nurse leaned to her right to address Robert.

"I'm ... I'm his father," Robert said, his voice cracking.

"Don't you worry," the nurse said. "He's doing much better. His vital signs are stable."

"Is he awake? Can we see him?" Sunday asked.

"I gave him a sedative thirty minutes ago," she said. "He'll be zonked out." She consulted her watch. "And visiting hours are over."

Lyla slid her arm around Robert's waist. "His dad came all the way from London. He just got here."

The nurse rocked back in her chair, studying them.

Lyla pointed to Sunday. "And she's been here quite a while, waiting to see him. We," she gestured to herself and Robert, "made her late getting back up here from the cafeteria."

"I'll let two of you go in for five minutes. It's only supposed to be one at a time—I'm not going to stretch the rules to make it three. You'll have to decide who stays back."

Sunday's heart sank as she stepped away. "It should be the two of you," she said.

"I saw him before you got here," Lyla said. "Why don't both of you go in?"

Sunday extended her arms to both of them. "Absolutely not. I'll come back in the morning. The fact that Josh now has both of his biological parents in his life is nothing short of a miracle."

"He won't know who's in the room," Lyla said. "The nurse just told us that."

"Yes, but you will. This will be the first time you'll see your child—together. I won't interfere with that." She squeezed their arms. "Maybe it'll be better that Josh doesn't know about Robert yet. You can share this experience, just the two of you."

Lyla swallowed hard.

"You weren't able to be with each other at Josh's birth, but you can be together now," Sunday added.

The nurse stood up from behind the monitor. "Have you decided?"

"See you in the morning," Sunday said, turning on her heel and walking quickly to the elevator.

Lyla put her hand on Robert's elbow, and they followed the nurse into Josh's room.

The nurse double-checked Josh's IV and the readout on his monitor before making room for them at the bedside.

"Five minutes," she said as she left the room.

Lyla pulled Robert with her to Josh's bedside.

Robert bent over his son, registering every detail of his face. He reached out with a shaking hand and gently brushed back a lock of Josh's hair.

"I've brought someone you've been wanting to meet," Lyla whispered as she lifted Josh's hand and placed it into Robert's. "Meet Robert Harris. He's your father."

The only sounds were the beeping monitors and Josh's steady breathing.

Tears spilled off of Robert's chin and landed on their joined hands.

Lyla stood shoulder to shoulder with Robert and they watched Josh's chest rise and fall in an easy rhythm.

The door to the room opened, and the nurse poked her head into the room. "I'm sorry, you two," she said in an authoritative tone, "but it's time for you to leave."

Robert brought Josh's hand to his lips and brushed it with a kiss before replacing it on the blanket. "I'll be back, my boy. Now that I've found you, I'm not going to leave you."

Lyla and Robert filed out of the room.

"Thank you for letting me see my son," Robert said to the

nurse.

They made their way to the elevator in silence.

"He's wonderful, isn't he?" Lyla said as they rode the elevator to the ground floor. "He looks so much like you when you were his age."

Robert rubbed his hand over the stubble on his chin. "I can't believe the changes in my life in just a few hours."

The elevator bumped to a stop at their floor, and they got off.

"I've found you again, and I have a son!"

Lyla grinned at him. "You're exactly as I remember you."

"Surely not," Robert said. "I'm much grayer and not nearly so agile."

"You look the same to me," she assured him. "Where are you staying? I'll give you a ride to your hotel."

"Can we go somewhere to talk? I've got so many unanswered questions. And I'm hungry. Would you like to get something to eat? That cafeteria food didn't look too appetizing."

"Aren't you exhausted from your flight?"

"I should be, but after all of this," he made a circling gesture with his hand, "I'm too wired to sleep."

"I don't think sleep is in the cards for me, either," Lyla said. She inhaled deeply. "Do you still like grilled cheese?"

Robert's face broke into a grin. "Like the ones you used to make?"

"You remember."

"I could never forget. I haven't had one like yours, since," he said, turning his head aside, "since forever."

"Let's fix that," Lyla said. "I don't live far from here. We'll have to stop at the store to get bread and cheese."

"And let's pick out a nice bottle of champagne," Robert said. "We've got a lot to celebrate."

CHAPTER 32

Chief Thomas came around the side of his desk, extending his hand. "To what do I owe the pleasure of a visit ... from both of you?"

John and Maggie each shook his hand and sat in the chairs across the desk from the chief.

"We've got something we need your advice on," John began.

"Police matters involving Rosemont?" The chief looked at Maggie.

"No," she replied. "Westbury Animal Hospital."

The chief's eyebrows shot up. "What's going on? Is one of your employees embezzling? Or helping themselves to your supply of controlled substances?"

"Nothing of the kind," John said. "We're here about property we've uncovered that may belong to a woman who was murdered in the seventies."

The chief jerked back in his chair. "You'd better start at the beginning."

"We found a woman's coat when we were cleaning out our

file room. We think it might have belonged to the victim," John said. "We've brought it with us."

Maggie removed the red coat from the shopping bag she'd set at her feet.

"Why in the world do you think this belonged to a person murdered more than forty years ago? Even if it did, what difference would that make now?"

Maggie laid the coat on the desktop, smoothing it into shape. She lifted the collar and pointed to the label.

The chief whistled. "This may have been a valuable garment, but I don't understand what it has to do with the police."

"The coat also had a brooch pinned to the lapel," John said.

Maggie scrolled to the picture of the pin on her phone and showed the chief. "I took the brooch to Burman Jewelers," she said. "Those are diamonds, and it was made by a very famous jeweler, Van Cleef & Arpels."

"Where's the pin, now?"

"In the safe at Burman's. Larry is preparing an appraisal."

"Did he give you a rough guess of its value?"

"A hundred thousand, maybe more," John said.

"Holy smokes," Chief Thomas said. "What a lucky find."

"That's just it," Maggie said. "We've got plans for this brooch, but we want to be sure it belongs to us. Harriet searched all the databases for lost or stolen jewelry, and it doesn't appear on any of those. I took the coat to Anita Archer and Judy Young to see if they might know who owned it."

The chief nodded. "You'd have made a fine detective," he said. "That's where I would have started. What did they tell you?"

"Anita didn't recognize it, but Judy thinks it belonged to her piano teacher. The woman was always very well dressed, and Judy remembers rumors that she was seeing Hector Martin."

"That would explain a coat like this and the brooch you described. Those wouldn't come with a piano teacher's salary."

"Exactly," John said. "The piano teacher's name was Elizabeth Filler. Judy brought us copies of old newspaper clippings detailing her murder in the late seventies."

Chief Thomas furrowed his brow. "I remember that from when I was a kid. Very sensational at the time. The killer was never caught."

"That's why we're here," John said. "Would you still have a file on the case?"

"We never destroy cold case files on a murder," the chief said. "There's no statute of limitations on that crime."

"We'd like to know if there's any mention of next of kin in the file," Maggie said.

"Judy's certain the coat belonged to the victim?"

John shook his head. "She can't say for sure."

"Then I'd say that coat—and the brooch—belong to the two of you," he said. "You're free to do whatever you want with them. Even if Elizabeth had family, there's no proof it was her coat and part of her estate that her heirs would have inherited."

"If she had family, we'll contact them to see if they can identify the brooch. We want to try," John said. "Unless we find the rightful owner or their heir, we're going to auction it off and use the money to fund a school to train guide dogs."

"That's a wonderful cause." The chief looked from John to Maggie. "You're always doing great things for our community."

"The school is David Wheeler's idea," John said. "He leaves for an apprenticeship at one of the premier guide dog training facilities this summer after he graduates from high school. He'll be there for two or three years. My goal is to raise the money he'll need to start his own school by the time he returns to Westbury."

"We want to be sure the pin is ours to sell before we tell anyone else about our idea," Maggie said.

The chief turned to his computer and began typing on the keyboard. "We've computerized most of our cold case files," he said, perusing the screen. "But not this one. We'd still have a paper file, somewhere in the bowels of our storage room." He looked at Maggie and John.

"You'd like me to dig it out to see if I can find anything about Elizabeth Filler's family? Or any mention of the coat or brooch?"

They nodded in unison.

"I can do that." He sighed heavily. "Give me a few weeks. I'm not going to pull anyone off of an active investigation for this, so I'll get to it myself."

"Thank you, Chief," John said. "We're in no hurry."

Maggie began folding the coat to put it back in the shopping bag when her ring caught on a small vertical slit in the side seam. She carefully extricated her ring.

"That's odd," she said. "This looks like some sort of hidden pocket. I think there's something in here." She inserted her fingers into the opening and withdrew a small, yellowed scrap of paper, creased in the middle. She unfolded the paper and placed it on the chief's desk.

All three of them leaned over to read the note written in neat, precise cursive.

I'm not asking. Get it for me. You don't want to say no.

The chief picked up the note. "You've never seen this?"

"No," Maggie said. "That paper is so old that it feels almost like fabric."

"Sounds threatening, doesn't it?" John asked.

"It's odd, that's for sure," the chief said. "You've piqued my interest. I'll go through the file and let you know what I find."

CHAPTER 33

The sun shone high in a cloudless sky, flooding Lyla's bedroom with light. The aroma of coffee beckoned to her from beyond her closed bedroom door. She propped herself on her elbow and checked her bedside clock. It was almost noon. She'd slept for six hours and felt like she needed another six. She yawned and stretched, then donned her robe and slippers and padded down the hall to the kitchen.

"Still an early bird, I see," she said, smiling at the mature man but seeing the younger version that she had carried in her heart all these years.

"Getting up after eleven hardly qualifies me as an early riser," he replied, pouring coffee into a mug and handing it to her.

"Thanks." She brought the mug to her nose and inhaled. "How did you sleep? That mattress in the guest room is pretty firm."

Robert shrugged. "As well as could be expected. The mattress was fine. My mind was still churning."

"It's a lot to take in," Lyla said.

"One thing still bothers me."

"What's that?" Lyla asked as she took a sip of her coffee.

"That I didn't try harder to get in touch with you after I went back to London."

"You've explained all that," Lyla said. "You were battling cancer, and you thought I'd," she swallowed hard, "forgotten you."

"I should never have thought that," Robert said. "That's not something you would have done. I should have known better."

"You were young," Lyla said. "We both were."

Robert slapped the countertop in frustration.

"We can't do anything to change the past," Lyla said quietly. "Let it go."

"Can you … let it go?"

Lyla nodded.

"I need you to understand that cancer left me a changed person. I recovered, but during the decade following my recovery, I was always waiting for the other shoe to drop—for the cancer to return. Waiting for the results of every follow-up test was torture. The disease stripped me of my self-confidence, too. I was damaged goods and convinced myself that you—or any other woman—wouldn't want me."

"Is that why you never married?"

"Partially. That and the fact that no other woman measured up to you."

They stood in silence and looked at each other.

Lyla sighed heavily. "We're making ourselves sound like characters in a Shakespearean tragedy."

"Star-crossed lovers?"

"Exactly."

"I'm so sorry that you had to endure giving up our child for adoption."

"You're not mad at me? Because I've spent most of my adult life being mad at myself."

Robert crossed to where she stood and took her into his arms. "Not for a moment. I know you made a selfless decision for him."

"And now, he's brought us back together again." Lyla tilted her face to his.

Robert bent and kissed the woman he'd been unable to forget.

***

"I'll bring you a burger from Pete's as soon as you're allowed to have solid food again," Sunday said, reaching for the cafeteria tray that held the remnants of Josh's lunch of broth and Jell-O. "I understand hospital broth is horrible."

He caught her hand and pulled her to him. "Don't worry about it. Now that you're here, I've got everything I'll ever want or need." He kissed her open palm.

"Oh, Josh," she replied. "I'm so sorry this happened to you. I was terrified that I was going to lose you. After waiting so long to find …" her voice caught in her throat.

"Your soulmate? The love of your life?" he supplied softly.

Sunday nodded.

Josh reached up and smoothed back the thick shock of hair that had fallen over her eyes. "You haven't lost me. I'm right here, and I'm not going anywhere."

She looked up, a question in her eyes.

"And I feel the same way about you."

A knock on the door alerted them to the nurse's presence. "I need to change his IV and do some other routine maintenance," she said with a smile. "Why don't you go get something to eat while I tidy him up; make him more presentable?"

"Great idea," Josh said, winking at Sunday. "I don't want her to have any second thoughts."

"Not a chance," Sunday replied.

"Give us fifteen minutes," the nurse said. "Go on, now."

Sunday brushed a kiss across Josh's lips and left the room, heading for the elevator. It was after one. She was hungry and decided to head to the cafeteria before they finished lunch service.

The elevator doors opened, and Lyla and Robert stepped out.

"How is he this morning?" Lyla asked.

"Much better," Sunday said. "He's sitting up and just ate broth and Jell-O for lunch. He complained about the food—kept asking the nurse if he could get a burger—so he's getting back to normal."

"The antibiotics must be working," Robert said.

"That's what the nurse told him," Sunday replied, noting that Robert was wearing the same clothes from the day before. Had he gone to his hotel, she wondered, or could he have spent the night with Lyla? She glanced at Lyla and thought she detected a new sense of contentment radiating from her. She forced her mind from her nosy thoughts—she'd ask her best friend about whatever was going on between her and Robert later.

Lyla put her hand on her heart. "I'm so relieved to hear it. He gave us quite a start."

"The nurse just went in to change his IV and help him clean up. She'll be done soon. They're talking of moving him out of ICU this afternoon," Sunday said. "I thought I'd get some lunch and come back to wait with him."

Lyla moved aside. "You go on. We had a late breakfast." Her color rose. "We were up most of the night, catching up on ... on old times."

"I can imagine," Sunday said. "Have you decided when you're going to tell Josh?"

Robert and Lyla exchanged a glance.

"We thought we'd tell him this afternoon," Robert said.

"Good. Now that you're here, I'm going to go home instead of heading to the cafeteria, make myself a quick bite, and take a nap. I wasn't up all night," she looked from one of them to the other, "but I still barely slept."

"Great idea," Lyla said.

"I'll call when I wake up," Sunday said. "I'd like to hear how Josh takes the news."

Robert's expression grew somber. "I hope we're not rushing it," he said. "Maybe we should wait."

Sunday patted his elbow. "I think you've waited long enough to be reunited with your son. My guess is that he'll be very receptive to learning you're his father."

She stepped around them and pushed the button to summon the elevator.

Lyla and Robert continued down the hall to Josh's room.

"Do you still want to proceed like we discussed?" Lyla asked Robert.

"Yes. You tell him about me, and if he wants to see me, I'll go in. His condition is the most important thing right now. If he's not feeling up to it, I can wait."

"You're a kind and patient man," Lyla said softly.

The door opened and the nurse stepped out. "He's all yours," she said.

Lyla pushed the door open and entered Josh's room.

The head of his bed was raised into a sitting position, and

Josh was watching a game show on television. He muted the sound as she approached.

"How are you feeling?" Lyla asked.

"Much better," he said.

She stood next to the bed and smoothed the blanket.

"Something is bothering me," he said. "I think I had a weird, painkiller-induced dream last night."

Lyla cleared her throat. "What're you talking about?"

"I dreamed that you brought a man into the room with you last night. You put my hand in his and told me that he was my father."

Lyla felt herself flush.

"And now you've got a strange look on your face." Josh fixed her with his gaze. "What's going on? Did you—?"

"It's true. It's all true. Your biological father is here, Josh."

"He didn't die?"

Lyla shook her head. "I only found out, myself, last night. Right before I brought him in to see you." She related the events of the prior evening.

Josh leaned back against his pillows. "This is a miracle. I kept asking myself what the reason was for my accident—what good could come of it." He looked at Lyla. "Now, I know. I might never have found my father if I hadn't been in the hospital."

Lyla's eyes were brimming. "He's waiting outside," she said. "We didn't want to push you if you weren't ready. Would you like to meet him? Are you up to it?"

"I don't want to wait another minute."

"I'll go get him."

Lyla hurried from the room.

Josh closed his eyes, suddenly very tired. He heard Robert's footsteps and forced his eyes open.

The two men looked at each other, their silence drawing them slowly together.

Josh lifted his hand, and Robert grasped it. "Hello, Josh. I understand you had an adoptive father who you loved. Why don't you call me Robert?"

Josh squeezed Robert's hand. "Thank you for understanding that."

Robert pulled Josh's hand to his chest and a long moment elapsed before he could talk. "We've got a lot to catch up on. I can't wait to learn all about you and your life."

CHAPTER 34

"It's been weeks since I've seen my girl," John said as he pulled into Susan's driveway. "I hope she'll remember me."

Maggie rolled her eyes. "Julia won't forget her grandpa. I can guarantee that."

John leaped out of the car. "I'll bring the food. You go on in."

"Can you get it all?"

"Of course I can," John said, motioning to Susan's front door with his head.

Maggie climbed the steps to the porch and rang the doorbell.

John lumbered along in her wake, brown paper shopping bags bearing the Pete's Bistro logo in each hand and a small bag from Celebrations tucked under his arm.

Aaron opened the door. Cooper stood behind his master, wagging his tail at high speed. Aaron bent to hug Maggie, then stepped onto the porch to take the bags of food from John. He noticed the Celebrations bag and laughed. "You can come over without a gift for Julia, you know."

Maggie spun to face her husband. "Honestly, John. You're spoiling her."

His face flushed. "That's not a crime, is it?"

Maggie put her arm around his waist and hugged him. "No. It's not a crime to be so tender-hearted. When did you have time to run out and buy this? We only decided to pick up dinner and come over a couple of hours ago."

"I might have a stash in reserve," John said, "in case of emergencies."

Maggie chuckled. "I'll bet you're Judy's favorite person in town."

John knelt on one knee to greet the golden retriever who was patiently waiting for attention. He ran practiced hands over the dog's back. "You're in fine shape."

Cooper raised his muzzle to John and licked his face.

John gazed into the dog's eyes. "You're happy here, aren't you, boy?"

Cooper emitted a soft "Whoof."

"Good boy," John said, patting Cooper's head as he got to his feet.

Cooper led Maggie and John into the family room.

Julia was happily ensconced in her swing. She took one look at John, and her face lit up. She began waving her arms and kicking her feet.

Susan poked her head out of the kitchen. "I always know when John's here," she said. "Julia doesn't react to anyone else like that."

John couldn't suppress a grin. "Can I ... ?" He approached the swing.

"Of course," Susan called from the kitchen. "Give her whatever you've brought her this time while Aaron and I set the food out."

"Looks like everyone's got your number, John," Maggie said.

John wasn't listening. He'd taken Julia out of the swing seat and held her on his lap. "How's my girl?" he asked tenderly. "Grandpa's missed you. I thought we could read a book together. The lady at the shop said you'd love this." He pulled a copy of Pat the Bunny from the Celebrations bag.

Julia poked at the fuzzy belly of the bunny on the cover.

"We're going to read lots of books together," he said.

Maggie stood and watched the man she loved without reservation forging an unbreakable bond with their granddaughter. It was a shame he never had children of his own, but he was making up for lost time with Julia.

John turned the page, and Maggie went to the kitchen. "What can I do to help?"

"Would you set the table? I'm going to stick these mashed potatoes into the microwave."

Maggie knew the layout of her daughter's kitchen as well as she knew her own and set to the task.

"Thanks for picking up all the food," Susan said.

"I'm glad it was meatloaf night," Aaron said. "That's my favorite special at Pete's."

"Mine too," Maggie said. "He gets the spices just right, and it's never dry or dense."

"And two pies?" Susan said.

"John loves coconut cream, and Aaron's favorite is key lime. We had to have both," Maggie said.

"I won't argue with that," Aaron said, winking at his mother-in-law. "Thank you for remembering. Julia's not the only one being spoiled over here."

"Of course." Maggie loved the kind man who had married

her daughter. "We've got to keep Westbury's newest—and best—orthopedic surgeon happy."

The microwave pinged, and Susan removed the now-steaming dish of potatoes.

"I'll go get John," Aaron said.

"We've got a lot to catch up on," Maggie said. "Did you hear about Josh's father?"

"Josh called me this afternoon," Susan said. "He's over the moon about it. We didn't talk long. He promised to call when he's out of the hospital. I can't wait to hear all about it."

"His infection in the hospital brought back some horrible memories," Maggie said quietly. "It's thrown me for a bit of a loop."

Susan put plates on the kitchen island, next to the takeout containers from Pete's. She came to her mother and put her arms around her, hugging her close. "That's understandable. I'm sorry, Mom. Remember, I recovered. Josh is getting better now, too."

"I know." Maggie touched her daughter's cheek. "I keep telling myself that. In the meantime, I've forgotten to tell you that Mike and Amy and the girls are coming to visit for Easter. They'll arrive the Sunday before and be here for the carnival."

Susan and Maggie served themselves and took their seats at the kitchen table. John and Aaron followed suit.

Aaron put Julia in her highchair, and John positioned it next to him.

"I heard about Mike's visit," Susan said. "From Marissa Nash."

"How did she know?" Maggie asked. "From Sophie and Sarah?"

"Exactly," Susan said. "When did you decide to do the carnival?"

"We didn't really decide," Maggie said. "Judy and Joan assumed we'd hold it as an annual event and had already organized a committee to plan it. Gloria, Tonya, and Nancy Knudsen are on the committee, too. They're almost all done."

"I love them," Susan said. "If you ever need to accomplish something, give it to those gals."

"You can say that again."

"What'll you do with the money you raise, now that the town workers' pension fund is solvent again?"

"Wait until you hear."

Maggie nodded encouragingly at John.

"We're going to use it as seed money for the guide dog training facility that David wants to start here in Westbury."

"That's a terrific idea," Aaron said.

Susan clasped her hands.

Cooper barked.

"I can't think of anything better," Susan said.

"We've got a lot to look forward to this spring," Maggie said.

"There's one more thing," Susan said. "Marissa and Nicole are teaming up with Sophie and Sarah to throw a baby shower for Loretta."

Maggie's chin came up.

"It'll be right here, at our house." She looked at her mother. "You don't mind, do you?"

"Not a bit. I'm thrilled for Loretta and Frank."

"Good because I offered to make all the food—except for the cake, of course—and could use your help."

"Count me in. I'm so impressed the girls are taking this on."

"Wait until you hear their ideas," Susan began.

Aaron and John smiled at each other across the table. Life was good when their wives were happy.

CHAPTER 35

*D*odger sat patiently next to the wheelchair while its occupant rubbed the back of his ears. David and Dodger never missed their weekly therapy dog visits to Fairview Terraces. Dodger's tail began to brush against the carpet as he looked toward the end of the long hallway.

David glanced up to see what had captured his dog's attention. He saw Glenn making his way toward them.

"I heard you were here," Glenn said. "The minute you and Dodger set foot inside Fairview Terraces, the news travels like wildfire."

"You can say that again," chimed in the man in the wheelchair. "It's the best part of my week."

David grinned. "Dodger's always a hit."

"We like you, too," the man said, looking up at David. "Everyone comments on what a nice young man you are."

"We're going to miss you when you and Dodger go off to school," Glenn said.

"Make sure you come see us when you're home," the man said.

"I will."

The man gave Dodger a final pat on the head and rolled away.

"Were you looking for me?" David asked.

"I was. Do you know about the surprise shower for Loretta?"

"Grace told me. She's taking care of Julia while Susan hosts it at her house. How did you hear about it?"

"Gloria's going to it with Joan and some of the other gals. It's all they talk about."

David looked at Glenn. "Do you have to go?"

"No. This isn't one of those new-fangled couples' showers. Sam and I were talking about doing something while our wives were there."

"That's nice."

"Sam said that the two of you got the nursery painted to Loretta's satisfaction."

"Finally," David said. "We had to paint it twice to get the exact color she wanted, even though they looked the same to me."

Glenn regarded the boy with great fondness. "That surely won't be the only time in your life when you'll repaint a room to make a woman happy. My advice—just go with the flow. It's easier to repaint than it is to argue about it."

"I'll try to remember that."

"Since the room is ready, we thought it would be a good idea to put the cribs together. One of the things I've learned the hard way is that an assembled crib may not fit through a bedroom door. It's better to put it together inside the nursery. And since they'll have two cribs, it's doubly important."

"Do they have the cribs yet?"

"I just got off the phone with Frank. They were delivered yesterday," Glenn said. "They're in big boxes in his garage. I asked him if it would be all right if Sam and I came over the night of the shower, and the three of us could assemble the cribs."

David chuckled. "I'm guessing he jumped at the chance to have your help. He's not very handy around the house."

"As a matter of fact, he did. He said he'd order in dinner for us. When I heard you were here, I thought I'd see if you wanted to join us. Sean will be there. It could be a fun guy's night."

"That sounds like a great idea," David said.

"Good. With all of us working, we'll have those cribs assembled before Loretta and the girls get home from the shower."

Dodger let out a soft "woof."

Glenn bent and patted the top of his head. "Are you getting bored, boy? Anxious to get back to your adoring public?"

Dodger swished his tail.

"I'll see you at Frank and Loretta's the night of the shower. We're going to meet there at five thirty."

"You can count on me," David said.

Glenn clapped him on the back. "I know that about you, son. I can always count on you."

CHAPTER 36

"I'd never been to the police station until I married you," John teased as they pulled into the parking lot of police headquarters.

"I wonder what he's found," Maggie said. "The chief sounded excited but wouldn't give me any hints."

"You tried to wrangle it out of him, didn't you?"

"Of course I did," Maggie replied as they got out of the car and headed to the entrance. "You know me."

"It's nice of him to stay late for us," John said. "I'm sorry I couldn't get away from the hospital any sooner."

"You're still looking for another vet, aren't you?"

"I am. I need to find the right fit."

"Good. You're working way too hard."

"That's the pot calling the kettle black."

Maggie opened her mouth to reply when Chief Thomas opened the door to the waiting area. "I saw you walking up," he said. "Follow me. I think you'll be interested in what I've uncovered."

Maggie and John exchanged glances behind his back.

Chief Thomas led them into his office and pointed to the chairs opposite his desk. He sat and tapped a tattered manila file folder. "This is our file on the Elizabeth Filler case. As you know, she was murdered—bludgeoned to death. The murder instrument and the murderer were never found."

Maggie and John nodded.

"It was in the newspaper articles Judy showed us," Maggie said. "Did you find anything in there that would tie our red coat to Elizabeth?"

He shook his head. "No mention of the coat or the brooch. As far as I'm concerned, they belong to you since she had no relatives."

"We can do what we want with them?" John asked.

"Yes."

Maggie cocked her head to one side. "That's not why you called us here. You've found something else, haven't you?"

"There were two things of interest in here," he said, opening the file. "More so now, in light of the note that you found in the coat."

"I thought you just said the coat can't be tied to her," Maggie said.

"It can't be, legally. There's not enough evidence. But that note you found in the hidden pocket of the coat, taken together with what's in here, may answer a lot of questions—including the identity of Elizabeth Filler's killer."

Maggie and John inched forward in their chairs.

The chief picked up a small packet of letters, tied together with a stained and frayed piece of ribbon. "These are letters from Hector Martin to Elizabeth."

"So it was true," Maggie cried. "Were they in love?"

"He was in love with her," the chief said, "at least for a time.

He even wanted to marry her. Evidently, she turned him down. We have to guess what she told him from his responses to her. He was more than thirty years older than she was—he writes about that—and begs her to reconsider. Tells her she'd be well provided for the rest of her life. He says that he doesn't need an answer right away. He'll give her time."

"Gosh," Maggie said.

"There's a gap in the letters of six months. When they resume, there's a much different tone. Hector has discovered that some of the books from his rare book collection are missing. In one letter, he mentions that fact, asking if she knows where they might be, and in the next letter—some three weeks later—he withdraws his proposal and breaks off all contact with her." He looked between Maggie and John.

"It sounds like Elizabeth's response to his letter convinced Hector that she had stolen the books," John said.

"That's my take on it," the chief said. "Hector was in his nineties when I first met him, but he still had all of his marbles and struck me as someone who wouldn't allow himself to be taken advantage of."

"This makes me very sad," Maggie said.

"You're a romantic at heart, aren't you, sweetheart?" John said.

"I never met the man, but my life has certainly been altered —for the better—because of him. I'd like to think of him as having been happy."

"How does this lead you to the murderer?" John asked. "Do you think it was Hector?"

"No. There's something else in here." He held up a small, tattered leather notebook. "Her address book."

The chief set it on the desktop and opened the spiral-bound

pages to the letter B. He turned it around to face them and tapped an entry.

Maggie and John leaned over to read it.

Maggie's eyebrows shot up.

"Nigel Blythe!" John exclaimed.

The chief nodded. "With the address of Blythe Rare Books in London." He allowed this revelation to sink in.

"Elizabeth knew Nigel?" Maggie sputtered. "And Hector apparently thought she had stolen rare books from him."

"It appears our Mr. Blythe knew about Hector's rare book collection long before Anthony Plume came along."

Maggie sagged back into her seat and put her hand on her heart. "What an uncanny coincidence."

"Maybe not," the chief said. "The rare book community isn't very large."

"So ... do you think Nigel wrote that note to Elizabeth?" Maggie asked.

"I think it's a good possibility."

"And he murdered her when he didn't get what he wanted," John supplied.

"Exactly. We'll never know for sure. I'd like to get a sample of Nigel's handwriting to compare to the note hidden in the coat."

"That note was written a long time ago. A person's handwriting changes over time," John said.

"The older the sample, the better," the chief said. "I called the attorney for Nigel's estate to see if she can send me an exemplar."

Maggie sat up straight. "I've got a better idea. The man who's been helping liquidate Blythe Rare Books is in town right now."

It was Chief Thomas's turn to look surprised.

"He brought the college's books back to us and is staying on for a while because he found his long-lost son here," Maggie exclaimed.

The chief raised an eyebrow.

"It's complicated," she said.

"I guess," he replied.

"The point is," Maggie continued, "Robert would be the best person to get you that writing sample once he returns to England. He's certain to have uncovered all sorts of old, handwritten lists and inventories drawn up by Nigel."

"That would be terrific. We may not be able to prove he killed her, but if we find that Nigel wrote that note, it'd satisfy me that the case has been solved."

John blew out a breath in a rush. "I never expected this. I thought you were going to tell us you'd found a reference to a distant cousin in the file and that we'd need to turn over the coat and brooch."

"Nope. They're all yours."

"Thank you," Maggie said.

"I'm the one who should be thanking the two of you," the chief said. "We may be able to finally solve this cold case."

***

"You're looking much better," Maggie said, smiling at Josh as he sat in a chair in his hospital room, his leg in a cast stretched out before him. "You gave us all quite a scare."

"I guess it was touch-and-go for a while with my infection. I'm glad I don't remember any of that."

"The important thing is that you're going to be fine."

"It'll be a while before I can come back to work," Josh said.

He gingerly lifted his arm in the sling. "I won't be able to use crutches until my broken collar bone heals."

"Don't worry about your job," Maggie said. "I'm managing with a temp. Come in when you're ready."

"I appreciate that," Josh said. "I'm anxious to get back to normal."

They heard a light knocking at the door. Sunday slipped in and joined them. She bent and kissed the patient.

"How are you today?" She smoothed a lock of hair off of his forehead.

"Great, actually," Josh said. "They're talking about releasing me tomorrow."

"That's terrific!"

"I'll need a lot of assistance for a while."

"Physical therapy?" Maggie asked.

Josh nodded. "And help with personal hygiene and getting in and out of my wheelchair." He sighed heavily. "I can't go home alone, so the hospital is finding me a spot in a rehab facility."

"I'm sure you won't be there very long," Sunday said.

"I agree," Maggie chimed in. "You're young and healthy. You'll be home in a couple of weeks."

"I hope so," Josh said. "I want to spend time with my father before he has to go back to England."

"That's a remarkable story," Maggie said. "It's the true blessing in all of this."

Josh grinned.

"Speaking of your father," Maggie said. "I'd like to ask him to do me a favor."

"Is it about the rare books?" Sunday asked. "I think we've got that wrapped up."

"It is—in a way. It's a long story."

"I'm not going anywhere." Josh gestured to his surroundings.

BARBARA HINSKE

Maggie looked from one to the other. "I don't want to monopolize your visit."

"Not at all," Sunday said. "Plus you've piqued our curiosity, so now you have to tell us."

Maggie motioned for Sunday to sit in the chair next to Josh while she perched on the edge of the bed. "John and I seem to have a weird knack for finding valuable things," she began, and launched into the story about the coat.

"We've got our answer about ownership of the brooch, but we may have uncovered information that could help clear up an old, unsolved murder."

Sunday pressed her fingers onto her temples as she shook her head. "This woman who was killed—Elizabeth Filler—may have stolen some of Hector's rare books before he donated his collection to the college. She sold them to Nigel, and he murdered her?"

"That's the theory."

"That's wild," Josh said.

"The police would like a sample of Nigel's handwriting—preferably from the seventies—to compare to the note you found," Sunday said. "You'd like to ask Robert if he can find something in the bookstore's records when he returns home?"

"Exactly," Maggie said.

"He's still in Westbury," Josh said. "He canceled his vacation plans so he can visit me every day. Would you like me to ask him?"

"Would you?" Maggie replied. "I'd appreciate that."

"I'm sure he'll do anything he can to assist the police," Sunday said. Her eyes grew large. "Who wouldn't want to help solve a murder?"

CHAPTER 37

Robert rubbed his hands together as he waited in front of his hotel for Lyla to pick him up. He hoped that Josh—and Lyla—would like the plans he'd made for them. He waved when he saw her turn onto the driveway from the street.

"I just got a call from Josh," she said as he got into her car. "He's going to be released from the hospital tomorrow."

"That's great news," Robert said. "It's a couple of days earlier than expected."

"Those antibiotics did the trick. Now they have to find a place for him. He can't go home alone. I'd offer to stay with him, but I'm not physically strong enough to help him."

Robert opened his mouth to speak, then thought better of it.

"What are his options?"

"There are convalescent centers where people go when they leave the hospital but aren't yet ready for home."

"That sounds promising."

"They're some good ones." She cut her eyes to his. "But I wish he could be with me."

"I know you do," Robert said. "I'm sure he doesn't think that's even an option."

"I wasn't with him when he was growing up. I wish I could make it up to him in some small way by being there for him now."

Robert put his hand over hers on the steering wheel. "You've been at the hospital night and day this whole time. I'm sure Josh knows how much you care about him."

She blinked rapidly. "I hope you're right."

"I understand how you feel," he continued. "I've only known I have a son for less than a week, and I want to help."

"He's been so happy about meeting you," Lyla said. "I know it sounds crazy, but I don't think your introduction to each other could've been any better. I'm just sorry that you'll be leaving soon."

She pulled into the hospital garage and parked the car. She was reaching for her door handle when he put his hand lightly on her shoulder.

"Can we talk for a minute? Before we go in?"

"Sure."

"I've contacted Cambridge and taken a leave of absence."

Lyla pushed back into her seat. "What?"

"I've been there for a long time and have never taken time off. I told them I have a family emergency." He studied her face. "I can take care of Josh. I'm strong, and, being a resourceful bachelor, I can cook and run a household. I'll rent a car and learn to drive on the right side of the road. I'll take him to physical therapy and his doctor's appointments."

Relief spread across Lyla's face. "You'd do all that?"

"Of course I would. I figure we could move into his apartment, and I'll take care of him there."

"That apartment of his is tiny," Lyla said. "You'll get tired of sleeping on his couch."

"I'll get a blow-up mattress."

She rolled her eyes. "That's probably worse. Why don't the two of you move in with me? I've got three bedrooms, and I can be there to help when I get home from work. I'll give you a break."

"I'm sure it won't be necessary. That's a lot to take on—two men who have only reappeared in your life in the last few months."

They sat in silence, looking into each other's eyes.

When Lyla spoke, her voice was soft and strong. "Those two men are my son and the only man I ever loved."

Robert took her face in his hands. "I would stay here solely to help Josh, but I also want nothing more than to spend time with you."

He pressed a kiss into her forehead. "I tried to forget you, but I never could. You've been in my thoughts every day since I left all those years ago. Now that I'm here with you, I don't want to let you go."

"Do you think we're being silly? It's only been a week—less than a week. And a very emotional one, at that. It's been such a long time. We're different people now," Lyla whispered.

"It was love at first sight for me before," Robert said. "And it's the same for me now. We've been given a strange gift, reuniting like this."

"I think so, too."

"Let's give ourselves a chance. I want to help our son, and I also want to see where we go from here." He lifted her chin, and they kissed, long and tenderly, releasing years of regret.

When they finally pulled apart, Lyla wiped a tear from the corner of her eye.

"It's a plan?" Robert asked.

Lyla nodded. "Now, let's see if we can convince our son to go along with it."

"I guess that puts us in the same shoes as most parents of adult children," he said.

Lyla chuckled. "Based on conversations with some of my friends, I'd say you've hit the nail on the head. Let's get up there before they've made arrangements to ship him off somewhere else."

They made their way through the hustle and bustle of the busy hospital to Josh's room. He was napping while Sunday sat in the chair, typing away on her laptop. She put her fingers to her lips as they entered and rose to meet them.

"He just got back from physical therapy. He's exhausted," she whispered.

Robert and Lyla huddled with her. "Have they found him a rehab center yet?"

"I don't think so," Sunday replied.

"Let me tell you our idea," Lyla said, outlining their plan. "What do you think?"

"It's a perfect solution." Sunday looked between them, unable to suppress a grin. "In many respects."

Lyla blushed, and Robert looked at the floor.

"Do you think he'll go for it?" Lyla asked.

"Do you think he'll go for what?" came a sleepy voice from the bed.

Robert went to the bedside. "We've got an idea to run by you—for when you get out of here. We all," he gestured to Lyla and Sunday, "think it's a wonderful plan."

Josh looked at Sunday, and she nodded vigorously. "Then I'm sure I'll like it. What've you got?"

Robert filled him in. "Lyla and I would be honored to do this for you," he stated quietly. "It would give us both great joy."

"I'm not going to be at my best," Josh said. "This may not be the time to get to know me."

"On the contrary," Lyla joined in. "This will be the ideal time. We know you'll face challenges—"

"I may get cranky, and I'll certainly be a burden."

"We don't care about that," Robert said.

Sunday spoke up. "It seems to me this gives you a unique opportunity to get to know each other. I can't imagine another time or circumstance where you'll live together under one roof." She took Josh's hand. "Why not give it a try?"

"If it doesn't work out—for any of us—you can still go to a rehab facility," Robert said.

Josh looked at the three anxious faces at his bedside. A smile started with his eyes and spread to his lips. "All right. Let's do this. I'm outta here tomorrow. Will you be ready?"

"I'll go tell your nurse," Lyla said. "I'm sure there's a number of things we'll need to do to get the house ready."

"I'll come with you," Sunday said. "I'll make a list."

They left the room.

"Thank you, Josh," Robert said. "For giving us a chance. You're going to be back to normal soon, and Lyla and I are excited to help."

CHAPTER 38

Mike Martin strode down the sloping back lawn of Rosemont, the early morning dew clinging to his shoes. "I thought I'd find you perched here, sipping your morning coffee," he said when he reached the low stone wall bordering the woods that flanked the back of the property.

Maggie patted a spot next to her. "Join me?"

"Sure. This is such a peaceful spot."

Maggie gazed up at Rosemont, its three stories of mullioned windows rising above them. "I never get tired of how beautiful she is," Maggie said, gesturing to her home with her coffee cup. "I love to sit down here, gathering my thoughts before the day starts. I haven't had time to do this since I became president of Highpointe."

"I'm glad. Once the twins are awake, I'm sure you'll be going a mile a minute." He put his arm around her shoulder. "What're your plans for us this week?"

"I thought you'd be jet-lagged after your trip from California. I was going to let all of you sleep in, and then I figured the five of us could have a picnic lunch in the country. Josh told me about a lovely spot he took Sunday to."

"That sounds like a nice idea. It's supposed to be a beautiful day. You're taking the week as vacation?"

"I am," Maggie said.

"I hope you stick to it." He gave her a stern look.

"I'll do my best," Maggie said.

"Why don't we have dinner at Pete's tonight? My treat. You can enjoy your day with us without having to worry about a thing."

"You're the best, you know that?" Maggie finished her coffee. "I'll take you up on it. Today may be the only chance we have to relax. The girls want to spend tomorrow and Wednesday with Marissa and Nicole, getting ready for Loretta's baby shower."

"That's right. I almost forgot about that."

"Once that's done, we'll be setting up for the Easter Carnival on Saturday." She cut her eyes to his and couldn't suppress her grin.

"Nothing makes you happier than throwing a big party, does it?"

Maggie shrugged. "Guilty as charged." She slipped off the wall. "I'd better get dressed and pack our picnic lunch."

Mike joined her, and they climbed the hill.

"What are you and John going to do while Amy and the girls and I are at Loretta's shower?"

"Funny you should mention that," Mike said. "John got a text from Frank inviting us to come over. Apparently, he's organizing some sort of 'nursery work party' while Loretta's out of the house."

"That's a nice idea," Maggie said. "The shower is a surprise.

Coming home to find the nursery done will make the evening that much more special for her."

"That's the plan."

"Who else will be there? Besides you, John, and Frank?"

"Do you mean, will there be anyone who knows what they're doing?"

Maggie opened her mouth, and Mike held up a hand to stop her. "No worries. John and I aren't known for our abilities as handymen. Sam, Glenn, and David will be there. Frank is providing food, and John and I will run out to the hardware store if they need anything."

Maggie rubbed his arm and leaned over to kiss his cheek. "As I said, you're the best."

CHAPTER 39

"You two are up early," Maggie said to her granddaughters as they entered the kitchen Tuesday morning. "We were just talking," she said, gesturing with her coffee cup to their parents, who sat with her at the kitchen table. "We thought we'd all go out to breakfast."

"No time," Sophie said, pulling a box of cereal out of the pantry. "But thank you."

"What're you in such a hurry about?" Amy asked her daughter.

"Marissa and Nicole are coming over in half an hour, and we're going to start putting the decorations together for the shower."

Sarah poured herself a glass of orange juice. "Can we use your color printer, Gramma? We've downloaded two shower games, and we need to print out sheets for everyone."

"Of course you can," Maggie replied. "Why don't you set up in the library? There's plenty of room to work in there."

"You girls have done such a nice job preparing for this

BARBARA HINSKE

shower." Amy rose from the table. "Let me make myself a piece of toast, and then I'll come help you."

"We don't need help, Mom," Sarah said. "We've got this."

"Oh … okay," Amy said. "I just thought—"

"I'm sure they do," Maggie said. She leaned toward Amy and Mike. "Why don't the two of you go out for breakfast and take the rest of the day for yourselves?"

Mike looked at Amy as a slow smile spread across his face.

"When was the last time you got away on your own?"

"I honestly can't remember," Amy said. "Maggie, are you sure?"

"Positive. I'll be here all day. If the girls need anything, I can help."

Mike shot out of his chair. "I'll go get the keys to the rental car."

"Let me grab my shoes and purse," Amy replied. "Thank you," she mouthed to Maggie. "You girls have fun and be good for Grandma. No fighting."

"We know," the girls moaned in unison.

Mike and Amy were pulling out of the driveway when Frank Haynes rang the front door.

Eve and Roman began to bark.

"They're here!" Sophie cried, racing to the front door with the dogs leading the way. Maggie and Sarah followed close behind.

Sophie opened Rosemont's massive front door, and Marissa and Nicole rushed inside. The four girls threw themselves at each other in enthusiastic hugs and greetings.

The dogs sat obediently, wagging their tails as they waited their turns for attention.

Maggie looked quizzically at Frank. He was laden with Celebrations-logoed bags clutched in both hands.

"Where do you want these?" he asked.

"In the library," Maggie replied, leading the way.

"Thank you for having them here, Maggie," Frank said.

"I love this sort of thing," Maggie said. "It'll be fun."

"If they need anything else, I told them to let me know, and I'll pick it up and drop it off," he said. "And if they get unruly and you want them out of your hair, just call me."

Maggie patted his arm. "Don't worry. Everything's going to be fine."

He bent to pat Roman. "I'd better get going."

The girls raced into the library and began to remove the supplies from the Celebrations bags.

"Have fun," he said as he left.

The girls were busy sorting the items they'd brought and didn't look up.

Maggie checked on them periodically. They'd needed her to change the magenta printer cartridge, but otherwise, they were getting along famously, and she became engrossed in a treatise on upcoming trends in higher education.

Maggie was surprised when she heard another knock on the front door. She found Frank on the doorstep, laden with yet another round of Celebrations bags.

"They needed these," he said simply as he stepped inside and walked directly into the library.

Maggie followed him.

Sophie, Sarah, and Marissa sat cross-legged on the floor in front of the fireplace, stringing together a banner of dancing frog princes and princesses. Nicole was curled up in the oversized chair by the French doors, staring into the garden.

"Thanks, Dad," Marissa said as Frank deposited his parcels on the floor by the desk.

Nicole uncoiled herself and walked over to Frank.

He put his arm around her thin shoulders and pulled her against him.

She whispered in his ear.

He leaned over to address her. "Are you sure you want to come back to the office with me?" he addressed her quietly. "There's nothing fun to do there."

Nicole's head brushed against his side. "I messed up," she said. "I cut the wrong place. That's why we needed you to get that stuff. They," she pointed to the older girls, "have to do it over again. It's all my fault."

"That can happen to anyone, sweetheart," Frank said, sending a stern glance at Marissa.

"That's what we told her, Dad," Marissa said.

Nicole pressed her face into Frank's side.

"We want you to stay," Sophie and Sarah said. "It's no big deal. Now that we have what we need, we'll be finished in no time."

"I can't do anything right," Nicole said. "I just have to sit here and watch them."

"Why don't you come into the kitchen with me?" Maggie asked. "I'm going to make my mango salsa for the shower—it's always better the next day. Would you like to help me?"

Nicole took a step forward and raised her face to Maggie.

"It'll be fun. You can learn how and make it for your family, later. You'll be the only one who will know how."

Frank looked anxiously from Maggie to Nicole.

"When we're done here, I thought I'd take us all for manis and pedis," Maggie improvised. "As a special treat for working so hard on the shower."

The four girls swung their heads to Maggie.

"That would be so cool," Sophie and Sarah said.

"You won't want to miss that," Maggie said as she knelt and took Nicole's hand.

Nicole nodded her agreement and nestled herself into Maggie's outstretched arms.

Frank winked at Maggie and gave her a thumbs-up.

She got to her feet and took Nicole's hand.

"Thank you, Maggie. You're a very kind woman," Frank said, his voice thick with emotion as she and Nicole walked him to the door.

"Bye, Dad," Nicole said, turning her back to him and heading for the kitchen.

***

"I know you think we've got plenty of time before my C-section." Loretta leaned against the kitchen counter and narrowed her eyes at Frank. "But I want to get these cribs set up and in place so I can finish decorating the nursery."

"I understand," Frank yawned. "I'll do it this weekend. It's been a long day, and I'm tired."

"That's what you said last weekend," Loretta said. "You can't be that tired."

"I've got to make dinner first," Frank said. "Let's see how I feel after we've eaten."

Loretta scowled at him.

Marissa burst into the kitchen. "I left my book report book at Susan's," she said. "I can't believe I forgot to put it back in my backpack."

"You're babysitting tomorrow, aren't you? Can you get it then?" Loretta asked.

"It's long, and I've barely started it. I have time to read tonight." Marissa's voice raised an octave. "I need it now, Mom."

"I'll take you," Frank said, reaching for his keys on the counter. "It won't take more than thirty minutes to run you over there and back."

"No," Loretta spoke sharply. "I'll take her. You finish making whatever you'd planned for dinner. We'll eat when we get home, and maybe you can start on those cribs."

"Suit yourself," Frank said.

Loretta shrugged into a ratty old jacket that hung by the back door and picked up her keys. "Let's go."

"You're wearing that?" Marissa asked.

"I'll wait in the car while you run in to get it," she said. "No one's going to see me."

Marissa glanced at Frank, standing behind Loretta. He shook his head slightly.

"Okay," Marissa said.

"Can I come, too?" Nicole looked up from where she had been coloring at the kitchen table.

"Sure," Loretta said. "Get your shoes on. The sooner we get out of here, the sooner we'll be back." She led the way to the garage.

Marissa snuck a look at Frank and gave him a thumbs-up as she followed her mother.

CHAPTER 40

"I have to go to the bathroom," Nicole said, squirming in the backseat.

"Marissa will be right back out with her homework, and we'll be home in fifteen minutes," Loretta said. "Can you wait?"

Nicole shook her head, vehemently.

"Okay. Go ring the doorbell and ask to use the bathroom."

Nicole shook her head again. "Can't you come with me? I don't want to ask Susan by myself."

"What are you talking about? You love your half-sister. She won't mind."

Nicole cupped her crotch with her hands. "Pleeeease," she wheedled.

"Oh … all right." Loretta released her seatbelt and threw open her car door. "Come on. Let's go."

Nicole followed her mother up the steps to the porch, placing one of her hands over her mouth to suppress a giggle.

Loretta rang the bell and waited until Susan came to the front door.

"I'm sorry," Loretta said. "We've got a bathroom emergency."

Susan swung the door open while Loretta stepped aside to let Nicole race into the house.

"Why don't you come in?" Susan asked.

Loretta shook her head. "Frank's making dinner. We need to get back."

"Julia's awake. Wouldn't you like to see her?"

"Well … yes." Loretta stepped into the foyer and turned toward the kitchen, which was in darkness.

Susan flipped a switch, and the room was suddenly flooded with light. Marissa and Nicole, together with the twins and six other assembled friends, cried, "Surprise!"

Loretta stepped back and rested one hand on her protruding baby bump. "What's going on?"

"It's a baby shower," Marissa cried. "For you."

"We wanted it to be a surprise. And I didn't spill the beans," Nicole added triumphantly.

"I'm completely … stunned. I can't believe you did this for me." She scanned the smiling faces trained on hers. "I … I don't know what to say." She swept the back of her hand across her eyes.

Gloria stepped forward and put her arm around Loretta's shoulders. "Come on in, dear. We're going to eat, and then play games and open gifts. They've got a buffet set up, so fix yourself a plate, and we'll get the party started."

"Look at all this," Loretta said, turning around. "Everything's beautiful. You've gone to so much trouble." Her voice caught. "And you're all here."

"We've got your daughters and my nieces to thank for this," Susan said. "They planned it and did all the work."

Loretta swung to face the four young girls who stood to one side, beaming.

"This is incredible." Her voice cracked. "I've never had a shower." She looked around the room. "Look at all the decorations."

"We downloaded them and printed them out," Sophie said. "They're a frog prince and princess. One's a boy and one's a girl."

"I can see that," Loretta said. "They're adorable."

The four girls vibrated with excitement.

"They were so cute at Celebrations," Marissa said.

Loretta opened her arms wide and hugged each girl, in turn. "So this is what you've been up to on your spring break vacation," she said to Sophie and Sarah. "What a kind and generous thing to have done. I'm touched."

"We had a blast doing it," Sarah replied as Sophie nodded her agreement.

"Wait until you see our gift," Nicole said. "You're going to love it."

"Don't tell her," Marissa said. "Let Mom unwrap it."

"I'm not gonna tell!" Nicole gave her sister a dirty look.

"Thank you," Loretta said to Susan as she made her way toward the buffet where the other women waited for her.

She hadn't taken more than eight steps before Joan came up from behind and whispered in her ear, "We're all so happy for both of you, my dear."

Judy squeezed Loretta's hand. "Aren't you glad you listened to me and registered?" she asked, puffing out her chest.

Loretta laughed. "You were right, Judy!"

Tonya caught Loretta's eye and winked at her.

Loretta grinned. This was what it felt like to have a group of supportive women friends. She stepped to the counter and took a generous serving of everything offered.

"I'll take your plate to your seat for you," Maggie said.

Loretta hesitated, looking into Maggie's eyes. "Thank you," she said softly. "For always being gracious."

Maggie flushed. "I hope you've saved room for cake," she said, gesturing to the confection at the end of the table. Laura had outdone herself. The two-tiered cake was covered in white marzipan and decorated with tiny frogs wearing purple cloaks and gold crowns.

"I'm eating for three now, you know. I'm sure I'll have room, but I think it's almost too pretty to cut."

"We've got to eat your cake," Nicole said from behind her. "It's red velvet—your favorite!"

Loretta and Maggie both laughed.

"I think your mother was kidding. We'll cut the cake after we've played games and opened presents," Maggie said.

Loretta inhaled deeply and marveled, as she often did, at the remarkable blessings that had come into her life since moving to Westbury.

***

"Thanks for picking up the food." Frank took three bags from John.

"After years of takeout as a bachelor, my car almost automatically heads to Pete's at dinnertime," John said.

"Here's the rest of it," Mike said, placing two more bags on the kitchen counter.

"Good to see you," Frank said to Mike. "The girls are having so much fun with Sophie and Sarah."

"We wouldn't miss the Easter Carnival at Rosemont. Our girls wouldn't stand for it."

"I'm glad they all had spring break from school at the same time."

"It worked out well, didn't it? They've loved planning this shower. Congratulations," Mike said, extending his hand to Frank.

"Thank you." They shook.

"Twins, isn't it?"

"Yes," Frank said, drawing a deep breath. "A girl and a boy."

"You're in for a wild ride, to be sure," Mike said. "I wouldn't trade the experience for anything, but your world is about to be turned upside down."

"That's what people say," Frank replied. "I can't believe it's all that much harder than having one baby."

Mike grimaced. "That's what I said when we knew we were having twins. I quickly found out how wrong I was."

Frank sucked air through his teeth.

"You'll be fine. If you ever want to talk to another dad who's been through it, give me a call."

"Thanks," Frank said. "I may take you up on that."

"Where's everyone else?" John asked.

"Glenn and Sam are in the nursery. They're trying to assemble one of the cribs," Frank said. "It's not going as easily as they expected. David and Sean are unboxing the other one and bringing the parts in from the garage."

"Let's all break for dinner," John said. "Things may look better after we eat."

"I can help them," Mike said. "I've got experience putting cribs together. I'll go tell them the food's here."

John pulled the lids off of steaming dishes of barbecue pork and chicken, beans, potato salad, and coleslaw. "Real guy food." He nodded his approval to Frank.

"We deserve it," Frank replied.

Dodger, Daisy, Sally, and Snowball were the first to arrive in the kitchen. Dodger and Daisy took up positions along the wall, keeping their eyes trained on the floor in case any food should drop. Sally put her front paws on the counter while Snowball milled around underfoot.

"Down," John commanded Sally, looking over at Frank. Sally reluctantly put her paws on the ground.

"I know, I know," Frank said. "Sean trained Daisy, but I could never get the hang of it with Sally or Snowball."

"What about Sally and Snowball?" Sean asked as he and David came into the kitchen.

"Looks like we've got some work to do with these two," David said to Sean, pointing to the two unruly dogs. "Let's put all of the dogs outside while we eat."

"Good idea," Frank said, handing Sam a plate.

"Thanks. I'm starved," Sam said.

"I hear you're having a bit of trouble," Frank said.

Sam waved his hand dismissively. "We'll figure it out. Don't you worry."

Glenn joined them and filled his plate. "Feed me like this, and I'll come over to help out anytime," he said, smiling at Frank.

John and Frank got their food and joined the older men at the kitchen table.

"Tell us all about this school you're going to in California," Glenn said to David.

"I leave this summer after graduation. I'll be working in the kennels for six months until I get into the apprenticeship program."

"And then you'll come back to Westbury in a couple of years when you're done with your training?" Glenn asked.

"Yep. To start a guide dog training school here."

"We're going to make it a division of Forever Friends," Frank interjected.

"That's if we have the money to start the school," David said.

Frank and John glanced at each other.

"Like we've said, Frank and I are going to worry about the financing," John said.

"I'm so proud of you," Sam said. "I'll volunteer my time to help with construction."

David leaned toward the kindly older man who had taken him under his wing as a helper. He'd learned a lot about home repairs—and life—from Sam. "Thank you," he said.

"Do you have a name for this new school?" Glenn asked.

"If it's all right with Frank," David said, "I'd like to call it Forever Guides."

"That's a terrific name," John said.

Frank put his fork down and reached over to clap David on the back. "I love it. We'll form a holding company and put both Forever Friends and Forever Guides into it as subsidiaries."

David raised both hands, palms out. "I don't know anything about the business stuff. I'll leave that to you."

"Fair enough," Frank said. "You'll be in charge of programs."

"I'll take on all veterinary services," John said. "And be in charge of the breeding program. If you'll have me."

"Are you kidding? Of course," David said.

Sam cleared his throat. "We may be getting ahead of ourselves, but I know that Joan and Gloria want to volunteer to be puppy cuddlers. Before the pups go out to their puppy raiser families."

"They'll be at the top of the list," David said.

"I'd like our family to be puppy raisers," Sean said, looking at Frank. "Could we?"

"We'll have to see what your mother says at the time," Frank said.

Sean's shoulders drooped.

"I think we'll be able to do that as long as you do most of the work. Your mother will have her hands full with the twins."

"That's exactly what I want," Sean replied.

Mike sauntered into the kitchen, a smug smile on his face. "I hope you guys left some of that for me. It smells amazing."

"I was wondering what was keeping you," John said.

"I was just putting a couple of cribs together," he replied casually.

Glenn and Sam snapped their heads to him.

"What? Are you saying you put a crib together?"

"Not one crib. Both of them."

Glenn and Sam looked at each other.

"How?" Sam asked. "We were having a terrible time. And we were following the instructions."

"Plus, we know what we're doing," Glenn said. "Or at least we thought we did."

Mike laughed. "That's your first mistake. Those instructions are worthless. We bought cribs from the same manufacturer for our girls. I had a devil of a time putting them together back then. These cribs aren't much different." He brought his plate to an empty spot at the table. "Once I got started, it all came back to me."

"Here's to you," Sam said, raising his glass to Mike in a toast. "I wasn't sure we'd get them done before Loretta and the girls got home."

"Thanks," Frank said. "You've saved my bacon. Why don't we finish eating and go watch the game on TV?"

"Now you're talking," John said, tucking into his food. "It's a good one tonight."

***

Loretta pulled her car into the garage and addressed her daughters. "Thank you for my shower. It's one of the nicest things anyone's ever done for me."

"You liked it? You really did?" Marissa asked.

"Of course! Everything was perfect. The food was wonderful, and the games were fun. Everyone had a terrific time."

"And you were surprised, weren't you?" Nicole asked.

"I most certainly was."

"See. I told you I could keep a secret." Nicole leaned forward from the backseat to address her sister.

"You did good." Marissa agreed.

"You got a ton of presents, too," Nicole said.

"That's for sure," Loretta said. "We couldn't even fit them all in the car. I'll have to send Frank over to Susan's tomorrow to pick up the rest."

"The clothes we got are so cute," Marissa said.

"I can't wait to dress the babies," Nicole chimed in.

"I can't believe how generous everyone was. I'm overwhelmed that Gloria made them each an oversized crib blanket and Joan knitted them sweaters." Loretta's voice caught, and she swallowed hard. "It's incredibly special, girls, when someone makes you a handmade gift." She hoisted herself from behind the steering wheel and leaned to her left, stretching out her right side. "We'd better get this stuff inside."

"It looks like the guys Frank invited over are still here," Marissa said.

Loretta stopped lifting a bag out of the trunk and looked at Marissa. "Frank had ... a party?"

"Sort of," Marissa replied.

"Is that why there are all those cars parked on the street?" Nicole nodded.

"I thought someone else was having company." She sighed

heavily. "I hope they leave soon. I'm exhausted. I want to unload the car and go to bed."

"We can take care of this," Marissa said. "You go on in."

Loretta straightened and put one hand on the small of her back. "You don't mind?"

"Go on, Mommy. We got this," Nicole said, trying to sound very grown-up.

Loretta opened her arms and drew her daughters to her. "I love you." She kissed them each on the top of the head and headed into the kitchen.

The faint sound of a referee's whistle emanated from the far corner of the house. She heard a spontaneous outburst of excited male voices. Loretta shook her head. It sounded like a group of guys enjoying watching a game together. After the lovely evening she'd had, it was nice to think that Frank had had fun, too. Even so, she hoped they'd go home soon.

Loretta took a deep breath and composed her features. What would they call this—putting on her game face? She squared her shoulders and walked into the family room.

Sam and Glenn rose from the sofa when she entered, and Frank, who had been deep in conversation with John about a recent play, turned to her.

"Sweetheart, you're home," he said. "How was the shower?"

"It was perfect." She crossed to him. Frank looped his arm around her waist.

"You knew all about this, didn't you?" she asked.

He shrugged.

Loretta addressed the room. "Hello, everyone. Thank you all for coming over to keep Frank company." She looked up at Frank and winked. "It looks like you had a wonderful dinner. You can't beat barbecue with all the fixings."

"I'm going to clean all that up," Frank said hastily. "Don't worry about it."

"Sophie and Sarah and our girls did such a wonderful job on the shower. You should be very proud of your daughters, Mike."

"I think they've inherited the entertaining gene from their grandmother," Mike replied, flushing with pleasure at Loretta's compliment of his daughters.

"I'll bet that Joan and Gloria helped with the food, too," Loretta addressed Sam and Glenn. "Please let them know how much I appreciated it."

"Do you need any help carrying in the loot?" John asked.

"No. The girls are bringing in what we could fit in my car. We'll get the rest tomorrow."

"Then I think we'd better be off," John said.

"The game's not over," David protested.

"We can find out who won on the news tonight," John replied, moving toward the door. "It's late, and we should clear out."

The others got reluctantly to their feet.

"I think Sam's got a question about the nursery," Frank said. He looked at the older man, who gave him a quizzical look.

"Can it wait until tomorrow? I'm bushed," Loretta said.

"It'll only take a minute, right, Sam?" Frank stepped behind Loretta and motioned to Sam.

"Not even," Sam said, nodding vigorously. "I need your advice on one thing, and I'll be able to get what I need to complete everything tomorrow." He looked at her kindly. "I'm sure you want to get the nursery finished."

"I most certainly do," Loretta agreed. She headed down the hallway.

Sam and the others followed her.

Loretta pushed the door to the nursery open and cast her

eyes over the room in front of her. Two fully assembled cribs stood against opposite walls, bathed in the warm glow of a pair of nursery lamps placed on either end of a chest of drawers. One light was a frog prince, and the other, a frog princess.

The scene was tranquil and welcoming, ready for the twins to make their appearance. She spun around. "You got the cribs put together!"

Everyone in front of her was grinning.

"Thank you!" she cried. "That's what this guy party was all about, wasn't it? To put the cribs together."

"That was one of the reasons," Frank said. "I guess my friends," he said, his voice wobbling, "know I'm not too good at that sort of thing."

"None of us were," Sam said. "Glenn and I were having a dickens of a time with them. Thank goodness Mike was here."

Loretta looked for Mike and found him leaning against the wall in the back.

"We had the same cribs," he said. "And the same assembly nightmare."

"I was getting so antsy about them. I'm very grateful to you —to all of you."

"You're welcome," Glenn said. "Thanks for having us over, Frank. We had a blast."

"I'm glad you came. Who knows how long those cribs would've taken me?"

"And those lamps," Loretta continued. "They match the décor from the shower. They're adorable. Where did they come from?"

"I picked up some stuff from Celebrations that the girls needed, and Judy showed them to me." Frank beamed. "I thought you'd like them."

Loretta threw her arms around his neck and hugged him.

"We'll have to do this again," John said. "Why don't you all come over to Rosemont for the playoffs?"

"It's a plan," Sam said. "And now, we'd better let this expectant mother get her rest."

Frank and Loretta saw their guests to the door and stood, arm in arm, watching them drive away.

"Thank you, Frank," Loretta put up a hand to cover her yawn. "I can't wait to show you the gifts from the shower."

"I think you're going to have to, my dear," he replied. "You're practically asleep on your feet. We'll look at them tomorrow, and I'll help you put them away. Right now, let's get you to bed."

Loretta leaned against her husband and they headed inside.

CHAPTER 41

Maggie rolled over and snuggled against John. He put his arm around her and drew her close.

"I thought you were awake," she said. "Can you see what time it is?"

John peered at the bedside clock. "It's almost four."

"I suppose I should get up and get busy," she murmured into his chest.

"I think you can stay in bed for a few more minutes. The carnival doesn't open until ten, and the committee has everything ready to go."

She swept her hair off her face. "Remember the first Easter Carnival here at Rosemont?"

"How could I ever forget? You and Susan pulled it together in under two weeks."

"With a ton of help from our friends."

"And you raised a lot of money for the town workers' pension fund. That was such a kind and generous thing to do—

especially for a newcomer to town. I think that's when everyone fell in love with you."

"Is that when you fell in love with me?"

"No. I was hook, line, and sinker the moment we met." John kissed the top of her head.

"When I brought Eve in—after I adopted her?"

"Yep. And, for the record, I think she adopted you."

Maggie chuckled. "You're right about that. And I'm so glad she did."

"Not as glad as I am."

"I'm surprised the twins are so excited about the carnival. I thought they'd be getting too old for it now that they're teenagers."

"If anything, I think they're more eager. This is going to be a big part of their childhood memories."

"Wouldn't that be wonderful? I'd love for them to remember Rosemont this way." She ran her hand over his chest. "I'm thrilled that we're donating the proceeds to fund Forever Guides. I hope we can pull in a significant amount of money. Do you think people are getting tired of the same old games and egg hunt?"

"Quite the contrary. My staff at the hospital, and everyone in and out of there for the past two weeks, has talked about nothing else. The carnival has become a tradition and a point of pride for Westbury. We have some new events this year, too."

"Really? How do you know about this, and I don't?"

John shrugged. "Maybe I'm involved in them."

"And you didn't tell me?"

"Need-to-know basis."

"I need to know—now. What've you got up your sleeve?"

"Since the proceeds are going to Forever Guides, we thought we'd include some dog events. David and Sean are setting up an agility track and will be doing demonstrations with Dodger and Daisy. For a suggested donation of a dollar, people can try it with their dog."

"That's a wonderful idea."

"Juan and one of the other techs from the animal hospital are going to do toenail trims for a five-dollar donation."

"How nice of them," Maggie said.

"Grace and her little brother Tommy are offering a one-mile dog walking service for a dollar, too."

"Let's make sure we buy a bunch of those," Maggie said. "We don't walk Eve and Roman as much as we should."

"Agreed. And there's one more event. We hope it'll be a big money-raiser." He took a deep breath. "At least I say that now."

"What do you mean?"

"We're having a dunk tank."

"No! For heaven's sake. Those are always popular. It'll raise a ton of money, depending on who's getting dunked. I'd hate to be that person."

John remained silent.

"Whose idea was this?"

"Mine."

"Oh my gosh. Are you the one getting dunked?"

"I'm one of the people. I won't be in the tank all day."

"Who else have you recruited for this folly?"

"Frank, Alex, Marc, Pete, and Tim Knudsen."

Maggie propped herself up on one elbow. "I love this! How much will it cost?"

"We're suggesting a donation of a dollar."

"A dollar?" She popped onto her knees. "This is the best thing I've ever heard. I need to see how much cash I have in my wallet." She threw the covers aside, jumped up, and headed for her purse.

"Are you telling me you'd like to see your dear husband drop into a tank of water?"

"You bet I am. You and all the rest." She rummaged in her purse and pulled out her wallet. She switched on her nightstand lamp. "I've got eighty-five dollars in here." She began to giggle.

"You don't have to try to dunk eighty-five times," John said. "You can donate more than a dollar a try."

"Not a chance," Maggie said. "I may need to slip out to the ATM to get more cash before the carnival starts. I'm rusty, but I pitched for my high school girls' softball team. I used to have a pretty good arm."

"You're kidding, aren't you?" John looked at Maggie with wide eyes. "Where's my sweet, kind, gentle wife?"

"She's right here, and she's on a mission." Maggie stood and made an exaggerated circling motion with her arm. "I need to warm up."

John groaned and got out of bed. "I'd better warn the others."

"Do what you've gotta do," Maggie said. "Tell them I'm coming for them."

John laughed.

"It's all for a good cause. I think you'll raise a lot of money today."

***

"You're sure this is okay?" Josh glanced over his shoulder at Sunday.

"Maggie saved that parking spot for us by the garage and told me to take your wheelchair around the back of the house," she replied.

"We can watch the festivities from her patio," Lyla said. "When you get tired, we'll take you home."

"I'm sure I'll be fine," Josh said. "I'm not that fragile."

"You're making great progress in your physical therapy since you've been out of the hospital," Robert said. "You don't want to push yourself too hard."

Josh scowled.

"Be patient a little bit longer, son," Robert said. "All in good time."

Sunday positioned his wheelchair in a shady spot that offered a full view of Rosemont's vast back lawn. "Look at all these people," Sunday said. "I've heard of the carnival, of course, but I've never been."

"I haven't, either," Lyla said. "Half of Westbury is here."

"Why don't the three of you go have a look around? I don't want to spoil your good time. You don't have to babysit me."

"You go," Sunday said to Robert and Lyla. "I'd rather sit here and observe."

"Why not?" Robert pointed to the lawn.

"I'm not sure—" Lyla began.

Robert stepped forward. "It'll be fun. And I think the kids need time to themselves."

Lyla cast a glance over her shoulder at the pair on the patio. "I hadn't thought of that. I guess you're right. We're always around when she stops by to see him."

"Exactly," Robert said. "Besides, I'd like to have you to myself." He glanced around. "Of course, I don't exactly have you to myself here."

"You know what they say—you can be alone in a crowd."

"I've certainly found that to be true." Robert took her hand in his, and they walked across the lawn. "What do you want to do?"

"I'd like to stop by the bake sale table and pick up something yummy for our dinner tomorrow. After that, I'd like to amble around. How about you?"

"As long as I'm holding your hand, I don't care."

Lyla squeezed his hand, and they set out for the large banner bearing the words BAKE SALE. They took their time perusing the choices, leaning over the table to inspect the baked goods before making their selections.

The woman behind the table put their baked goods into a clear cellophane box. Robert handed her a twenty-dollar bill and pointed to the tip jar for his change as she passed the box of pastries to him.

Lyla took his free hand again, and they set out, skirting the section of the lawn reserved for the three-legged race and other games. They meandered through the crowd until they came to the low stone wall at the bottom of the lawn that flanked the woods.

"Look at that," Robert said, drawing Lyla with him to the wall. "This must be built of stone that was quarried in this area." He set the cellophane container on the wall. "Maybe even from this site. It reminds me of the stone walls separating the fields back home in rural England."

"It's beautiful, isn't it?" Lyla ran her hand over the smooth stones that formed the wall. "I would never have noticed this if you hadn't pointed it out." She rested her shoulder against his. "You always opened my eyes to the beauty around us. I've never forgotten that."

Robert flushed. "Everything seems beautiful around you."

They stood with their backs to the chaos on the lawn behind them, observing the woods on the other side of the wall.

"The first leaves of spring are such a vibrant shade of green, aren't they? Hopeful and promising," she said.

BARBARA HINSKE

"That's poetic," Robert replied. "I'm not the only one who appreciates beauty."

"I'd love to come out here to paint this," Lyla said. "I didn't tell you that Josh and I first met—before we knew we were mother and son—in a painting class."

"That's interesting. It's like the universe was trying to throw you two together."

"I've thought that," Lyla replied. "We hit it off right away in class and found ourselves together one morning at dawn, painting the same tree." She glanced aside, remembering. "His adoptive father had just died, and we had a deep conversation about his desire to find his birth mother." She swung around and perched on the wall.

Robert joined her. "And neither of you had any idea, at the time, that you were talking about each other?"

"Not a clue."

"Anyone who doesn't see the hand of God in this—all of this," he said as he rested his hand on her shoulder, "isn't looking."

"I agree with you."

"I'm sure Maggie and John would be happy for you and Josh to come back here to paint the woods," Robert said. "When he's out of his wheelchair."

"I don't think I'd want to impose on her." Lyla looked back over her shoulder. "There's something special about this spot, though. Just sitting here makes me feel calm and happy—optimistic about the future."

"About the future," Robert began, turning to her as a soccer ball zoomed past them and ricocheted off the wall, sending their baked goods flying.

"Sorry!" cried a pack of elementary school children as they chased after the ball.

Lyla leaned back and surveyed the scene. The cherry pie they'd just purchased was a red smear on the dirt. The only remains of the dozen chocolate chip cookies were two specimens that sat on a clean patch of grass and looked as if they had been placed there for a photoshoot.

"Will you retrieve the cookies for us?" she asked. "I think the only thing to do now is to eat them and head back to the bake sale table."

Robert swung his legs over the wall and retrieved the cookies. He held them both out to her. "Take your pick."

She selected the smaller cookie and took a bite. "Mmmm ... these are good. I hope they still have some. What were you going to say about the future?"

"I think that's a conversation for another time," he replied, nibbling at his cookie. "When we're not being bombarded by soccer balls and children. These are good," he said, helping her off the wall.

They joined hands again as they finished the cookies and made their way back to the bake sale.

***

Sunday tapped Josh on the shoulder and pointed into the crowd. "Do you see them? Robert and Lyla?"

Josh squinted.

"They're walking up to the bake sale."

"Swinging hands? Like teenagers?"

"Yes. That's them."

"Whoever would have thought that this stupid accident of mine would have brought my biological father back into my life?"

"Let alone reunite him with the love of his life—your mother," Sunday replied. "They seem happy as clams whenever I'm at Lyla's. She's been my closest friend for the last five years, and I've never seen her so contented."

"They're getting along famously, all right," Josh said. "I haven't heard one harsh word."

"I worry that she'll be heartbroken when he goes back to England," Sunday said. "Has he said anything about when he'll return?"

Josh shook his head. "I know what you mean. I've even thought about not working so hard in physical therapy so that I'll stay in this wheelchair longer. I don't think he'll leave until I'm on crutches."

"That's so sweet! But don't you dare do that," Sunday said. "You have to put yourself first." She watched Lyla and Robert. "I have a feeling we don't need to worry about them. They're going to work something out."

Josh studied his biological parents in the distance. "I think you might be right about that."

CHAPTER 42

"You think you can really do this—" Alex taunted as Maggie wound up and released the ball. Her pitch hit the center of the metal plate, a bell rang, and the mechanism released Alex into the tank of water below.

Alex sputtered and stood, smoothing his wet hair back from his face.

Maggie chortled, then fished a twenty-dollar bill out of the pocket of her jeans and shoved it into the slot of the donation jar.

"John tried to warn me," he called to her. "I just didn't believe you were that accurate—or had this much stamina."

"Hah! Now you know," Maggie said.

"You've already dunked your husband, Frank, and Tim. Unless I'm mistaken, you're even more accurate with me."

"My muscles are warmed up. I'm in the zone. Get back up there."

Alex grinned, shaking his head. "This is a whole new side of you I'm seeing. How much money do you still have in your pocket?"

"I just put a twenty in the jar, and there's more where that came from."

Alex pointed to a line of high school boys forming behind her. "Better let them take a turn," he said.

Maggie glanced over her shoulder. "Sorry, I didn't see you there. I don't mean to monopolize this," she said to the boy at the front of the line as she stepped aside.

"We don't have any money," he said. "We came to watch you. One of the guys," he gestured behind him with his thumb, "said there was a lady over here with a killer arm."

Maggie's cheeks grew pink. "Thank you. I used to pitch. Back in the day."

"No kidding? You're really good. We're the Westbury High School baseball team," the boy said.

Maggie's head snapped to Alex and then back to the boy. "All of you?" She stepped aside and counted twelve boys in line.

He nodded.

"My arm's getting a bit tired," she said, "but I've got a lot of money I'd like to contribute to the cause." She pointed to the donation jar. "How about I pay, and you take the throws for me?"

A grin spread across the boy's face. "Sure," he said. "We'd be happy to help."

"What?" Alex made a show of being outraged. "I guess I'd better get prepared to hold my breath." He climbed back onto his perch.

"No one ever accused you of being a dummy," Maggie called to him. She caught his eye and winked at him. "Or of being a bad sport."

She spoke to the boys lined up behind her. "Give it your all," she said.

The first boy sent a ball sailing, and seconds later Alex plunged into the dunk tank.

The afternoon unfolded under a cloudless sky. Sophie and Sarah won the three-legged race for the third year in a row. "Twin power," they declared to their competition. The Easter egg hunt saw two hundred children scrambling over the lawn in search of a thousand eggs.

Josh had finally given in to fatigue and asked to leave after the last egg was found. Maggie was saying goodbye to the four of them when Tonya signaled to her from the check-in table.

"We've counted the admission fees and the proceeds from all of the booths."

Maggie raised her brows. "And? How'd we do?"

"Best year yet!" Tonya replied. "Admissions were up from last year by eighty people, and the booths all did very well. Especially the dunk tank." She removed her glasses with one hand. "I think the lion's share of the donations at that booth came from you."

Maggie chuckled. "Best money I've spent in years. There's something satisfying about sending a person into the water. It's a classic. You can't beat it."

"I guess not." Tonya rolled her eyes. "Would you like George to announce the results like he's done other years?"

"You bet," Maggie said. "No one can command attention like George."

"It helps that he's six foot eight, is standing on a tree stump, and has a megaphone," Tonya said. "And he genuinely loves to do it. Says he feels like a ringmaster in a circus."

"I love that husband of yours," Maggie said. "Would you tell him that John would like to say a few words about the money when he's done?"

"Sure. They're both standing by the stump. Marc and Mike have been rounding up people for the announcement."

They wove their way through the crowd milling around on the lawn. Excited children chased and called to each other. Dogs barked. Families and friends chatted in amiable groups, relishing the mild spring afternoon.

Maggie found John and Frank huddled together in deep conversation. She put her hand on John's back.

He looked up and smiled at her, then quickly made a show of scowling. "Here she is—the woman who showed us no mercy."

"Whoever would have guessed you were a major league pitcher in a former life," Frank teased.

"It wasn't that bad, and you know it," Maggie protested. "I think you both sort of enjoyed it."

"I'll neither admit nor deny," Frank said.

"The important thing is that you've raised a lot of money."

Both men grinned.

"George is going to announce the total funds raised. He knows you want to say a few words when he's done," she said to John.

John looked at Frank, who nodded.

George Holmes climbed onto the stump, towering over the crowd. He raised the megaphone and began. "Ladies and gentlemen, boys and girls of all ages." He paused. "I love saying that. Thank you all for attending the annual Easter Carnival at Rosemont. Have you had fun today?"

The crowd cheered.

"It looked to me like everyone was having fun. I'm thrilled to tell you that we've broken all records for donations again this year." He made his voice even louder. "We've raised twenty-two thousand seven hundred thirty-five dollars!"

The crowd roared and erupted into applause.

"We can be so proud of our community. You're all very generous. And this year we've got something more to celebrate. Here to tell you about it is someone you all know and love: a son of Westbury and our own veterinarian, John Allen." George led the crowd in clapping as he stepped down to make way for John.

"Thank you, George." John looked out at the sea of faces trained on him. "I think you all know David Wheeler. He and his therapy dog, Dodger, are recognized all over town and were part of the dog agility booth many of you enjoyed this afternoon. What you may not know is that David will be going to California this summer to begin his career as a guide dog trainer."

A murmur went through the crowd.

"David's dream is to start a guide dog training school right here in Westbury. There's a huge need for guide dogs in this part of the country, but the schools that provide them to people are located on each of the coasts. He plans to change that."

John pointed to Frank.

"Frank Haynes has pledged to donate space at the Forever Friends facility for a new wing to house Forever Guides. It'll encompass a breeding program and training facilities for the guide dogs and their handlers. It's a very ambitious—and worthy—goal."

He searched the crowd. "David, would you come up here, please?"

David and Dodger made their way to the stump.

"The proceeds of today's carnival will serve as the first

deposit into the fund to make Forever Guides a reality," John said, looking down at David as the crowd clapped.

"There's more," John said. "Frank has offered to match today's receipts, so that brings the total of your seed money to forty-five thousand, four hundred and seventy dollars!"

The crowd whistled and cheered.

David looked at Frank, shock registering on his face. "I … I can't believe this," he sputtered.

"Believe it, David," Frank said. "You're going to make this school a reality. I'm thrilled to be a small part of it."

David stepped toward Frank and put his arm around the older man. "Thank you. I'm going to work super-hard in California. I won't let you down."

"You're a good bet, David," Frank said. "I have no doubts."

CHAPTER 43

"Ms. Martin," came the familiar voice on the other end of the line.

"Maggie, please," she replied. "How are you?"

"I'm very well, thank you, madam," Gordon Mortimer said. "I'm calling about the two photos you sent me."

"I'm glad you received my email. I know you only got the photos this morning." She drew a deep breath. "You're still acting as a fine art appraiser and dealer, aren't you?"

"I most certainly am, madam."

"Good. You were so helpful to us when we sold all that vintage silver we found in the attic a couple of years ago."

"It was my pleasure. I must say, working with that Martin-Guillaume Biennais tea set was one of the highlights of my career." He cleared his throat. "You said in your email that you found this Van Cleef & Arpels brooch at your husband's animal hospital and that the painting you sent the picture of used to hang over your living room mantle before you replaced it with the artwork you purchased in Cornwall?

"That's right. We put the landscape in the attic when we hung the one we bought on our honeymoon. We've been thinking of getting rid of it. We wanted to see if it has any value before we donate it to the church rummage sale."

"I see."

"We're in no hurry for a response. Take your time."

"I can advise you right now to hang onto that painting," he said quickly.

Maggie's pulse raced. He'd used the same tone of voice when he'd told her about the value of her silver.

"I'll need to inspect it, of course, and I believe it will need to be cleaned by an expert."

"It's so dark and dreary," Maggie said. "That's the reason neither of us likes it. Is that because it's dirty?"

"I suspect so. It's been hanging over a working fireplace for many years. That's not the best place for a masterpiece."

"Masterpiece? I don't think it's even signed."

"I suspect that the frame is covering up the signature."

"Do you have any idea who painted it?"

"I'll need to see it in person. The man your late husband inherited the house from—Hector Martin—was it? He was a wealthy collector of many fine things, as I recall. The silver, of course, and I remember that Rosemont was furnished with many fine antiques. I also read about his rare book collection—"

"Yes. Hector had a refined eye and wonderful taste," Maggie interrupted him. She remembered how long-winded Gordon could be when he got onto a tangent. "Who do you think the artist is?"

"Well..." He hesitated.

Maggie held her breath.

"Don't hold me to it, but I suspect your landscape was painted by Thomas Cole. Are you familiar with him?"

"Only vaguely. What can you tell me about him?"

"He was an American painter who lived between 1801 and 1848. He's the founder of the Hudson River School of painters."

"I've heard of them."

"They were primarily landscape painters and are known for their glowing, almost romantic, use of light. That's one of the reasons I think your painting needs to be cleaned."

"Do you have any idea of the value of our painting, if it really is a Thomas Cole?"

"Without seeing it, I'd only be speculating. The condition of the piece will be critical. If it is a Thomas Cole and is in relatively good condition, it could bring several hundred thousand dollars at auction."

Maggie gasped.

"I'm assuming you don't have it adequately insured?"

"No," Maggie said.

"I'd like to take a look at it as soon as possible," he said. "That's why I'm calling—to coordinate our calendars. I could be with you next Tuesday."

Maggie didn't bother to check her schedule. Whatever she had planned, she would move. "That'll be fine."

"Good. I can get the first flight out in the morning and be at Rosemont by noon."

"Thank you," she said, her mind still reeling.

"What will you do with the painting if it's what I think it is?"

"John and I are raising funds to start a guide dog training school in Westbury. That's why I emailed you about the Van Cleef & Arpels brooch. We've had it appraised by our local jeweler and thought we'd sell it and donate the funds to the new school." She took a deep breath. "I never suspected the painting could be far more valuable. I'll need to talk to John, but I'm sure we'll want to sell it, too."

"That would be most generous of you both," he said. "My favorite cousin is blind and has had guide dogs all of his adult life. I've witnessed, firsthand, what a difference they've made in his independence. I'd like to contribute to your cause by donating my commission on any sales and waiving my fees."

"That's awfully kind of you, Gordon."

"Not at all."

"What do you think about the brooch?"

"It's a lovely piece, to be sure," he said. "The market for brooches isn't as strong as it is for necklaces or bracelets. Still, the diamonds are extraordinary, and it's a Van Cleef & Arpels—very collectible. You may want to have it authenticated by the maison, itself. I'll get you the cost—it won't be cheap. Between the painting and the brooch, I believe you'll be able to fund this new school of yours."

Maggie rested her elbow on her desk and cradled her forehead in her hand. "I can scarcely believe this," she said.

"It's the most thrilling email I've received in a long time," Gordon said. "I'll look forward to seeing you next week."

"Yes," Maggie said.

"One more thing," he said. "I'd like to look in the attic at Rosemont this trip. Who knows what else is lurking up there?"

CHAPTER 44

"Look at you!" Sunday cried as Josh rose from Lyla's sofa to greet her.

He positioned the crutches under his armpits and swiftly traveled the distance to where she stood in the entryway.

"Whoa. You're good with those. I thought it would take a while to get used to them."

"Not my first rodeo," he said, a note of pride in his voice. "I was a jock in high school, remember?"

"I believe you've mentioned that, yes." She leaned in and kissed him squarely on the mouth. "I guess you're putting your experience to good use."

"I am. It couldn't come at a better time. I was so tired of that wheelchair, I was ready to scream."

"You may still need it," Sunday said. "I wouldn't get rid of it just yet."

"That's what Lyla said." He shook his head. "Too late. I've already sent it back."

"I see. Pretty confident, aren't we?" She cuffed his shoulder playfully.

"I'm moving back to my apartment this weekend, and I'm starting work again on Monday."

"Are you sure you're ready for that?"

He moved back to the sofa and sat. "I withdrew from all my classes, so I won't have any schoolwork until next semester. I can't just sit around doing nothing. I'm going crazy with boredom."

"I understand," Sunday said. "How will you get there? You can't drive with a broken right leg."

"I'll figure something out."

"Why don't we carpool? That way, if you need anything from the store, we can stop on the way home."

"I don't want to tie you up."

"Nonsense. I come here every day after work as it is right now."

"We can pick up groceries and cook dinner together," he said. "I'll amaze you with my culinary skills."

Sunday snuggled next to him. "Everything about you amazes me."

Josh drew her to him and kissed her.

Lyla leaned her head into the room and cleared her throat. "Dinner's ready. Just come in whenever you're ready." She headed back to the kitchen. "It's chili in the crockpot, so it'll stay warm. No need to hurry."

Sunday and Josh giggled like teenagers.

"That's another reason for me to go back to my place," he whispered in her ear as he kissed her temple. "We need some privacy."

Sunday rested her forehead against his. "I can't argue with that. I also think Lyla and Robert need time alone, too." She sighed heavily. "I wonder if he'll go home, now that you're moving out."

"That's the only reason I hate to leave," Josh replied. "They're so happy together, but I can't stay here forever."

"I know," Sunday said. "They have to work this out for themselves, and we have to let them do it."

CHAPTER 45

"Deidre," Robert said, "thanks for returning my call."

"I was delighted to hear from you," the attorney for Nigel Blythe's estate replied. "How's your son?"

"He's made remarkable strides after his infection cleared up. He's out of the wheelchair and getting along quite nicely on crutches. In fact, he's moved back to his apartment and returned to work."

"That's wonderful news. I'm happy for you."

"Thank you. How are things with the estate?"

"I was going to call you about that. The heir is anxious to liquidate the inventory and close the shop."

"He doesn't want to find someone to take it over?"

"I made inquiries among the rare booksellers in the UK and on the Continent and came up empty-handed. The heir is in a hurry to get his money and asked me to call you." She barreled on. "He's hoping you'd be interested in it," she said. "He'd be willing to make you an outstanding deal."

Robert sank back into his chair. At one time in his life, being the proprietor of his own rare book store in London would have been a dream come true. He swallowed hard. Not anymore.

"Robert? Are you there?"

"Yes. I'm ... I'm here."

"It's just a suggestion. Take some time to think it over. If anyone could make a success of taking over Blythe Rare Books, it's you."

"I'm sure I could," he said. "I wouldn't want to do it out of his shop."

"Too much notoriety over the murder and attempted murder he confessed to?"

"That's part of it," he replied. "We've also found out that he might have murdered another woman in Westbury."

"What are you talking about?"

Robert supplied the details about Elizabeth Filler and the possible connection to Nigel.

"Good heavens! Who knew that the seemingly stodgy world of rare books could be so salacious?"

"That brings me to the reason I called. As I said, Elizabeth's murderer was never found. If handwriting experts can verify that the threatening note was written by Nigel, the police will consider the case closed."

"Do you want me to see if his cousins have some old letters from him? They weren't close, so I very much doubt they'll have anything."

"That's not necessary. Nigel kept detailed records of his inventory dating back to when he opened Blythe Rare Books. I found them when I was going through the shop. There's a filing cabinet in his office. The old handwritten inventories are in the bottom drawer. Would you mind going to the shop and pulling out a handful of pages from the late seventies?"

"I can do that." Deidre paused as she checked her calendar. "I'll be in the area on Wednesday. What do you want me to do with them?"

"Scan them and send them to me and Chief Thomas of the Westbury Police Department. I'll send you his email address."

"Will do. You'll have to let me know what they come up with. You've piqued my curiosity."

"That's why I want to look at the records, too. I've seen the note, and it looks like Nigel's handwriting to me, but I'd like to compare it myself."

"Do you have a copy of the note?"

"Yes."

"Scan it and send it to me, and I'll compare them, too. I'll let you know what I think."

"Good. I'd value your opinion."

"It's a plan. And think about whether you'd like to buy the inventory of the shop even if you don't want to take over the space. If you're not interested, we'll auction off what can be sold and donate the rest."

"Give me a few days to get back to you," Robert said. "I have some ideas, but I need to talk to someone first."

"Of course. In the meantime, let's solve the murder of Elizabeth Filler."

"Thank you. I'll be in touch." Robert punched off the call and scooped the keys to his rental car off of the counter. He'd better hurry if he was going to be ready by the time Lyla got home.

***

Robert stood back and observed Lyla's living room. He'd lined the mantle with candles, and their flames flickered in the breeze from an open window. He'd lit a fire for ambiance, but the late afternoon was too warm, and he'd been forced to turn on the air conditioning and open the window.

He raked a hand through his hair, which over the years had grayed at the temples and thinned in the back. Why had an old bachelor like himself thought he'd be any good at creating romantic ambiance? Still, he had to try. What he had planned was long overdue, and Lyla deserved the very best.

He'd pushed her sofa against the wall and moved her coffee table into the dining room. The bistro table and chairs from her porch now sat in front of the fire. He'd covered the table with a white tablecloth he'd found in her linen closet, and from the bush in the backyard, he'd cut massive branches of lilacs that now stood in a vase dominating the center of the table. He was pleased with the overall effect and hoped she wouldn't be annoyed that he'd messed with her things. He sighed heavily. The die was cast. She'd be home soon, and he'd know her reaction as soon as he saw her face.

Robert retreated to the kitchen. The Chantilly cream layer cake, topped with berries, that he'd picked up from Laura's bakery, stood on the counter. He'd window-shopped at the jeweler across the square on his way home and hoped he'd be taking Lyla there very soon. Steaks were marinating, potatoes were baking, and a wheel of brie stood ready to pop into the oven. He'd chopped a salad and it was now chilling in the refrigerator.

Robert stepped to the mirror. He straightened his tie and smoothed his hair. The reflection that greeted him gave evidence to his years, but the feelings in his heart were unchanged from decades ago.

Car tires crunched across the gravel driveway. Lyla was home.

Robert put the tray with the cheese into the oven and held

the back door open as Lyla mounted the steps, her purse over her shoulder and a heavy satchel bumping against her leg.

"I've got a ton of work to do tonight," she began as she ran her eyes over him. "You look nice," she said. "Were you at a job interview?"

He drew his brows together as he stepped aside to let her enter.

"That's a joke," she said. "About the interview. You do look very handsome."

He bent to kiss her. "Let me take that from you," he said, lifting her satchel from her arm.

Lyla inhaled deeply. "It smells heavenly in here!" She placed her purse on the counter. "A cake from Laura's?" She looked around the kitchen, then to Robert. "You've made dinner, haven't you?"

He clasped his hands in front of him. "I want tonight to be special."

She removed her coat, and he took it from her. "Let's go into the living room. You can relax, and I'll open a bottle of wine. I've got a brie in the oven."

Her eyes widened as she preceded him. "Look at this!" she cried.

"Do you like it? I tried to make it look nice."

"You succeeded." She put her hand on his arm. "It's lovely. Lilacs are my favorite."

He passed his hand across his brow. "I thought I remembered that. After I did all of this, I worried that maybe I'd gone too far."

She looked into his eyes, then dropped her gaze. "What's the occasion? Now that Josh is on his own again," her voice wavered, "are you headed back to England?"

Robert stepped in front of her and put his hands on her arms. "No. That's not what I want."

She lifted questioning eyes to his.

"What I want is to stay here."

"With your son?"

"With you, Lyla. You've always been the only one for me. My whole life, there's never been anyone else." He inhaled slowly. "I'd planned to do this later, but I think now's the time." He dropped onto one knee and took her hand in his.

Lyla held her breath.

"Lyla, I once wanted to spend my whole life with you—and I still do. We've missed out on too many things. I don't want that to continue a moment longer. I want us to enjoy our son and, God willing, grandchildren together. I want to greet every sunrise and sunset by your side."

He pressed a kiss into her hand. "Lyla Kershaw, will you marry me?"

Lyla dropped to her knees and threw her arms around Robert's neck. She pressed her lips to his ear and whispered, "Yes."

He encircled her with his arms and brought his lips to hers. They kissed deeply, only breaking apart when a strong burning smell enveloped them.

"The cheese!" they cried in unison.

Robert reached the kitchen first, as black smoke seeped from the vents in the oven. He lunged for the pair of oven mitts he'd deposited on the counter and opened the door. The cheese had caramelized into a black bubbly mess. Robert pulled the baking sheet from the oven.

"The sink," Lyla directed.

He dumped the sheet and its smoking contents into the sink, and she ran the faucet. Steam shot off the hot sheet, and the offending cheese crackled and popped before the cold water had its desired effect.

They looked at each other and laughed. "So much for the appetizer," Robert said. "I guess my meal's gotten off to an inauspicious start."

Lyla circled his waist with her arms and hugged him from behind. "This evening could not have gotten off to a better start. I don't care if we even eat dinner."

"Don't say that," he said. "I've been working on it all day."

"I'm sure it'll be wonderful. What can I do to help?"

"Can you get the salad out of the fridge? I'll go light the grill."

"Sure," she said. "We've got a lot to talk about." She glanced at him as she tugged at the refrigerator door.

He stopped on his way to the backyard grill. "If you're worried about where we're going to live, I'd like to relocate here."

Lyla's shoulders relaxed. "What about your position at Cambridge?"

"I've got an opportunity to start a rare book brokerage. I'd do it online—from here."

She raised her brows. "How long have you been considering this?"

"I've always wanted to own my own shop," he said, "but times have changed. Everything's done through the internet now. I had a very interesting conversation with the attorney for Nigel's estate this morning."

"I can't wait to hear about it."

He stepped through the door, then stuck his head back into the kitchen. "One more thing. I want you to have an engagement ring."

"Oh … I wasn't even thinking about that. At my age? We can just get wedding bands."

He shook his head, emphatically. "Nope. That won't do for my girl. I'll want you to pick it out. There's a jeweler near the bakery," he said.

"Burman Jewelry."

"Are they any good?"

"Absolutely. They're the best in town."

"Good. I know you're busy at work," Robert said, pointing to her satchel with the toe of his shoe, "but clear your calendar so we can go ring shopping. Tomorrow."

Happiness took hold of her. "I think I can make that happen."

"I thought maybe you could. Now, let's get dinner on the table and start planning the rest of our lives."

***

"Thanks for picking up a pizza," Josh said. "I haven't had a Tomascino's five-meat supreme in ages. It's my favorite."

"I'll have to remember that," Robert said as he put the box on Josh's kitchen counter.

Josh reached for his crutches and began to get to his feet.

"Sit," Sunday commanded. "I'll bring you a slice."

Lyla opened the pizza box with her left hand.

Sunday gasped and grabbed her friend's hand. "Is this what I think it is?" She pulled Lyla's hand to the vent hood over the stove and switched on the light.

"It is," Lyla said. She rotated her hand back and forth under the intense halogen lights of the hood. The emerald-cut center diamond sent rainbows around the kitchen.

"Congratulations!" Sunday said, drawing Lyla into a hug. "I'm so happy for you."

Josh looked from the scene in the kitchen to Robert. "What's going on?"

"We're getting married," Robert said. "Your mother and I are getting married."

Josh grabbed his crutch and shot out of his seat. "What? When did this happen?"

"I proposed last night … and she accepted." Robert looked at Josh. "What do you think about this?"

"I'm thrilled!" Josh replied. He pointed to Sunday. "We watched the two of you together at the Easter Carnival at Rosemont and could see the love you share."

Sunday sniffled and fished in the pocket of her jeans for a tissue. "I was hoping for this. You're perfect for each other."

"I'm so glad you approve," Lyla said.

"That's a gorgeous ring," Sunday said. "I love the sapphire baguettes surrounding the center stone. It's breathtaking."

"Thank you." Lyla shot Robert a dazzling smile. "I said I didn't need a ring, but he insisted. We went to Burman's this afternoon. They had this in the case, and I knew right away that it was the one. I tried it on, and it was my size, so I got to wear the ring out of the store."

"Sounds like it was meant to be. Well done," Sunday said, looking at Robert.

"Let me see it," Josh said.

She extended her hand, and Josh made a show of covering his eyes. "You could blind people with that thing."

Lyla laughed and pulled her hand back.

"It's beautiful. I'm so happy for both of you."

"What are your wedding plans?" Sunday asked.

Robert and Lyla exchanged a glance. "We wanted to talk to

you about that," Robert said. "I'm going to move here and start an online rare book store. I'm buying the inventory of Blythe Rare Books and have to go back to England to deal with all of that, plus pack up my place in Cambridge."

"Wait a minute," Sunday said. "You're leaving Cambridge and coming here with Nigel's inventory? Explain."

"We'll get to all of that over dinner," Robert said. "I'm planning to head home week after next, and Lyla is taking a leave of absence to come with me. We'd like to get married here before we go. We'll handle our business in England and then take a proper honeymoon in Europe."

Sunday sighed heavily. "That sounds fabulous."

"We're going to get married at the courthouse," Lyla said. "There's no time to plan anything else. We were hoping you'd agree to stand up for us," she said. She turned to Sunday. "You'd be my maid of honor."

Robert addressed Josh. "Would you do me the honor of being my best man?"

Sunday moved to stand next to Josh and slipped her arm around his waist. They looked at each other, and Josh responded. "We'd be honored. Just let us know when and where to be."

"Thank you," Robert said.

Lyla drew in a ragged breath. "We certainly have a weird love story. Our birth son reunited us after decades apart."

Sunday's eyes glistened. "It's so beautiful."

"Oh, blimey!" Robert said. "You don't want your pizza to get soggy. Let's eat, and we'll fill you in on everything."

CHAPTER 46

"Welcome back," Maggie said as she walked to her assistant's desk outside her office.

Josh looked up at her and grinned.

"How are you doing? You gave us all quite a scare."

"I gave myself a scare," he said. "I'm doing well."

"You're on crutches?"

"Yes. For eight to ten more weeks."

"I've never been in a cast. How is it?"

"The worst part is when it starts to itch." He pulled an unbent wire coat hanger from under his desk. "I'm prepared for when it does."

Maggie laughed. "I'm thrilled to have you back. Don't overdo. If you need to leave early, feel free."

Josh shook his head. "I'll be fine. How have things been here? How are the trustees?"

"It's been interesting. I think we've come to an understanding."

Josh waited, but Maggie didn't elaborate.

"I know I've just come back to work, but I need to take the afternoon off—a week from Friday."

"Take whatever time you need. I'm sure you'll have follow-up doctor appointments and physical therapy sessions."

"I will, but I need the time off because I'm going to be the best man in a wedding at the courthouse." He watched her face and waited for her question.

"That's so nice. Who's getting married? Do I know them?"

"Lyla and Robert."

"What?" Maggie brought her hand to her heart. "That's the most wonderful news! John and I talked about how happy they seemed together at the Easter Carnival."

"You saw them there?"

"They spent a lot of time by that low stone wall at the bottom of the lawn. I love that space. I sit on the wall whenever I need peace and quiet or to think something through."

"Robert mentioned it looks like the stone walls that divide farms in rural England, where he grew up."

"Is that right?"

"He said it made him feel right at home."

"I'm so pleased to hear that."

"Lyla said she'd like to paint the wall and the woods behind it this fall, but she didn't want to bother you."

"I forgot—you met Lyla in a painting class before you discovered you were mother and son."

Josh nodded.

"You're both welcome at Rosemont any time. You don't need to ask. If I see people with easels on the lawn, I'll know it's you and Lyla."

"Thanks, Maggie." He picked a small stack of phone messages from his desk and handed them to her. "You've had some calls while you were in your meeting. Nothing urgent."

Maggie leafed through them. "I'd better get busy," she said, turning to her office. She had her hand on the doorknob when she halted abruptly and retraced her steps to Josh's desk.

"You said that they're getting married at the courthouse?"

"Yes. It's just going to be them plus Sunday and me as the maid of honor and best man."

Maggie rolled her lips into a line. "Hmm..."

"Robert is buying the inventory from Blythe Rare Books and will operate an online rare book business from here in Westbury. He and Lyla are leaving for England on the Sunday after they get married to package the inventory for shipment, close up his house in Cambridge, and then take a honeymoon."

"That's all so exciting!"

"They wanted to get married before they leave."

"Makes sense," Maggie said. "I was just thinking that they should get married at Rosemont." She set the phone messages back on his desk and began gesturing with her hands. "You know—in front of that low stone wall, facing the woods. It's so pretty this time of year."

Josh stared at her. He could see she was on a roll.

"I've still got an aisle runner from when John and I got married on the back lawn."

"That's very nice, but I'm positive they wouldn't want you to go to any trouble."

Maggie waved her hand, dismissively. "Nonsense. Rosemont is the perfect place." She stared at him. "I'm sure Susan would love to help me with this."

"They're going to have the town clerk marry them," Josh said. "That's why they're going to the courthouse."

"Not a problem," Maggie said. "The clerk's married people at Rosemont before."

Josh couldn't suppress a grin. "How many weddings have you had there?"

Maggie laughed. "We've hosted several over the past few years. I love throwing a party, and a wedding is my favorite kind." She looked at him. "I think the low stone wall is an auspicious place to start their marriage. Admit it—both Lyla and Robert were drawn to it."

"You're right about that," Josh said.

"I'm going to write a note to them," Maggie said, "inviting them to get married—no, insisting on it—at Rosemont. Can you deliver it to them tonight?"

"I sure can."

"And take Sunday with you when you do. She'll talk them into it."

"I'll bet she will."

"Good. We've got a plan." She snatched the phone messages off his desk. "I'd better get through these. I've got a wedding to think about."

CHAPTER 47

Gordon pointed to a spot in the upper right corner of the painting as it rested on the floor of the library, leaning against the wall. "It's dirty, but you can get a glimpse of Cole's masterful use of light."

Maggie narrowed her eyes and tilted her head.

"You'll see—once it's cleaned."

"I'm sure you're right." She glanced at him. "You're certain this is a Thomas Cole?"

"It'll need to be authenticated, of course, but yes—I'm sure."

She inhaled deeply. "And the value?"

"It looks to be in good condition," he said. "We'll know more after it's cleaned, but I'm guessing it would go at auction for between two hundred fifty and three hundred thousand dollars."

"That's just crazy," Maggie said.

"Maybe you'll change your mind and keep it after it's cleaned."

"No. John and I will stick with our decision to sell it."

"Still intent on raising money for that guide dog school?"

"Yes," Maggie said.

"That's a wonderful cause. I'll be thrilled to help you." He grasped the frame at either end and turned the painting to the wall. "Can you store it this way until I make arrangements to ship it to the restorer who will clean it?"

"Of course. I don't think we should haul it back to the attic. It'll be safe right there."

"Thank you, madam. I'm sorry that my plane was delayed, and I arrived so late this morning."

"You had no control over that."

"Indeed."

"You mentioned going through the rest of the attic while you were here to see what else might be lurking up there. Do you have time?"

Gordon looked at his watch. "I'm afraid not," he said. "My return flight is in two hours. I should be leaving here shortly."

"Another time, then," Maggie said, swallowing her disappointment.

"Maybe just a quick peek," he said. "I must confess, I'm very curious to see what's up there."

"Follow me," she said, rushing to the staircase. "I unlocked it and left the door open this morning, so it could air out."

"Thank you, madam. My dust allergies get going in an attic."

They hurried to the second floor and took the steep, narrow stairs to the attic at a slower pace.

Maggie stepped into the attic and wedged herself between an umbrella stand full of fishing rods and a dress form hovering to the right of the door.

Gordon squeezed past her. "My word," he said. "I'd forgotten how much—"

"Junk?" Maggie supplied.

"How many fine pieces of furniture and household items you have up here." He gingerly slid a trunk out of his way and headed for a highboy in the corner. "I wish I had more light," he said, edging his way in the dimly lit space.

"I promise I'll have the windows washed, and we'll bring portable lights up here if you'd like to come back."

Gordon had reached the highboy and inspected it by the light of his cell phone flashlight. "This is a magnificent piece, madam."

"I've never made it back that far into the attic to look at it," she replied.

He removed a drawer and examined its construction. "Eighteenth-century." He glanced at her. "This attic isn't the place to keep it," he said, a note of reproach in his voice.

"We'll move it downstairs. Right away," Maggie said.

"No. Why don't you wait to do anything until I come back."

"All right. Whatever you say."

Gordon sneezed loudly into his handkerchief.

"I'll bring a mask with me," he said, looking at this watch. "And now, I really must be on my way." He began retracing his steps to the door. He was halfway there when a furry object launched itself from a tall stack of boxes, landing briefly on his shoulders before sliding down his back, nails catching on the fine wool of his suit jacket.

Gordon lurched forward and swung an arm in self-defense, barely missing the creature, who let out a high-pitched screech. He stumbled, then caught himself. "What in the devil was that?"

Maggie swallowed hard. Now was not the time to laugh. "That was one of my cats. Bubbles. I believe you've met her before?"

He mopped his brow with his handkerchief. "I believe you're

right. That feline delights in terrorizing me, doesn't she?" He smiled wanly at Maggie.

"I shouldn't have left the door open. This attic is irresistible to cats. I think she must have been asleep, and you startled her when you sneezed," Maggie said.

"Cats don't like me," he said, making his way to her.

"Bubbles likes everyone."

Gordon stepped around her, and they descended to the library.

"Do you have the brooch?" she asked.

"Yes." He patted the inside breast pocket of his suit coat. "I have special TSA Precheck boarding clearance, so I won't have to remove my jacket. It'll be safe here."

"And it's insured," Maggie said.

"That, too, but I don't want anything to happen to it. I've placed it in an auction in London at the end of next month. I inquired about obtaining a certificate of authenticity from Van Cleef & Arpels. It would cost two thousand dollars, and they said it would take months to obtain."

"You don't recommend waiting to obtain a certificate? Or am I pressuring you to sell it too fast?" She bit her lip. "Like I did with the Martin-Guillaume Biennais tea set?"

"No, madam, you are not. This upcoming auction should be the ideal venue for your brooch."

"Good. We're not in a rush this time."

"Let me write you a receipt for this," he said, crossing the library to the desk where he'd deposited his satchel. He sat and took out paper and a fountain pen. He removed the cap from the pen, and ink began to leak onto the paper.

He quickly recapped the pen, cursing under his breath. "This pen always leaks after I've been on an airplane. I forget to replace it with," his tongue curled around the words with disdain, "a gel pen."

Maggie snatched a tissue from the holder on the edge of the desk and handed it to him. "There are lots of pens in the lap drawer of the desk."

"Thank you," he said, pulling the drawer open. He began shuffling papers right and left, looking for a pen.

"I thought there were pens in there," Maggie said, leaning over him and peering into the drawer. "They must have rolled to the back. Pull it out farther."

"It's stuck on something," Gordon said, tugging at the drawer. It finally came free, dislodging a yellowed envelope that had been jammed in the back. The drawer fell into Gordon's lap, and a pen rolled into his open hand.

"Well, at least we've found a pen," Maggie said.

Gordon set the drawer on top of the desk and picked up the yellowed envelope. He flipped it over in his hands. Two strips of cellophane tape that had lost their stickiness long ago ran the length of each side of the business-sized envelope.

Gordon looked up at Maggie.

Her pulse began to race at the excitement in his eyes.

"At one time, it was common for people to tape valuables to the underside of a desk," he said. "I always check when I acquire antique furniture."

"I wonder what could be in there?" she replied, trying to temper her excitement.

"Let's find out. May I?"

Maggie nodded.

Gordon picked a letter opener out of the drawer and carefully released the seal of the envelope. He squeezed the short ends of the envelope, and he and Maggie peered inside.

"It's a stamp," she said, her tone tinged with disappointment. "An old postage stamp."

"My guess is that this is a rare, old postage stamp," he said. "It was almost certainly secured to the underside of the desk for safekeeping." He shook the envelope, allowing the stamp to slide onto the desktop.

Maggie reached for it.

"No!" he cried. "This should only be handled with stamp tongs."

"I don't have stamp tongs."

He looked up at her. "There may be some in that attic of yours. Possibly more stamps, too. Do you have any gloves? White cotton gloves."

"I think I still have a pair," she said.

"They'll do for now." He leaned over the stamp. "It's a Canadian stamp. 1878."

"That is old," Maggie said, trying not to squeal. "Maybe it's valuable."

"Stamps are not my area of expertise," he said. "Why don't I take a photo of the stamp and consult one of my colleagues?"

"That would be fabulous," Maggie said.

He pulled his phone out of his satchel. "Can you get those gloves and put the stamp back in the envelope? I'd suggest you move it to your safe."

Maggie was already headed to the stairs. "Will do. This gives us something else to investigate when you come back."

She ran up the stairs to her bedroom and returned with the gloves. Under Gordon's supervision, she replaced the stamp in the envelope.

"And now, Madam, I must be going. I'll have to make haste to catch my flight." He picked up his satchel and headed for the door.

Maggie went ahead of him. "Thank you for making the trip and for," her voice grew soft with emotion, "everything. Good things always turn up when you're here."

Gordon cleared his throat. "You're most welcome, madam. I'm glad to do it. Rosemont is a fascinating home, and you and your husband are most kind."

Maggie hesitated, then gave him a swift hug before opening the door. "You're becoming like family to us, Gordon. Come back soon, and plan to stay here—at Rosemont."

He flushed and dashed down the steps to his rental car.

CHAPTER 48

"I appreciate your coming by the station." Maggie and Robert took seats in the chairs in front of the chief's desk.

"I've received preliminary results from the handwriting expert," he continued, looking at Robert. "I see you were copied on Deidre's email."

"Yes. I was curious to see the sample of Nigel's handwriting for myself."

"Did you reach a conclusion?"

"I did," Robert said. "So did Deidre. We both think—"

"Let's see what Maggie thinks before we share our conclusions," the chief said. "Would you like to compare the note you found in that jacket pocket to the handwriting samples?"

Maggie slid to the edge of her seat. "You know I would."

The chief withdrew two sheets of paper from a file on his desk, which he placed in front of her.

Maggie bent over them.

"Here's a magnifying glass," the chief said, handing it to her.

She hovered over the papers. "I don't need this," she said, setting the magnifier aside. "Even to the naked eye, it looks like the same handwriting."

The chief spoke to Robert. "What did you think?"

"The same. Both Deidre and I believe Nigel wrote that note."

"The handwriting expert reached the same conclusion," the chief said. "Nigel had some unique aspects to his penmanship."

"The below-the-line parts of the Y's and G's all had very distinctive tails on them," Robert said.

"The expert mentioned that to me. He's going to provide an opinion that the note was written by Nigel."

"That's wonderful," Maggie said. "Will you consider the case of Elizabeth Filler's murder solved?"

The chief nodded. "We'll close our file. I thought you'd want to know."

Robert rested his fingertips on his chin. "Unbelievable. It's like something on television."

"I have to admit, this is a first in my career." He rose from behind his desk. "You've helped the Westbury police solve a cold case. Thank you."

Maggie and Robert followed him out of the station and stood in the warm sunshine on the front steps.

"I never—in a million years—thought I'd help solve an American cold case," Robert said.

Maggie chuckled. "Me, either. I'll tell you something—I've done a lot of things since moving to Westbury that would have seemed impossible in my old life."

They ambled toward their cars.

"Maybe it'll be the same for you when you move here."

"My life's already turned upside down since I arrived. I've got a son, and I'm marrying the love of my life tomorrow." He stopped walking. "Are you sure about having the wedding at

Rosemont? We're fine with getting married at the courthouse. We just—"

Maggie held up her palm to stop him. "Of course I am. Look at this day," she said, raising both hands over her head. "It's a perfect spring day, and tomorrow's supposed to be the same. That area by the wall is in shade at four o'clock. You couldn't ask for a lovelier spot to get married."

"I agree, but you barely know us."

Maggie grew serious. "John and I were both touched by your love story. We didn't find each other until later in life, and you're reconnecting with each other decades after you should have been married. We feel a sort of—kinship—with you." The breeze blew her hair into her eyes, and she brushed it back. "We were fortunate enough to join our lives on the back lawn of Rosemont, and we'd love for you to do the same."

Robert swallowed the lump in his throat. "That's a lovely thing to say, Maggie. Lyla and I are thrilled to be getting married tomorrow—at Rosemont."

CHAPTER 49

Maggie carried her coffee down the back lawn toward the figure perched on the low wall. Roman and Eve zigzagged across the lawn in front of her, chasing birds they had no chance of catching.

"You beat me to it," she said as she sat next to John.

"I couldn't sleep," he said. "I didn't want to disturb you, so I got up."

"You're taking the day off," Maggie said. "I thought you might want to sleep in."

"Too many years of getting up at the crack of dawn. That's what veterinary practice does to you," he said. "I'm glad I'm up. I've been thinking about our wedding." He put his arm around her and drew her close. "Reliving the best day of my life."

Maggie pulled his face to hers, and they kissed long and slow. "You still make me feel like my shoes are going to fly off my feet when you kiss me," she said.

John laughed. "I hope that's a good thing."

"It most certainly is," she said, resting her head on his shoulder.

"What do you have planned for the day? Do we have much to do to get ready for the wedding?"

"Not really."

"Is it still going to be just Lyla and Robert with Sunday and Josh standing up for them and the clerk officiating?"

"That's the plan. Susan is coming over on her lunch hour to help me put flowers out on the wall. I want to look for the aisle runner from our wedding. I think it's in the basement."

John surveyed the area around him. "I'll trim the weeds from the other side of this wall and mow the grass in front of it."

"That'd be nice," Maggie said. "I wasn't going to ask you to do it on your day off, but I forgot to call the landscaper. It'll be much prettier if you do." She slipped off the wall. "I'm also going to pick up a small cake at Laura's. Sunday dropped off champagne. I'd better shine up our champagne flutes and polish the ice bucket."

She looked at John. "What are you laughing at?"

"The two of us. We both love to get ready for a party—whether it's large or small."

"Guilty as charged." She snatched her coffee cup from the wall. "We'd better get busy. Race you to the house," she said as she sprinted up the slope.

***

"You've got more flowers in the car?" Maggie asked.

Susan nodded, her arms full of pots of white tulips.

Maggie helped her place them along the wall. "Do you need a hand with the rest?"

"I can manage, but can you carry the organza and ribbon?"

Maggie raised an eyebrow as they hurried up the lawn, skirting the house, to the driveway where Susan's SUV sat with the hatchback open.

Susan smiled at her mother as she leaned into her car and pulled out two large Celebrations bags, handing them to Maggie.

"I thought you were only going to swing by the grocery to get a few flowers," Maggie said.

"I'm your daughter, Mom," Susan said. "Why would you think that?" She loaded her arms with the remaining pots of tulips from the backseat and kicked the door shut. "It's a Rosemont wedding—a certain amount of style is required."

Maggie grinned. "I can't deny that."

They began to retrace their steps to the wall.

"I see you found the white aisle runner from your wedding," Susan said. "It looks nice."

"Thank you. I appreciate that you took care of the flowers."

"You're welcome. I wish I wasn't so busy at work, so I could do more." She set the pots on the ground as Maggie removed a bolt of organza from one of the bags. "I figure you've got all sorts of errands to run this afternoon, to get ready."

"They have to have a wedding cake. I'm going to swing by Laura's," Maggie said.

Susan fished a pair of scissors out of her purse. "I came prepared, in case you weren't home," she said, holding up the scissors. "I'll cut the fabric and ribbon, and you can put them on the pots."

"Sounds like a plan," Maggie said, taking the piece of organza that Susan held out to her. "We'll have this done and you'll be back to work in no time."

Mother and daughter bent to their task, working steadily in companionable silence.

***

"Can you help me zip this?" Maggie spun her back to John.

He stopped buttoning his shirt collar and tugged at the zipper. "It's stuck."

"I know it's stuck. That's why I asked." She glanced over her shoulder at him. "I'm sorry I snapped. It's just that we're running so late. They should be here any minute. It's probably caught on the lining. Try to hold the fabric out of the way and inch the zipper up."

John did as he was instructed. The zipper remained unmovable. "Sorry, sweetheart."

"If I hadn't been in such an all-fired hurry, this wouldn't have happened." Maggie began trying to wriggle out of the dress. "I'll wear something else."

"We did get carried away cleaning up the yard, didn't we?"

"And then I had to wait at Laura's for them to finish decorating the cake." She slapped her hands on her thighs in frustration. "I can't get it off."

The doorbell rang.

"That'll be them. Would you answer the door and then come back up. You're going to have to cut me out of this dress."

"I thought you loved that dress," he said, making his way toward the hallway.

"I do, but there's no other choice," she called after him.

Maggie twisted herself into a pretzel and tugged at the recalcitrant zipper until she heard footsteps on the stairs. She retrieved a pair of scissors from her nightstand drawer. "It's no use," she said.

Lyla entered the room, calling softy to Maggie.

Maggie's breath caught in her throat. "Oh, Lyla! You look stunning."

"Thank you, Maggie. I've always thought any woman in a wedding dress looks beautiful."

"There's some truth in that, but you are stunning." She stopped and looked at Lyla. A floor-length lace sheath in a creamy hue hung gracefully on Lyla's thin frame. A satin belt adorned with seed pearls accentuated her narrow waist. Her hair was freshly styled and curved around her chin. "I'm so glad you're wearing a wedding gown."

"I wasn't planning on it when we were going to be married at the clerk's office. But when we changed the venue to here," she looked around the room, "to Rosemont, I decided I wanted something more … traditional."

"It's perfect. Where did you find it?"

"Sunday took me to Archer's Bridal."

Maggie grinned.

"Do you know them?"

"Quite well, actually."

"This was a floor sample—on sale, no less. It fit without any alterations."

"Meant to be," Maggie said.

"That's what Sunday said. I have her to thank for insisting I get a gown and having my hair and makeup done, too."

"I'm so glad," Maggie said. "John's got a nice camera and wants to take pictures."

"Gosh, we'd forgotten all about a photographer. We've been focused on getting ready to leave for England."

"We've got you covered." Maggie gestured behind her back. "I need to get out of this dress."

"That's why I came up. John told us what happened. I'm a

dab hand at zippers. Let me give it a go before we take drastic measures." She eyed the scissors in Maggie's hand.

"Thank you," Maggie said, presenting her back to Lyla. "John and I weren't getting anywhere."

Lyla inserted her fingers behind the fabric and fidgeted with the zipper.

Maggie held her breath.

The zipper lurched forward and then finished its smooth ascent to her neckline.

"There," Lyla said. "Got it."

"Thank you! You saved me and the dress."

"You're welcome. I'm glad we had a moment alone. I wanted to thank you for providing us such a lovely spot to get married."

Maggie smoothed her dress into place and smiled at Lyla. "You're most welcome. Now let's get down there. I think this wedding's been delayed long enough."

***

Robert stood next to the town clerk in front of the low wall. Josh finished securing the boutonnière to the lapel of his father's neatly tailored blue suit and stepped aside. Robert straightened his tie. Pots of white tulips, wrapped in organza and tied with lilac ribbons, lined the top of the wall. A light breeze rustled through the leaves, chasing dappled sunshine across the white runner that led from Robert to the top of the lawn.

Maggie stood off to one side. She narrowed her eyes and scanned the rear façade of the house. Where was John? He was supposed to be here with her.

All three of them stared at the top of the lawn and Rosemont.

The light glinting off the French doors from the library scattered as the doors opened, and Sunday stepped out. She wore a tea-length satin dress in a rich shade of coral. Her blond hair bounced against her shoulders. She walked to the runner and made her way down the slope to the small group assembled at the wall.

Maggie glanced at Josh as Sunday approached. He kept his eyes riveted on the beautiful young woman. Maggie felt a surge of happy anticipation. She hoped there'd be another wedding in the near future.

Sunday nodded to Josh as she came to the end of the runner. He winked at her in return. She took her place on the other side of the clerk.

The French doors opened again, and John stepped out. He turned and extended his elbow to Lyla.

She emerged and slipped her hand into the crook of John's elbow. Her timeless lace gown was luminescent in the sunshine. She, in her dress, and John, dressed in a classic dark blue suit, made the perfect picture against the warm stone backdrop of Rosemont.

Robert gasped.

Josh and Sunday exchanged smiles.

John leaned over and said something to Lyla. She nodded, and they proceeded to the aisle.

Maggie studied Robert. She'd seen that expression on a man's face once before. John had looked at her that way as she'd come down the aisle, across this very lawn, to join her life with his.

She blinked rapidly and reached for the tissue she'd tucked into her sleeve before she and Lyla had come downstairs. No matter what Robert and Lyla's future held, she felt sure the love they shared would see them through.

John and the bride walked slowly, in regal unison. Her bobbed hair brushed against her shoulders and her smile outshone the sun.

Maggie swore she heard Robert's heart hammering in his chest.

When they reached the others, Lyla leaned toward John. "Thank you for walking me down the aisle."

"It was my honor," John said, his voice husky with emotion.

Robert held out his hands, and Lyla placed hers into them.

John went to stand with Maggie. She leaned into him, and he put his arm around her, brushing a kiss on the top of her head.

"Dearly beloved," the clerk said. "We are gathered today ..."

The brief ceremony continued under a cloudless sky.

"You may now kiss the bride," said the clerk.

Robert swept Lyla into his arms, and they shared the kiss that had been delayed too long. Maggie, John, Sunday, and Josh clapped along with the clerk.

Josh stepped to his parents and opened his arms to hug them both.

John hurried to the stone wall and retrieved his camera from the backside of the wall.

"I thought you'd forgotten," Maggie said.

"No way. I'm way ahead of you," John replied. He moved to the wedding party. "Stay like that," he said. "Let me get a picture of the three of you." The newly reunited family smiled at the camera. John snapped the photo, then began posing and photographing the wedding party.

Maggie contemplated the happy scene unfolding in front of her before she headed up the hill to Rosemont's covered patio. While John took photos, she busied herself with the simple reception she and Sunday had planned.

On a round table draped in a floor-length antique tablecloth adorned with embroidered roses, Maggie set out the small, tiered wedding cake she'd picked up earlier at Laura's Bakery. The lacey sugar work on the side of the cake was accented with piped icing pearls. It seemed as if Laura had copied Lyla's dress, Maggie thought, although she knew that wasn't possible.

Next to the cake, she placed cut crystal champagne flutes she'd polished to a high shine. The bottle of Dom Perignon Sunday had supplied rested in a gleaming silver ice bucket, next to Maggie's Botanic Garden Portmeirion dessert plates, which were perfect for a garden reception. Silver dessert forks shone in the bright afternoon.

Maggie sighed in satisfaction. It might not be elaborate, but it would certainly be a lovely reception.

She spun around at the sound of her name being called.

Lyla and Robert approached, walking hand-in-hand.

"Maggie—what have you done?" Lyla cried.

"You mean, what have Sunday and I done?" Maggie replied. "We both thought you needed a cake and champagne."

"It's stunning!" Lyla gushed, pointing to the table. She tapped John's shoulder. "Would you take a picture? Before we disturb anything."

John did as she requested.

Sunday pointed to the champagne as she spoke to Josh. "Would you do the honors?"

Josh picked up a cloth napkin, wrapped it around the neck of the bottle, and deftly opened it without spilling a drop.

"Well done!" Robert said, clapping him on the back.

Josh filled seven flutes and handed them around.

The clerk shook her head. "I'm working."

Josh cleared his throat and raised his glass. "To my parents,

Robert and Lyla. May your future be filled with the happiness and love you both so richly deserve."

"Here, here," cried the others, raising their glasses.

Robert winked at his bride as everyone drank their toast, and he and Lyla started this welcome new chapter in their lives.

CHAPTER 50

David still had a ton of homework and wanted to get home. Frank caught him as he was closing up Forever Friends.

"David, I just ordered takeout from Pete's for Loretta. Their delivery person called in sick. Do you mind picking it up and dropping it off at the house? She's been working like mad all day, setting up the nursery and putting away the gifts from the shower. I'm taking the kids to dinner and a movie to get them out of her hair."

Frank's house was on his route home, so stopping by was easy. But he would have happily driven out of his way to help out, no matter how late he would have to stay up to get his homework done.

He rang the doorbell and waited. He knew Loretta was home, but she wasn't answering the door. He placed the bag containing her meal on the doormat and listened at the door. He heard nothing.

David rang the bell again. When Loretta still didn't answer, he knocked loudly in case the doorbell didn't work.

Dodger, who was waiting in his customary spot in the front passenger seat, began to whimper.

A sense of unease began to rise in David. What if something was wrong?

He left the bag of food on the doormat and gestured to Dodger to stay before letting himself into the backyard through the side gate. The kitchen door was slightly ajar.

"Loretta?" he called, pushing the door open farther. He stepped into the kitchen and raised his voice. "Loretta?"

"In … here …" came a gasping response from the front of the house.

David ran in the direction of her voice. He found her, on her knees and bent over, in the foyer. A pool of clear liquid surrounded her.

She looked up at him. "I couldn't get to the door." She doubled over and grasped her protruding stomach.

"Oh, my God! What's going on? I'll call the paramedics!"

Loretta held out a hand. "No. My water broke, and I've gone into labor."

David pressed both hands against the sides of his face. "What should I do? Call Frank?"

"I texted him, but he took the kids to a movie they wanted to see that was only playing in the next town. They're on their way home, but I need to go to the hospital." She grimaced again.

He dropped to his knees next to her. "Are you in pain?"

"They're labor pains. Nothing to worry about. Help me up, David. You're going to have to take me to the hospital." She flinched again. "Now."

David put his arms around her shoulders and helped her

stand. They made their way slowly to his car. He gingerly placed her into the backseat and secured her seat belt.

Dodger squeezed through the opening between the front seats and took up a position next to Loretta.

She put a free hand on her forehead. "Listen to me, David."

He gulped back his rising panic.

"Go back inside. Close the doors and lock up."

"Okay."

"Be fast," she said. "But drive carefully to the hospital. Don't speed. We need to get there in one piece."

"Sure," he said, turning and running back into the house.

Dodger sniffed along her body and gave her ear a tentative lick.

David accomplished his mission at lightning speed and flung himself behind the wheel.

"One more thing," Loretta called from the backseat. "If I start screaming, just ignore me."

He whipped his head around to look at her with wide eyes.

"Go!" Loretta commanded. "I'm having these babies!"

THANK YOU FOR READING!

Thank You for Reading!

If you enjoyed *Restoring What Was Lost*, I'd be grateful if you wrote a review.

Just a few lines on Amazon or Goodreads would be great. Reviews are the best gift an author can receive. They encourage us when they're good, help us improve our next book when they're not, and help other readers make informed choices when purchasing books. Goodreads reviews help readers find new books. Reviews on Amazon keep the Amazon algorithms humming and are the most helpful aide in selling books! Thank you.

To post a review on Amazon:

1. Go to the product detail page for *Restoring What Was Lost* on Amazon.com.
2. Click "Write a customer review" in the Customer Reviews section.

THANK YOU FOR READING!

3. Write your review and click Submit.

In gratitude,
    Barbara Hinske

JUST FOR YOU!

Wonder what Maggie was thinking when the book ended? Exclusively for readers who finished Restoring What Was Lost, take a look at Maggie's Diary Entry for that day at https://barbarahinske.com/maggies-diary.

ACKNOWLEDGMENTS

I'm blessed with the wisdom and support of many kind and generous people. I want to thank the most supportive and delightful group of champions an author could hope for:

My insightful and supportive assistant Lisa Coleman who keeps all the plates spinning;

My life coach Mat Boggs for your wisdom and guidance;

My kind and generous legal team, Kenneth Kleinberg, Esq., and Michael McCarthy—thank you for believing in my vision;

The professional "dream team" of my editors Linden Gross, Jesika St. Clair, and proofreader Dana Lee;

Elizabeth Mackey for a beautiful cover.

BOOK CLUB QUESTIONS

(If your club talks about anything other than family, jobs, and household projects!)

1. Do you know anyone who has an adoptive family?
2. Have you parented an adopted child? If so, what prompted your decision to adopt? Would you adopt again if given the chance?
3. Have you known anyone who has reunited with a birth parent or family member? How has the relationship developed over time? How has it affected relationships in the adoptive family?
4. How do you feel about the confidentiality of the adoption process?
5. Now that genetic medical history can be so helpful, should that impact an adoptee's rights to information?
6. Do you have a service dog, or have you ever seen one in action?

7. Do you know anyone who has reunited with someone from their high school or college years? Has the rekindled relationship worked out or, as the saying goes, can you 'never go home again'?
8. Do you ever wonder whether a relationship with an old flame might have led to lasting happiness if something had been different in your youth?
9. Is there anyone from your romantic past that you've reconnected with and are now just friends?
10. What one person from your past would you like to come in contact with now?

RECURRING CHARACTERS

Recurring Characters
   ACOSTA
   Grace: older sister to Tommy; David Wheeler's high school sweetheart; plans to attend Highpointe College upon graduation; babysits for the Scanlons
   Iris: mother to Grace and Tommy with husband, Kevin
   Kevin: professor at Highpointe College
   Tommy: became friends with Nicole Nash and David Wheeler while an in-patient at Mercy Hospital
   Alistair: butler at Rosemont for over fifty years, now a friendly ghost who lives in the attic
   John Allen: veterinarian and owner of Westbury Animal Hospital, Maggie Martin's husband, adopted grandfather to baby Julia and twins Sophie and Sarah
   Anita Archer: owner of Archer's Bridal
   Kevin Baxter: member of Highpointe College Board of Trustees
   Marc Benson: partner of Alex Scanlon, musician

RECURRING CHARACTERS

Nigel Blythe: owner of Blythe Rare Books in London, bought books stolen from Highpointe College Library, poisoned Hazel Harrington, attempted to kill Sunday Sloan and Anthony Plume

Harriet and Larry Burman: owners of Burman Jewelers

Jeff Carson: Widower; former wife, Millie, died 3 years ago; son Jason and daughter-in-law Sharon; grandchildren Tyler and Talia; cares about animal shelter; mother, Alma, uncle, William Olsson

Charlotte: owner of Candy Alley Candy Shop

DELGADO BROTHERS: involved in scheme to embezzle money from the Westbury Town Workers' Pension Fund

Chuck: former Westbury town councilmember; owner of D's Liquor and Convenience Store

Ron: investment advisor and CPA; married to William Wheeler's sister

FITZPATRICK

Laura: owner of Laura's Bakery; mother of one with husband, Pete

Pete: owner of Pete's Bistro, a popular lunch spot for Westbury town councilmembers

Gloria Harper: resident of Fairview Terraces, married to Glenn Vaughn, acts as surrogate grandmother to David Wheeler

Hazel Harrington: deceased rare-book librarian at Highpointe College, poisoned by Nigel Blythe

Robert Harris: rare-book librarian at Cambridge University, friend to Sunday Sloan

Frank Haynes: repentant crony of the Delgados, Westbury town councilmember, owner of Haynes Enterprises (holding company of fast food restaurants), founder and principal funder of Forever Friends dog rescue, grandson of Hector Martin, married to Loretta Nash

HOLMES

George: emcee of the annual Easter Carnival, father of three with wife, Tonya

Tonya: Westbury town councilmember; close friend of Maggie Martin

Russell Isaac: Westbury town councilmember, inherited auto parts business, former acting mayor of Westbury, involved in scheme to of Delgado brothers

Lyla Kershaw: works in accounting department at Highpointe College Library; close friend of Sunday Sloan; birth mother of Josh Newlon

Tim Knudsen: realtor, Westbury town councilmember, married to Nancy

Ian Lawry: former president of Highpointe College

MARTIN

Amy: Maggie Martin's daughter-in-law; mother to twins, Sophie and Sarah, with husband, Mike Martin

Hector and Silas: deceased town patriarchs; Silas (Hector's father) amassed a fortune from the local sawmill, real estate, and other ventures and built the Rosemont estate; Hector donated his rare book collection to Highpointe College and left his estate to his living heirs—grandnephew, Paul Martin, and grandson, Frank Haynes (Frank's father was Hector's illegitimate son)

Maggie: current owner of Rosemont and president of Highpointe College; widow of Paul Martin; former forensic accountant and mayor of Westbury; married to John Allen; mother to Mike Martin and Susan (Martin) Scanlon; grandmother to Julia Scanlon and twins, Sophie and Sarah Martin

Mike: Maggie Martin's adult son, lives in California with wife, Amy, and twin daughters, Sophie and Sarah

RECURRING CHARACTERS

Paul: Maggie Martin's first husband, deceased; embezzled funds while president of Windsor College; father of Susan (Martin) Scanlon and Mike Martin; had an affair with Loretta Nash and fathered Nicole Nash

Sophie and Sarah: twin daughters of Amy and Mike Martin; close friends of Marissa Nash; Maggie Martin's granddaughter

Gordon Mortimer: antiques dealer and appraiser

NASH

Loretta: current financial analyst at Haynes Enterprises; married to Frank Haynes; mother to Marissa, Sean, and Nicole, with baby number four on the way; former mistress of Paul Martin

Marissa, Nicole, Sean: Loretta's children, adopted by stepfather, Frank Haynes; Marissa (oldest) babysits for the Scanlons and is friends with Maggie Martin's twin granddaughters; Nicole (youngest) received a kidney from Susan Scanlon after it was discovered that they had the same father, Paul Martin; Sean works as David Wheeler's apprentice at Forever Friends and the animal hospital

Josh Newlon: Maggie Martin's administrative assistant; Lyla Kershaw's birth son; Sunday Sloan's boyfriend

Juan: veterinary technician at Westbury Animal Hospital

Anthony Plume: professor and dean of English Literature at Highpointe College; stole rare books from the college library and sold them to Nigel Blythe

SCANLON

Aaron: orthopedic surgeon; married to Maggie's daughter, Susan; father to baby Julia; brother to Alex

Alex: attorney who succeeds Maggie Martin as mayor of Westbury; partner of Marc Benson

Julia: infant daughter of Susan and Aaron Scanlon; Maggie Martin's granddaughter

RECURRING CHARACTERS

Susan (née Martin): Maggie Martin's adult daughter; attorney works at brother-in-law Alex's firm; helped Josh Newlon find his birth mother; nearly died donating kidney to stepsister, Nicole Nash

Sunday Sloan: rare-book librarian at Highpointe College; friend of Lyla Kershaw; Josh Newlon's girlfriend

Forest Smith: attorney at Stetson & Graham; assigned to assist Alex Scanlon; died in a suspicious fall off a bridge

Bill Stetson: partner at Stetson & Graham, Westbury's outside law firm

Chief Andrew (Andy) Thomas: Westbury's chief of police

Joan and Sam Torres: wife and husband; Maggie Martin's close friends, who befriended her on her first day in Westbury; Joan works as a police dispatcher, Sam as a handyman

Lyndon Upton: professor of finance at University of Chicago, former colleague of Maggie Martin's; volunteered to help with Westbury's embezzlement case

Glenn Vaughn: resident of Fairview Terraces; married to Gloria Harper; acts as surrogate grandfather to David Wheeler

WHEELER

David: works with therapy dogs; helps at Forever Friends and Westbury Animal Hospital; son of William and Jackie Wheeler; Grace Acosta's boyfriend

Jackie: wife of disgraced former mayor William Wheeler; mother to David

William: former mayor of Westbury convicted for fraud and embezzlement; committed suicide in prison; father to David and husband to Jackie

Judy Young: business-savvy owner of Celebrations Gift Shop and town gossip; close friend of Maggie Martin; maiden name Jorgenson

WESTBURY'S FOREVER FRIENDS

<u>Westbury's Forever Friends</u>
Blossom, Buttercup, and Bubbles: John Allen and Maggie Martin's cats, named after PowerPuff Girls
Cooper: the Scanlons' male golden retriever, a gift from David Wheeler to help baby Julia fall asleep
Daisy: Sean Nash's female Aussie-cattle dog mix
Dan: Josh Newlon's large black Labrador, who has a calming effect on baby Julia
Dodger: David Wheeler's constant companion, a mid-sized mutt with one eye, who works as a therapy dog at Fairview Terraces and Mercy Hospital
Eve: Maggie Martin's faithful terrier mix; found shivering in the snow, outside Rosemont, on Maggie's first night in Westbury
Jolly: Jeff Carson's schnauzer mix, adopted on Christmas Eve with Judy Young at the Olsson house
Magellan: Tommy Acosta's cat
Namor: David Wheeler's gray cat with four white paws;

brother to Blossom, Buttercup, and Bubbles; was named after John Allen's dog, "Roman" spelled backwards

Roman: John Allen's gentle golden retriever

Rusty: Sam and Joan Torres's dog

Sally: Frank Haynes' overweight border collie mix

Snowball: Marissa and Nicole Nash's male terrier-schnauzer mix

ABOUT THE AUTHOR

USA Today Bestselling Author BARBARA HINSKE is an attorney and novelist. She's authored the Guiding Emily series, the mystery thriller collection "Who's There?", the Paws & Pastries series, two novellas in The Wishing Tree series, and the beloved *Rosemont Series*.

Two of her works have been adapted for the screen. *Guiding Emily* debuted to great acclaim on Hallmark Movies & Mysteries in September of 2023. Her novella *The Christmas Club* was made into a Hallmark Channel movie of the same name in 2019.

She is extremely grateful to her readers! She inherited the writing gene from her father who wrote mysteries when he retired and told her a story every night of her childhood. She and her husband share their own Rosemont with two adorable and spoiled dogs. The old house keeps her husband busy with repair projects and her happily decorating, entertaining, and gardening. She also spends a lot of time baking and—as a result—dieting.

Please enjoy this excerpt from *No Matter How Far*, a Rosemont series novella by Barbara Hinske:

Prologue

Judy Jorgensen turned into the alley and picked her way carefully across the rutted snow, packed with gravel and bits of broken twigs. A fall on this terrain was sure to tear a hole in her tights. An icy wind blew under her skirt and bit through the thick Fair Isle scarf that her mother had made her last Christmas. She should have listened to her mother and worn the snow pants, but at twelve, she felt too old for unfashionable practicalities.

One mittened hand tucked a loose strand of her waist-length dark hair into her collar as she ran the other along the smooth stones of the wall that bracketed the alley. She leaned forward, keeping her eyes on her footing. She knew every inch of the passage from the school to the back gate of her mother's shop.

Celebrations, located on Westbury's town square, had been the community's source for stationery, gifts, and invitations since her grandmother had founded the business decades ago. When school was over, a snack would be waiting for her, along with the back inventory she'd have to help her mother stock. Judy kicked a rock down the alley. It landed in front of the wrought-iron gate that sat across the alley from Celebrations.

The street behind the shops on the town square was lined with charming historic homes, including the one that Judy and her mother had inherited from her grandmother. The residence on the other side of the iron gate was the grandest of them all. The towering, three-story Victorian—built by the first president of Highpointe College—was now home to the man's reclusive great-grandson.

Uncharitable rumors swirled around town about the elderly man, but William Olsson had never been anything but kind to Judy and her mother.

"He's just a private soul," her mother would say whenever she heard one of these rumors. "He's never hurt anyone. And he keeps me in business! His house and that beautiful garden of his bring in tourists every year!"

After church, Judy's mother would wrap up a serving of Sunday dinner and hand it to her. "Leave it in the stone wall's alcove next to the iron gate." She said it *every* time—even though Judy had been doing this for what felt to her like her entire life.

The next day, William would leave something from his gardens in the alcove for Judy and her mother. In spring, Judy would find fresh-cut flowers tied up with twine. Summer brought hydrangeas, fresh herbs, and strawberries. In fall, there'd be apples, chrysanthemums, pansies, and, as it grew colder, root vegetables and exotic hothouse blooms. But today, like every Monday before Christmas, Judy would find the best gift of all.

She stopped to claw at the hair the wind held plastered to her face and stepped closer to the nook and released the breath she'd been holding.

It was there. In the alcove.

She reached up and removed the package wrapped in tissue and tied with a thin red ribbon. She tucked it inside her coat and turned toward her gate.

She hoped that her mother wouldn't be busy with customers. They always unwrapped his gift together. She didn't want to wait.

Chapter 1

Judy Young stepped onto the sidewalk and inhaled deeply.

ENJOY THIS EXCERPT FROM NO MATTER HOW FAR, A ROSEMONT...

The scent of apple blossom hung heavy on this spring morning. The tree in her front yard was thick with pink and white blooms. She'd have a bumper crop of Pink Ladies in the fall—enough to make pies for the church bake sale and to can for applesauce.

She set out for her shop at a quick pace. Walking the short distance to Celebrations when the weather was fine was one of her favorite things, especially since she could look at her neighbors' homes as she passed by. She recognized every plant in the well-tended gardens and knew which shutters had just received a fresh coat of paint or which porch swing needed repair. She'd lived on this street for more than forty years, inheriting the family home and the shop when her mother had died.

Judy clipped along, avoiding familiar cracks where roots of the now-mature trees lifted the pavement, until she came to the Olsson house. The old Victorian home rose three stories, towering over its neighbors.

She squinted and tilted her head upward, inspecting the gabled roof and the windows that circled the turret. Each time she passed, Judy noticed small changes and grieved the home's steady decline. After William Olsson's death in the early 1990s, the house was left vacant but well maintained—until four years ago. She was running her eyes over the façade when she spotted a white piece of paper with the word "NOTICE" in heavy black type affixed to the front door. She'd have to get closer to read the words that followed.

Judy looked at her watch. She really shouldn't dally—the delivery service would soon be at the back door of Celebrations with her weekly shipment of cards and stationery.

She pushed against the wrought-iron gate that hung crookedly on its rusty hinges. It screeched open a mere twelve inches before it caught on a high spot on the sidewalk. Judy squeezed herself through the opening and picked her way carefully through the weeds and brambles that had taken over the once manicured lawn. A branch caught at her cardigan, and she pulled it away, tearing a small hole in her sleeve.

"Darn it," she muttered. She mounted the stone steps to the double front door and leaned in to read the piece of paper that was stapled there.

Judy gasped. The Olsson house was going to be auctioned off for back taxes. What did that mean? Her stomach lurched, and for a moment, she worried that she might be sick. Judy had never been inside the house, but it had been a special part of her life. Every Christmas, her mother and Mr. Olsson had exchanged gifts through the alcove in the alley. This notice felt like a leech on the house—a violation of her past. She grasped the offending paper and began to tug but stopped herself. Pulling it down wouldn't accomplish anything—and was illegal. It said so on the notice.

She took several deep breaths to steady herself, then snapped a photo of the offending notice with her phone. She'd text the photo to Susan Scanlon. Her young friend was a brilliant lawyer and could explain what this tax sale meant.

∽

"You're sure I'm all set to bid?" Judy curled the papers she was holding into a tight cylinder and tapped it against her leg.

The tall, blonde woman in her tailored blue suit, crisp white blouse, and high-heeled pumps turned to her friend. "You're qualified. We've filed all of the required paperwork and financial assurances." Susan smiled encouragingly at Judy.

"Okay. Good." Judy shifted her weight from foot to foot.

A man approached a podium set up on the courthouse steps

ENJOY THIS EXCERPT FROM NO MATTER HOW FAR, A ROSEMONT...

and tapped on a microphone, sending sharp crackling sounds into the air. The sunny spring morning was cool, and a light breeze ruffled the papers he set onto the podium. "Ladies and gentlemen, we're here for this afternoon's tax auction. If you've prequalified to bid, you'll have a number on a sheet of paper. Hold it up, and we'll take your bid. Our first address is …"

"How many did you say are ahead of us?" Judy asked.

Susan consulted her copy of the papers that Judy clutched in her hand. "Six. We shouldn't have long to wait."

"What happens if nobody bids?"

"The unpaid taxes continue to pile up," Susan said.

Judy nodded. "Do you think I'm the only bidder for the Olsson house?"

Susan looked at the others around them. "I recognize one of the bidders. He's a real estate developer. I suspect he's here to bid on the Olsson house. It's a double lot—prime property. He could tear the house down and put up eight patio homes without having to rezone it."

Judy groaned. "That would be a travesty—like trading the family silver for plastic cutlery."

Susan put a protective arm around Judy's shoulder. She loved all of her mother's close friends but felt a particular affinity for Judy. "Why don't you watch these other auctions—get a feel for how they go. It'll be your turn soon enough."

Judy inhaled sharply and nodded.

As the auctioneer droned on, she wrung the papers in her hands, rolling them tighter and tighter. When they finally announced the sale she was interested in, the papers fell to her side and she stepped forward.

"You've got this," Susan said. "Remember, the first bid has to be for the full amount of the back taxes." She handed Judy a three-by-five card where she'd printed the correct amount.

ENJOY THIS EXCERPT FROM NO MATTER HOW FAR, A ROSEMONT...

Judy nodded, raised her number, and made the required bid.

The auctioneer repeated the amount and asked for additional bids.

Judy focused on the real estate developer and held her breath.

The man raised his number and added a thousand dollars to Judy's bid.

Judy thrust her number in the air and added another thousand dollars.

She and the developer continued, raising each other by a thousand dollars each time for the next five minutes.

Susan leaned close to Judy's ear. "You're now at the maximum bid that you decided on before we got here."

The developer added another thousand, and so did Judy.

"It's easy to get carried away in an auction," Susan said.

"I can't let that bastard tear it down and turn the place into … God knows what."

"We don't know what he plans to do with it."

The developer increased his bid by two thousand.

"So that's how he intends to get the better of me." Judy's face grew red.

"Don't let your emotions take over!"

Judy raised her number and yelled, "Ten thousand more!"

Susan swung to her friend and client, who looked as surprised by her most recent bid as Susan did.

They both turned to the developer. He crumpled the paper with his number on it and turned to smirk at Judy. "Lady, you have no idea what you just stepped in. When you're done throwing your money into the financial abyss, give me a call."

The auctioneer gaveled the sale, announcing that that was the last item on the day's agenda. The crowd of bidders began to disperse.

Judy reached out a hand and grabbed Susan's arm to steady herself. "What in the hell did I just do?"

"You bought yourself that gorgeous Olsson house. Congratulations."

"I spent *way* more than I intended to. I don't want to even think about how much."

"You got an incredible property at a remarkably good price."

"You tried to stop me." Judy sounded close to tears. "Why didn't I listen to you? The place is a wreck—it'll be a complete money pit."

"Stop it," Susan said firmly. "You were going on your gut instinct. Don't second-guess yourself now. Enjoy this moment —you got what you came here for."

"I don't really own it for another six months, right?"

"Yes. Parties in interest can redeem the taxes and retain ownership."

Judy's breathing was coming in fits and starts. "So, I may not ever own it—the real owners could still come forward?"

"It's possible." Susan took Judy by the shoulders and turned her toward her. "I don't think that's likely. If the real owners were interested, they wouldn't have let the property go to tax sale."

Judy moaned. "I can't believe I just did this."

"Listen to me." Susan's tone was firm. "Pay the auctioneer and then forget all about this for the next six months. There's nothing you can do about it now. When you get the deed, you'll go through the property, assess its condition, and decide what to do with it. If it's too big a job to tackle, you can put it on the market. I'll bet you'll get an offer from that developer the moment you list it."

Judy swallowed hard. "That's comforting. I'd have a tough

time selling to anyone who wanted to tear it down, but at least I have a few ways out of this mess."

"You do. And stop thinking of it as a mess! Buying this house might be the key to something unexpected and wonderful."

Judy grinned. "You're just like your mother, with all of that hopefulness. That's why I love both you and Maggie!"

Read more here: *No Matter How Far*

ALSO BY BARBARA HINSKE

Available at Amazon in Print, Audio, and for Kindle

The Rosemont Series

Coming to Rosemont

Weaving the Strands

Uncovering Secrets

Drawing Close

Bringing Them Home

Shelving Doubts

Restoring What Was Lost

No Matter How Far

When Dreams There Be

Novellas

The Night Train

The Christmas Club (adapted for The Hallmark Channel, 2019)

Paws & Pastries

Sweets & Treats

Snowflakes, Cupcakes & Kittens

Workout Wishes & Valentine Kisses

Wishes of Home

Novels in the Guiding Emily Series

Guiding Emily

The Unexpected Path

Over Every Hurdle

Down the Aisle

Novels in the "Who's There?!" Collection

Deadly Parcel

Final Circuit

Connect with BARBARA HINSKE Online
Sign up for her newsletter at **BarbaraHinske.com**
Goodreads.com/BarbaraHinske
Facebook.com/BHinske
Instagram/barbarahinskeauthor
TikTok.com/BarbaraHinske
Pinterest.com/BarbaraHinske
Twitter.com/BarbaraHinske
Search for **Barbara Hinske on YouTube**
bhinske@gmail.com

Made in the USA
Middletown, DE
24 June 2024